Vengeance

A Sean Colbeth Mystery

Sean Colbeth Investigates

Book Six

Christopher H. Jansmann

Ephram Cotte
& Company
Publishing

ISBN: 978-1-960914-09-5 (Kindle Edition)
ISBN: 978-1-960914-10-1 (Paperback)
ISBN: 978-1-960914-11-8 (Hardcover)

Library of Congress Control Number: 2023919052

Printed in the United States of America

For Paula:

My love only grows stronger each day we are together.

Books by this Author

Chronological Order

Blindsided

Pariah

Outsider

Peril

Ditched

Bygones

Downhill

Duality

Focus

Bewitched

Requiem

Vengeance

Mirage

Solitude

Sean Colbeth Investigates

Blindsided

Outsider

Downhill

Duality

Bewitched

Vengeance

Solitude

Vasily Korsokovach Investigates

Pariah

Peril

Ditched

Bygones

Focus

Requiem

Mirage

Shorts

Snow Drifts

Baubles

Contents

One

Norm Thomas was waiting for me on the sidewalk when I pulled up in my departmental SUV. At least, I *thought* it was my number two; the flickering light from the faux carriage lamps the Village Council had planted along Main Street did little to illuminate anything, a complaint I had made from the moment their installation had been proposed. My desire for something that might contribute to the safety of our citizens had lost out to one of the village elders and their fond memories of a time that had never really existed; according to my cousin, Windeport had never had gas lamps nor someone who had dutifully gone around lighting them each evening. Sliding out of the driver's seat and into the sultry mid-July air, I glanced at one of the offending lamps and shook my head yet again.

Stepping up from the street, I ran a hand through my unkempt curls. "Norm, it's two o'clock in the morning," I said as I tried to stifle a yawn. "What's so important that it couldn't wait until the sun was up?"

Even in the half-light coming from the flickering lamps, I could see that Norm was uncomfortable. "I debated about calling you," he replied. "But I think I need a second set of eyes to confirm what I've got."

Trying — and failing — to stifle a second yawn, I nodded. "You were just as vague over the phone," I pointed out. Like me, Norm appeared to have rolled out of bed and tossed on whatever had been at hand; that we had both apparently settled on workout apparel spoke to our mutual off-duty obsession. "You're my second-in-command," I reminded him. "I thought you knew by now that you don't always have to get my approval."

He rubbed a hand along his chin which had a slight haze of stubble. "I know," he sighed. "I guess I'm not all that comfortable with that level of power in my hands." His boyish smile appeared, a subtle reminder he was about as old as Vasily had been when he'd joined me a decade earlier. "That and I didn't want to have to ask for forgiveness later."

I stepped closer and put a hand to his shoulder. "I wouldn't have hired you if I didn't think you could handle it."

Norm nodded. "I keep forgetting *that*, too."

"No, you don't," I smiled. "You just like having me remind you."

The smile reappeared. "Maybe."

"Now, tell me why I am here and not snuggled next to my girlfriend."

Norm frowned. "Snuggled? In this heat?" he asked incredulously.

"Metaphorically speaking," I replied.

It was hard to ignore the sudden memory of my girlfriend's damp skin against mine, though, for in truth we *had* been snuggled together atop a comforter I'd spread across the wooden slats of my back porch when the call had come in. The cool ocean breeze my bungalow enjoyed had brought some small measure of relief from the brutal heatwave, making it possible to sleep — or get up to whatever mischief Suzanne Kellerman, M.D., might have had planned for us. Norm caught the smile that appeared on my face and grinned, a clear indicator he'd seen through me completely.

"It's this way," he said, pointing toward the double glass door entrance to the building before handing me a pair of latex gloves. "You'll want these, I think."

My eyebrow arched but I withheld comment as I pulled the gloves on and followed him toward the entrance.

Glancing at the sign for Route One Hobbies hanging out over the sidewalk above us, we walked past the massive display windows, a signature feature for a store that had been in that location since the early 1940s. The building itself was a mirror image of the one a few blocks north that had originally been my family's pharmacy and was now home to Suzanne's medical practice. About the only difference between the two were those very windows, a holdover from the haberdashers that had been the first business in the space. Stepping up toward the double glass doors, I was struck by how they still had the very mid-century angled handles in stainless steel; for some strange reason, they fit the store perfectly despite being worn by age.

Norm held a door open for me and I stepped through to the hobby store proper. My nose was immediately accosted by a pungent, acrid odor, one strong enough that my eyes began to water. It was a far cry from the normally eclectic smell of a space crowded with items as diverse as oil paint supplies and the latest in remotely controlled scale vehicles. A single bank of florescent lights was on in the back of the store, though several of the fixtures were flickering in a way that indicated bulb changes would soon be necessary. What bulbs *were* operational provided far more illumination than the silly carriage lamps on the sidewalk outside, for I could easily make out the half-dozen aisles of perfectly organized merchandise stretching away from me plus the various model airplanes and rockets hanging from the ceiling. Still, I pulled my phone out of my microfiber shorts and kept it handy, suspicious that I might soon need a flashlight to see finer details.

Officer Lydia Smart was standing in the small open space between the door and the first set of aisles, causing me to raise my eyebrows; I was aware that she was on standby that week, so the fact that Norm had felt compelled to call in extra help was intriguing. Continuing to keep his own council, he pointed toward the plate glass windows and the massive model railroad layout that was stationed just in front of them. A sense of dread filled me as I looked at the dark bulk of the diorama, for while I'd never had occasion to take in the detailed miniature version of Windeport that had been created, I'd passed the window with enough regularity to be familiar with the bespectacled figure who could be seen laboring over it daily. Or, as I feared, *had* labored over it.

I caught Norm's arm as he started toward the layout. "Walter Guernsey?"

In the half light of the space, I could see Norm was surprised by my question, but quickly recovered. "Yes."

"Who found him?"

"Caitlyn," he replied.

My eyes widened. "Is she still here?"

"Upstairs in Walter's apartment, with Officer Napier," he nodded. "She called it in; Mark was the responding officer."

"Shit," I breathed. "How is she?"

"Unsettled," he replied. "She found him when she got back from working the swing shift."

I nodded at the oblique reference to Caitlyn's recent divorce; I had no idea what had led to the split that had been formalized in late April. With a pang of guilt, I also realized I'd not known she'd had to move in with her father as a result and presumed that meant Walter had been helping take care of her two children. "Are the kids with her ex-husband?"

"Yes," Norm confirmed. "That was the main reason she came into the store before going upstairs — since the lights were on, Caitlyn assumed Walter was working on the layout and had lost track of time. He's apparently done that before when the kids aren't here."

I glanced at the layout. "I take it she smelled whatever that is when she entered?"

Norm nodded. "And like any good investigator, traced it to the source," he added, nodding to the layout.

"Damn," I breathed.

"Yeah," Norm agreed before turning back toward the diorama.

The layout itself stretched the entire length of the plate glass windows but didn't appear to be more than a few feet wide; the entire base was wrapped in a dark curtain to hide the infrastructure holding the diorama up. Overhead, a valance of sorts hid spotlights that must have highlighted important areas on the layout, though none of them were currently on. Taking it all in at once, I was impressed with the way the layout had essentially been framed to focus the attention on the scale rolling hills and small structures that were scattered across the surface; it had an almost museum-level quality to the presentation.

Kneeling, Norm pulled back a portion of the curtain before looking at me. "There's not a lot of clearance under here, so watch your head."

I nodded and dropped into a crouch, then followed Norm underneath the surface of the layout. He'd found some sort of makeshift tunnel between sets of two-by-fours that served as legs to the structure; snapping on the flashlight from my iPhone, I played the light over tidy bundles of wiring that were neatly tacked to the underside of the styrofoam base for the layout, providing the power and/or magic for the diorama. Shelves had been erected between the two-by-fours, allowing stacks of small boxes to be carefully stored out of sight of the store's patrons. Running my light down the boxes told me little other than they seemed to be in as perfect order as the merchandise out in the store proper. Norm moved out into an opening and stood, then stepped aside so I could enter the same space; it was a small rectangle in the center of the layout, barely large enough for one, let alone two plus a dead body.

Shifting our positions slightly, I was able to crouch beside the lifeless form of Walter Guernsey; he was slumped against an exposed two-by-four, dressed in an apron bearing the logo for Route One Hobbies, a white button down, jeans and sneakers. His balding head of white hair was resting against the wood and was turned slightly away from me, his eyes, sightless, staring into the darkness below the layout. Those trademark spectacles of his were missing, though, which made his face seem more youthful in some way. Playing my iPhone's light along the commercial tile, I couldn't see where the glasses had gone, nor was there any indication of broken glass. Returning to Guernsey, the state of what little hair he had seemed unusual to me on second glance, for every one of them seemed to be standing on end as though a staticky balloon had been run over his head.

The pasty complexion of the face told me he'd been in that position long enough for the blood to have begun to pool in his lower sections; even with my gloves, I was reluctant to press a finger to his face to gauge the body's temperature, but I figured at that point he was quite likely already at room temperature. I did reach to an arm and gingerly tried to move it; there was some resistance, possibly indicating that rigor had already passed. My eyes traveled down the arm to the hand that was holding a small rectangular box with a round dial on the face; it was connected to a cable that ran back to a receptacle embedded inside of the layout. The skin surrounding the box had been blackened severely; leaning closer, I took a cautious sniff and unscientifically concluded it was contributing to the acrid smell in the store. Shifting my position slightly, I could see similar singe marks on the other hand as well, a clear indicator that Walter had been holding the device in both hands when whatever happened, happened.

Following the cable back to the layout a second time, I shined my flashlight around the plug and saw how the wood around it had telltale burn marks. Looking back at Walter, I examined first one sneaker, then the other before locating the scorch marks around the big toe of the right foot. Leaning back on my haunches, I slowly nodded; while I wasn't an expert by any stretch, I was seeing all the classic hallmarks of an electrocution. Standing, I turned to Norm.

"Unless I'm wrong, it looks like a rather sizable current travelled through his right hand, across his body to the ground via his right foot."

"That's my read, too." Norm waved at the ceiling. "The short appears to have taken out a portion of the electrical system for the store. The POS systems are fried, as are most of the circuits for this end of the building."

My eyebrows went up. Looking at the store anew, I started to run the possibilities. "Was it a problem with the wiring? It is an old building."

"I'm not sure it was," Norm said. "The panel looked fairly new. Caitlyn might know if work had been done recently."

"It might be worth having the electrical inspector for the Village take a look," I mused.

"I can talk to Hank and see when he can get here."

"Good. Was there a surge from the power company?"

Norm shifted on his feet. "I've not called them yet," he replied. "Mostly because something that large from the street would have toasted the *entire* building, not just the forward end."

I frowned. "The apartment was unaffected?"

"Yes," Norm confirmed.

I looked back at the body of the former proprietor and the small device he was holding. "What is that, exactly?"

"Throttle controller for the layout," Norm replied. "My father was into model railroading," he explained when I turned toward him again. "I've spent many an hour working on miniature steam engines and planting scale pine trees. It's plugged into a transformer that powers the layout; it's a melted mass just behind that piece of wood."

"Can they overload?" I asked, kneeling to look where he'd indicated. There was a twisted pile of something on a small shelf behind the wood that was the definitive source of the melted plastic smell.

"No," Norm replied. "And *that* is why I called you."

I looked at him. "Tell me more."

Kneeling next to me, Norm tapped at the gizmo with a gloved finger. "This is actually a fairly modern configuration; the transformer automatically shuts down in cases where there is an overload in order to protect the sensitive electronics of the layout." He beckoned me to stand, and I did; leaning across the layout, he picked up a small train. "Want to guess how much one of these little beauties costs?"

I shrugged. "A hundred bucks?"

Norm smiled. "Maybe back when this store was founded. Try three to five."

My eyes widened. "What's inside that thing?"

"All sorts of electronics," he replied as he carefully set it back down on a small track. "Electronics that control speed, sound, direction, lighting, you name it." Norm pointed back to the transformer. "Which is why those things are not supposed to short out like that; you'd be looking at thousands of dollars of damage."

"That looks to be a pretty serious short," I said. "This entire layout might be toast, too," I added sadly.

"Possibly," Norm agreed. "We may know more after we go through it."

I looked at him for a long moment. "You don't think this was an accident," I said. It was a statement, not a question.

"No," he replied. "Suspicious for sure. Malicious, well," he sighed, "I'm not there. Yet."

"All right," I nodded. "Then let's begin. Call the State and have them send the wagon for our victim, then see if you can reach Heather Graham at the Crime Lab. If she's available, we can have her team go over everything with a fine-tooth comb."

Norm smiled that boyish smile at me. "I was hoping you'd say that."

I rolled my eyes. "You already called them, didn't you?"

"I've been getting better at asking for forgiveness," he chuckled.

"That you have," I replied as I shook my head. "It's a good thing I like you, Norm. Otherwise, you might find yourself on the graveyard shift over Christmas."

"Understood," he replied. "Heather should be here in less than an hour; the morgue van was coming with her."

"Come on, then," I said, nodding at the apartment above us. "Let's go talk to Caitlyn before the techs arrive."

I followed Norm back through the small makeshift tunnel and into the store proper; from there, he led me to a door set between two shelves of magazines that led to the stockroom. The space was much as I remembered the pharmacy had once been like, with rows of boxes stacked in informal aisles on one side, and a small work area to the other. A large rolling door was at the far end, perfect to receive larger deliveries; closer to us was a standard metal exit door that we pushed through to the tiny rear parking lot behind the building. Caitlyn's car was parked beside the SUV Norm was driving; two patrol cars were on the street behind them. A large floodlight pointed the way to the exterior staircase leading to the apartment above the store, and I followed Norm up to the very attractive front door. It was slightly ajar, so we pushed through into the short hallway beyond. The general floorpan was incredibly similar to Suzanne's apartment, and for a moment, I half expected to see the Disney-themed cozy covering a teapot in the kitchen as we passed it.

Like the store below it, the apartment was scrupulously arranged though it was spare in appointments. We found Caitlyn sitting at a cottage-style dining table sharing a cup of coffee with Officer Napier; at our approach, he nodded and stood to retreat into the living room just beyond the table. My ace administrative officer looked up at me, her red-rimmed eyes telling me everything I needed to know. Death was never an easy subject; in my years as an investigator, I'd always found it emotionally wrenching talking to loved ones who had lost someone so suddenly, and usually, so violently.

It was several magnitudes more difficult when you knew the loved one personally.

I gestured toward a chair. "May I?"

"Please," she said.

Pulling the chair out, I settled in beside her; Norm remained standing but took up a position leaning against the island for the kitchen, his omnipresent tablet unobtrusively ready to take notes. I reached for Caitlyn's hand. "Cait, I am truly sorry. I can only imagine what you're going through."

"Thanks, Chief," she said, her voice a bit ragged.

"I know this isn't an ideal time, but I need to ask you a few questions if you feel up to it."

A tired smile appeared. "I know the drill," she replied. "Probably better than most."

"That you would," I smiled back. "I didn't know your father as well as I could have, but he seemed like a gentle soul," I began, easing into the discussion. "Did I ever tell you that he came to me after you interviewed?"

Caitlyn's eyes widened. "No," she replied.

"Yeah," I nodded. "He asked me some tough questions about the life of someone working in the department. Walter was worried I was going to put you into harm's way, but I reminded him that anyone who graduated in the top five percent of the Justice Academy was exceptionally equipped for anything I might throw at them."

The smile I'd hoped to see appeared on her face. "That sounds like my dad," she said softly. "He never gave the slightest indication he was worried about my choice of vocation, though he did take an insane amount of pride over my achievements at the Academy."

"That he did," I said.

"He did make it clear how much happier he was when I took over Dispatch/Intake," she continued. "Especially after I had Daniel."

"Our industry isn't terribly family friendly," I sighed. "You shouldn't be on swing."

Caitlyn squeezed my hand. "It's the only way I can make this work," she replied. "The child support from Nick doesn't go that far."

I nodded again, unwilling to voice my dismay that her ex-husband's lawyer had successfully portrayed Caitlyn as the breadwinner in the family owing to how variable Nicolao Romero's income was as a general contractor. That she had managed to get *any* money out of him seemed to have been a miracle, though the fact he was still somehow able to pay the mortgage on their three-bedroom home on the outskirts of town still galled me. "Norm told me the lights in the store caught your attention," I said, moving our conversation closer to the subject at hand.

She nodded. "I saw it on my walk back from the station. I assumed Dad was focused on his latest addition to the layout and didn't realize how late it was, though I was surprised the spots over the diorama were off."

"You couldn't see him from the street?"

"No," she shook her head. "That made me think he'd gone to bed and just forgotten to turn off a bank of lights. I went in through the stock room to turn them off myself, but then I caught a whiff of that smell."

I nodded at Norm. "You touched the door on the way in?" I asked.

"Yes," she nodded. "Plus the light switches by the rear door, and the larger bank of switches just inside the store. I grew a bit more worried when I couldn't get anything to turn on, so that's when I started to search the store. I didn't touch anything else other than the curtain around the layout."

"Good," I said. "We'll still need to take your prints, but I imagine they will be all over the store."

"Probably," she agreed. "Mostly around the checkout counter, though. I've not had a lot of time to help Dad with the store like I used to."

"Understandable." I paused again. "I'm sorry this will be your last memory of your father."

"You know, when you have an older parent, you tend to think about all of the ways that you might find them, when the time comes," Caitlyn replied. "I'm not sure I had 'electrocuted by a toy train' on my list, though."

"We don't always get a chance to choose when it happens," I said softly. "Given how he loved to work on that layout, hopefully he died doing what he loved."

Caitlyn chuckled. "I suppose he did. My grandfather started the store back in 1943," she continued, her eyes going distant with memory. "The first version of the layout appeared within a year. Dad updated it when he took over, then continued to revamp it as the times changed."

I felt myself frown. "It's supposed to be a hyper-accurate model of

Windeport, right?" I asked. "Our village hasn't changed enough since your grandfather's time for that many adjustments."

"As an Olympic swimmer, you probably didn't have much time to pick up a hobby when you were a kid," Caitlyn said, her brown eyes narrowing with humor.

"*Other* than swimming? Guilty as charged," I smiled.

"I figured. One thing to understand is that with something like model railroading, the work is never actually complete. It wasn't *just* that there were updates to the Village that he wanted represented; no, with each change in technology, Gramps would update his layout accordingly. My father did the same thing." She smiled again, this time fondly. "Dad was never happier than we he had the entire electronics torn apart."

"He was pretty good at it, then?" I asked carefully. "The electronics?"

"Yes," she nodded, her expression turning serious. "*Especially* the electronics. He got his degree in Electrical Engineering from UEM." Caitlyn paused. "Sean, I know what it looks like downstairs, but I just can't accept Dad died as a result of an accident."

"It does happen," I replied gently.

"I know that," she said. "But I'm telling you, it's not possible in this case. Dad had *just* finished rewiring the layout; part of that work was updating the main panel for the store to something more modern."

I thought back to the tidy bundles of wire I'd seen beneath the diorama. "Did he update the transformer, too?"

"Yes. *Everything* was new."

I glanced at Norm, who was leaning against the half-wall for the kitchen. "Everything?"

"Everything," Caitlyn replied.

I squeezed her hand. "Then we will dig into this a bit more. We'll need access— "

"You'll have it," she replied promptly. "To anything you need. I'm on the business and deed to the building, so there won't be any issues."

I nodded. "The State will be here soon and will need to turn everything inside out. And you know the other part of the drill, I'll need you to formally identify your father for us, either here or down at the morgue."

"Here would be easier," she replied. "Unless I can find someone to take the kids if I have to go to Augusta."

"We'll try and keep it here, then," I said, making a mental note to see if Charlie might be able to recommend someone who could do childcare in a pinch. Movement at the edge of the kitchen caught my attention; Officer Smart had appeared, and I nodded at her. "Speaking of the State," I continued as I stood. "I'll head down and get them going, then I'll have someone come and get you when we are ready. Will that work?"

"Yes," Caitlyn said. "Thank you."

I nodded and turned to go but paused at the hallway. Turning back, I looked at Caitlyn. "When was the electrical work completed?"

"This spring," she replied. "Nick—oh, shit," she breathed, her eyes going wide. "Nick was the one doing the work. He's going to be sick when he hears what happened."

I tried to keep my face impassive but traded a look with Norm who subtly nodded. "Did Nick to the *actual* work?" I asked.

Caitlyn looked at me and frowned. "I understand why you had to ask that," she replied, "but whatever else my ex-husband is, his professionalism is second to none."

"You told me earlier that it couldn't be an accident," I reminded her. "That doesn't give me a whole ton of wriggle room here. At the very least, something was done incorrectly during the update."

She sighed and pinched the bridge of her nose. "Yes, I suppose you're right; I'm too close to this, I think. And to answer your other question, Nick would have used a subcontractor for the electrical work. His talents are more on framing and cabinetry."

"Got it," I said, looking at Norm again before turning back to Caitlyn. "Do you have anyone that can stay with you? Besides the kids?"

"No."

"Then why don't you pack a few things and come stay with Suzanne and me," I offered. "Just for a few days — until the crime scene techs are done."

"I'm not sure — I'm supposed to have the kids tomorrow," she replied. "I don't think your bungalow is big enough for all of us."

"We'll deal with that tomorrow," I said gently. "After you've gotten a bit of sleep and a good meal or two."

Caitlyn smiled tiredly. "I won't refuse a comfortable bed and a warm shower at this point."

"Good. I'll run you over after we've spoken with the M.E., okay?"

"Okay," she replied.

I went over to her and leaned down to give her a quick hug. "We'll get you through this. Trust me."

"Of that, I have no doubt," she chuckled.

Two

As it turned out, the Medical Examiner arrived first, allowing me to get Caitlyn's official identification of the victim taken care of straight away. I left Norm to oversee their activities so I could take my administrative officer to the bungalow and a waiting Suzanne; my girlfriend quickly took charge of our temporary house-guest, ushering her straight to our guest room and a few hours of rest. By the time I returned to Route One Hobbies, the first glow of sunrise had begun to appear on the horizon, a gentle reminder that the day was moving forward whether I wanted it to or not. I'd intended on parking at the rear of the store only to find my plans thwarted by the large, unmarked van the crime scene techs used; while the driver had tried to keep one space open in the small lot, the only vehicle I knew to be small enough to fit would have come from the Disneyland Autopia. Though traffic out on Route One was still light, it still took me a few minutes to circle around and claim a spot on the curb in front of the store.

I found Norm standing in front of the layout talking to Heather Graham, the senior field tech for the State. Multiple portable work lights had been stationed around the diorama, flooding the area in brilliant white; a crew was setting up another handful along the aisles of the store, finally giving us some much-needed illumination. The cables snaking out the rear of the store to the generators powering everything were a bit of a hazard, though, despite the yellow-and-black tape that had been used to fasten them to the commercial tile. Glancing at the layout, I realized the harsh white of the portable lamps made the details seem less than carefully crafted; the tall steeple for the tiny replica of Saint Catherine's By-The-Sea looked as though it was bent slightly. I wondered if the selective spots in the valance overhead and been designed to hide such flaws.

"Suzanne's making sure Caitlyn is settling in," I said to Norm before shaking Heather's hand. "Good to see you again, Heather."

"It's been a busy few weeks here in Greater Windeport, hasn't it?" she smiled.

"That it has," I nodded. "The Village Council isn't my biggest fan right now."

"I imagine not," she replied. "How's the lawsuit going?"

"Just awesome," I frowned. "I'm meeting with their lawyers later today to discuss options for settlement."

Her eyebrows went up. "Settlement? What's there to *settle*?"

I shrugged. "Who knows. I suspect they want my head on a silver platter, along with some unspecified, albeit massive, amount of money."

"You're not going to do it, are you?" Heather asked quietly. "You didn't do anything wrong."

I shrugged again. "That's for Professional Standards to decide still. I meet with the panel formally tomorrow."

"Shit," she breathed. "This is shaping up to be the week from hell for you."

"Yeah, no kidding."

In truth, I'd been trying to block out the twin threats of the Professional Standards investigation into my handling of the Brogan case and the wrongful arrest civil lawsuit my prime suspect, Shelly West, had filed over it. If not for a rookie mistake on my part, the confession I'd gotten on tape from Shelly would have ensured her spending twenty-five to life as a guest of the State of Maine; without it, all I had was decades old circumstantial evidence Shelly's high-priced lawyer had successfully argued was just that — circumstantial. The District Attorney had therefore passed on pressing charges, and I'd been forced to watch Shelly walk out of my jail and straight into civil court, intent on extracting some sort of retribution. The Village Council had quickly informed me that Windeport would not be defending me, another sign of the continuing erosion of their faith in me; fortunately, I had enough stashed in my savings to pay the initial retainer for the lawyer my friend, State Police Captain James Roberts, had recommended but knew that was a one-time thing. If the case dragged into the fall, I'd have to start making some drastic choices financially.

Hence why I was blocking it.

"I've got some prelims for you, if you're ready," Heather said, pulling me out of my thoughts.

"That was fast," I said.

"Sort of," she replied. "The medical examiner has already done most of the legwork; we're still going through the store, but honestly, I'm not sure what we'll find."

"I figured as much," I nodded. "Time of death?"

"Best estimate from liver temp is between six and eight last night," she replied. "COD seems obvious — electrocution — but I'll leave that delineation to Lou."

"Don't tell me — the Chief Medical Examiner herself will be doing the postmortem?"

"You know it," Heather laughed before sobering. "If it helps, now that we know you have to be in Augusta tomorrow for the Professional Standards hearing, we can schedule the autopsy around it."

"It would," I nodded. "I can't believe I'm saying this, but the PM is likely to be the highlight of my day."

"Insane." Heather pointed to the layout and the several techs that were dusting it for prints. "There's plenty of evidence pointing to some sort of massive electrical short," she said. "We're still tracing the lines to get the full picture."

"We're going to bring in an expert to look over the electrical," I said.

"Hold off on that, actually," Heather replied. "We have one that works with our office; I've already contacted him. With luck, he should get here mid-morning and can do a thorough once-over."

"All right."

"To my untrained eye, though," she continued, "that box you and Norm found beneath this diorama—"

"The transformer," Norm interjected.

"Yes," Heather nodded. "That seems to have been the major source of the malfunction. We've bagged and tagged it and will have the nerds back at the lab go through it."

"There wasn't much left of it," I said.

"We've worked with far less," she reminded me. "We've also taken the small control box that the victim was holding. I'm less certain if that was a contributing part, or just a conduit. Again, the techs — and our expert — will be able to piece that part of the story together far better for us."

"Here's hoping." I watched one of the techs for a moment. "Did you find a pair of spectacles under there?"

Heather looked at me. "Not yet. Why?"

"Victim normally wore a pair," I said, "but they were missing when we found him."

"We'll be on the lookout, then," she said thoughtfully before turning toward the layout. "This is a rather remarkable piece of work. I can't believe how detailed it is."

"It is," I nodded.

"Looks like someone broke the steeple to the church, though," Heather observed, drawing my attention back to the miniature of Saint Catherine's.

Moving closer, I realized that what I'd written off as a flaw was, in fact, damage. "Huh," I muttered as I squinted at it. That close, the intricate detail of the church was quite visible, including what looked like individually placed stones for the walkways and realistically crafted stained-glass windows. Even the grass looked as though it had individual blades. The door to the parish hall beside the church was open slightly, too, and I could just make out a tiny poster for some social event. The detail was quite remarkable. "Can you get prints or trace off any of that?"

"Sure," she replied. "Why?"

"Tell me if that looks like someone brushed against it," I said as I stood to the side.

Heather stooped down and squinted. "Huh," she repeated. "I see what you mean. It would be in the right line for someone reaching across the table from this side."

"That's what I thought, too," I said. "Can you photograph everything? Top and bottom?"

"Already on our list," she replied, arching an eyebrow at me. "What are you thinking?"

"Nothing, yet," I demurred. "Anything else of interest?"

"Not really, no," she replied. "We still have a few more hours of work ahead of us, though. Don't you normally do a morning workout?"

I glanced at my smart watch. "Yeah," I sighed. "Practice started twenty minutes ago."

"Then go and come back when you're finished," she encouraged. "Or at the very least, get some breakfast."

Knowing what kind of a day was still ahead, I thought a few thousand meters in the pool might be rather beneficial. "If you insist," I said, looking at Norm.

"I'll stay," he replied to my unasked question. "I can run at lunchtime."

"Then I am out of here," I said. "See you in few hours."

Truth be told, given the kind of day I'd had so far — hell, the kind of *month* for that matter — sneaking off to the pool for a few hours was exactly what I needed to keep some semblance of balance; my increasingly aggressive workouts, when combined with Suzanne's nightly ministrations had gone a long way toward maintaining my sanity. Taking a last long look at the scene, I bowed to Heather and Norm, then made my way out the front of the store and to my waiting SUV. I spied my swim backpack in the back seat as I slid behind the wheel and smiled at the prospect of the momentary respite it represented before pulling out into traffic. The lights were on inside Suzanne's practice as I drove past the old pharmacy building; a quick glance at the clock on my dashboard only confirmed that she'd gone to the office way too early once again in her continuing efforts to get ahead of the never-ending insurance paperwork that threatened to drown her. Suzanne's dedication to her patients was extraordinary, though I knew the effort it took to keep her practice going was beginning to wear her down. I'd noticed the first traces of gray in her otherwise raven head of hair around Valentine's Day and had begun my own campaign to try and keep her de-stressed.

We're a matched set, aren't we? I thought as I turned onto Route 203. *Perfect mirrors.*

Triggering the Bluetooth function for my phone, I speed-dialed my girlfriend; she picked up on the first ring. "Hey, kitty," she said brightly. I'd never gotten tired of the nickname she'd tagged me with after that first night she saw me in the Chat Noir costume. "Was that your vehicle that just went by?"

"It was, Milady," I replied, staying in character. "The crime scene nerds are working their way through the store, so I've got some time to kill."

"Which means you're probably headed to the pool," she laughed.

"Exactly," I chuckled. "Unless you want to make me a better offer."

"I do have a new exam table in room three," Suzanne mused. "Why don't you make a U-turn and let me test it out by examining you from head-to-toe?"

"You did that last night, Doctor," I reminded her.

"I might have missed something. It wouldn't hurt to be thorough."

"I suppose not," I chuckled. "As tempted as I am to be your test subject, I suspect professional ethics would rule out such activities during business hours."

"Maybe for police officers," she replied. "We physicians have a far simpler creed: do no harm."

"I don't think Hippocrates was referring to you jumping your boyfriend in an exam room."

"I hear he was an advocate for the healing power of sex," Suzanne chuckled.

"Well, as much as I hate to disagree with the head of your order, so to speak, I will take a rain check on your kind offer — one that I will cash in this evening."

Suzanne chuckled. "That's rather presumptuous of you. What if I had other plans?"

"That would be too bad," I replied before going in for the kill. "So much for modeling that new competitive swimsuit I bought for regionals."

"Well, if you put it that way," she chuckled. "Enjoy your time at the pool; I suspect you could use the workout. How bad is it, anyway? Caitlyn only told me a little before I tucked her into bed. The poor woman was exhausted."

"I'm not surprised. She worked the swing shift last night before coming home to find her father dead."

"Oh *shit*," she breathed. "You left that little detail out when you asked me to take her in."

"That's my fault," I sighed. "I've got a lot on my brain these days."

"Don't I know it. Look, Sean," she added with a note of seriousness, "don't overdo it in the water, okay? It would be just like you to tear a rotator cuff or something in your pursuit of tranquility."

"I'll be careful, Doctor," I chuckled as the campus of UEM appeared. "See you tonight."

"Hugs and kisses," she replied before the line went dead.

The parking lot for the aquatics center was modestly full when I pulled in; at that part of the summer calendar, my Masters swim team owned the space until the age group swimmers arrived at seven and kicked us out. Glancing at the clock on my dashboard once more, I calculated whether I had enough of a margin to still squeeze in a full workout before I'd need to clear the deck myself and judged it might *just* be possible — though it would come at the cost of possibly not being able to use the locker room afterward. Enough scandals had rocked the swimming world over the past few years to have created a sizable set of new rules governing how those under eighteen interacted with adults, including ensuring they would never share the same space at any time. I didn't disagree with the new rules by any stretch; rather, I was incensed that they were necessary in the first place. There had never been any room in my world for those who preyed on children.

Parking the SUV, I grabbed my bag out of the backseat and fairly dashed through the side door to the center. One quick change in the locker room later and I was striding across the deck toward the bleachers in my swimsuit, cap and goggles looking for a place to stash my backpack. Owing to my unique position as the only former Olympian still in town, Coach always set aside a lane for me and anyone else that wanted to partake in the brutal workout he put me through daily. Vasily had been the only other person who'd ever shared the lane with me; since his departure a year earlier, I'd pretty much been guaranteed clear water and the freedom to run the workout at my own pace.

After greeting Coach and waving to a few of my fellow swimmers, I moved over to my lane and then paused for a moment to do a quick set of stretches; despite having healed remarkably well, the bicep where I had taken a bullet didn't always want to release properly, though that morning it seemed to be behaving itself. Pressing the goggles to my eyes to ensure they had sealed properly, I stepped up to the block for my lane and did a quick racing dive into the cool water of the pool; stretching my arms forward, I dolphin-kicked to the ten-yard mark before breaking the surface and beginning my first set of the morning.

We were doing short course that day, so I hit the wall at twenty-five yards and flipped, then came up and continued the long strokes of my freestyle. After the first six hundred yards, I switched to butterfly and felt the tension along my spine as my back muscles were pushed into overdrive; the ache always felt invigorating, though at my age it also meant I'd probably want a few minutes in the hot tub later, too. Four hundred of fly had me pleasantly warmed up and ready for the main set of the day; it appeared to be focused on the upper body, which equated to a ton of pulling and not a lot of kicking. It also meant it was fairly easy for me to shift the workout to autopilot and allow my brain to begin to process the events of the morning.

I couldn't deny that Norm seemed to be on to something, for I too had come away from the scene at Route One Hobbies thinking how improbable Walter Guernsey's death had been. It wasn't much more than a gut feeling at that point, with little to support it other than a general unease at what we had found; if the proprietor did indeed have a background in Electrical Engineering, it would be beyond ironic for him to have electrocuted himself. Then again, I had dealt with several dozen accidental deaths during my career in Windeport; strange things *did* happen, and, appropriately, often took place when you least expected them to be.

Wasn't it just last summer that Bernadette Gardner had leaned too far into her chest freezer and accidentally fallen in? I asked myself. *Reaching for that five-pound pack of hamburger may have cost her everything, but I didn't immediately think she'd been murdered, either. And yet... I do think this was suspicious.*

Shifting from being on my stomach to my back for the next set, I stared at the skylights of the aquatics center while I mused on what was troubling me the most.

Caitlyn says the wiring was just updated, so that rules out some flaw in ancient cabling from being the culprit. But that does bring her ex-husband into the picture, doesn't it? Would he have had anything to gain from offing Walter?

I didn't know enough about the divorce to say it had been without acrimony; neither did I know Nick well enough to gauge whether he'd been bitter enough to take out his ex-father-in-law in retribution. I thought I had met him a time or two at various social gatherings we'd had for the department, but my memories of him were a bit fuzzy, like he'd been a wallflower unwilling to fully participate. As I hit the wall again, I was forced to remind myself I had no idea what had triggered the split in the first place, nor had I been aware that Caitlyn had moved in with her father. Apparently, I'd been way too focused on my recovery from the gunshot wounds I'd received in California to have even had a quiet conversation to see how my ace admin was handling her situation. I suspected Suzanne probably knew everything, given how connected she was to the community; if not her, my cousin Charlie likely had heard a thing or two in her capacity as Director of the Windeport Public Library. More than once I'd swung by her cozy office to get the pulse of the Village, for nearly everyone came through her impressive structure at one point or another.

Thinking about Charlie reignited my personal curiosity over the layout featured in Route One Hobbies; in the short time I'd spent looking it over that morning, I'd come away impressed with the level of detail and felt badly that I'd not checked it out before. Considering I'd grown up in Windeport, it was kind of sad in a way. A part of me was seriously looking forward to making up for that oversight when I returned to the hobby store to review Heather's findings; it didn't hurt that her crime scene techs would take extensive photos of it as part of their process, either, a perk that would allow me to pour over the layout in far greater detail later.

That triggered a thought. *Caitlyn mentioned that the layout was started when Route One Hobbies opened back in the 1940s; I wonder if the library has any newspaper clippings of the opening? I'd love to see how the layout started versus where it is today.*

Hitting the wall, I paused and looked at the massive clock hanging on the wall. I'd been in the water a bit longer than I'd realized — long enough that I had missed my window to use the locker room. Pushing myself out onto the deck, I pulled off my cap and goggles and walked over to my waiting backpack; fishing around the bag, I quickly toweled off the worst of the chlorinated water with one hand while I dialed my cousin's cell phone. She picked up on the third ring.

"Hey, cousin. You're not calling me at this ungodly hour to say you and Suzanne are bailing on dinner?"

I frowned, having completely forgotten the cookout her daughters had insisted we do despite it being in the middle of the week. Apparently, s'mores weren't just for weekends anymore. "It's barely six-thirty, Charlie. Ungodly is two; I should know, I've been up since then. And yes, if you don't mind an extra guest."

"Heavens, no," Charlie replied. "I presume it's Caitlyn; you'll have to warn her how the twins hog the chocolate. She's likely to just have melted marshmallow between two wafers of cookie."

I felt my eyebrows go up. "News travels fast," I replied, looking at the clock again.

"Not as fast as an angry Chair of the Village Council," Charlie chuckled. "Apparently, the vehicles from the state are a tad obvious along Main Street; she was pounding at my door a bit past five to see if I knew what was going on."

I rolled my eyes. "Violet has my cell phone," I sighed. "She could have called me directly."

"Maybe she doesn't like confrontation?" Charlie asked innocently.

"Clearly you've never seen my new boss during Council meetings." Violet Kepler had been elected to the Windeport Village Council the prior November and had been rather outspoken about how much it cost to run the public safety services. I thought it was wise we didn't have a live feed of the meetings.

"I hear it's a hot ticket," Charlie laughed.

"It's a matter of perspective," I sighed. "What did you tell her?"

"That my cousin was a paragon of truth, justice and the American Way and would never gossip about a case."

I felt a smirk on my face. "Did you crib that from Superman?"

"Yes," Charlie replied. "I'm impressed — I didn't think you read comic books."

"Suzanne has been helping me catch up. I'm not sure Violet would have gotten the reference, though."

"Highly doubtful, based on her response to me." Charlie paused. "So, what *is* the scoop?"

"Wouldn't telling you that make me a hypocrite?"

"I have no idea. Spill."

I glanced at the pool and saw that for the moment, I was reasonably alone. I quickly gave my cousin a sanitized, light on the details overview of what had happened; much like Suzanne, I had often leaned on her as an informal consultant and trusted her implicitly. "It was kind of depressing, actually," I said as I finished my summary. "Caitlyn seems to be handling it pretty well, but Suzanne and I are going to keep an eye on her for a bit just in case."

"She's strong, but that's also wise. Does she have the kids this week? Maybe you should send her my way."

"I was thinking of asking you, actually, but that's not why I was calling."

"Oh?"

"No. Are you already at the library?"

"Not yet," she replied. "I am barely halfway through prepping my angels for art day camp, which doesn't start until eight. Besides, we're still on summer hours."

"Ah," I deadpanned. "So, you open at eight-thirty instead of eight?"

"Very funny, wise guy," she chuckled. "Why do you ask? Did you need something?"

"Kind of," I said as I put the towel down on the bleacher seat and then sat. Idly whirling my goggles on a finger, I watched as the pool tech began his daily ritual of dipping the chemistry unit into the far end of the pool as I spoke. "As you can imagine, I spent more than a few minutes taking in that incredible layout Walter was always working on while I was at the store this morning. It got me thinking it would be interesting to see how it had changed from the original version his grandfather built when the store opened back in the 1940s."

"You're wondering if the library has any historical photos of the layout over the years?" Charlie asked. "We probably do. I'll look when I get in and call you if I find anything."

"I'd appreciate that," I said.

"Are you looking for anything specific?"

The pool tech had been holding the plastic gizmo up to the light, checking the colors of the water inside against the key on the side of the device. Based on how he was shaking his head, I began to wonder if my brown hair was about to become a shade or two lighter. "I'm not sure," I said. "Maybe? I guess I'll know it when I see it."

There was a long pause at the other end. "You really do think Walter's death is suspicious, don't you?"

"Yeah," I sighed as the tech knelt again and started to test the water once more.

"Why? If you don't mind my asking."

"I don't know," I replied. "A hunch, I guess."

"Your hunches are usually right."

"Don't remind me," I sighed again.

"I'll call as soon as I've located what we have in the archives."

"Thanks, Cousin. I owe you."

"I'll put it on your tab," she chuckled.

Three

The rather loud rumble my stomach issued when I slid behind the wheel of my SUV had me detour through Calista's to pick up a freshly-baked blueberry muffin and an extra-large coffee to go; while not exactly the best way to refuel after a grueling workout, I was on a bit of a schedule and had no time for my usual oatmeal (or a shower, for that matter). Heather had texted me just as I was pulling my muscle t-shirt back on that her team was nearly done at Route One Hobbies — and that they were needed down in South China for a floater that had popped up on Three Mile Pond. I managed to polish off the muffin before pulling into a miraculously open slot just behind the van from the Crime Lab, but the coffee was still white hot, owing to it having come from a freshly made pot. Grabbing it from the cupholder in the SUV, I thought it was entirely on brand for me to tote it to the scene; as I entered the store, I could see from the slight smirk on both Norm *and* Heather's face they agreed.

"It's my first of the day," I said defensively.

Heather's eyes danced with merriment, but she passed on any further comment. "I'm sorry to skip out on you so quickly, but I think we've covered what we needed to here. I wouldn't be upset, though, if you kept the space on ice for a day or two."

I arched my eyebrow. "We can do that," I replied. "Why?"

"My electrical guru can't get here until tomorrow," she apologized. "Though it might be the day after. I didn't know he was working on a big case out in Western Maine; it's taking longer than he expected, but he's promised to drive to Windeport the moment he gets free."

"That's not a problem," I nodded. "Unless Caitlyn's insurance carrier needs access right away."

"They don't," Norm interjected. "I've already spoken with the adjuster from Allied Mutual; *they* are also tied up on a microburst down in Raymond that took out a slew of high-priced waterfront homes along Sebago."

My eyebrows went up. "Did I miss a memo? Are we at the end of times?"

"Don't worry, I've not seen any locusts," Heather laughed. "Not yet at least."

"What have you got?" I asked, keenly aware that aside from Heather and a single tech packing up a small toolbox, the store was quiet.

"Not much," she replied. "We took prints from almost everything and uploaded them to the State system; any hits will appear in the case file you have not yet created for me."

"Ah," I smiled. "I knew I'd forgotten something."

"It was an early morning," Norm offered with a slight trace of a smile.

"That it was."

"Caitlyn's prints are already on file since she's part of the department, so we'll run those as an exclusion right away," Heather continued before taking us to the checkout counter and the point-of-sale system. "One oddity came up over here," she said, picking up a small plastic evidence bag that had been left on the counter and handing it to me.

Holding the bag by an edge, I could easily see it held a pair of glasses. "Walter's?"

"I think so, yes, but we'll check both with Caitlyn and the eye doctor."

I looked to the counter. "They were over here?"

Heather nodded. "On top of the cash drawer, actually."

My eyebrows went up as I looked between the counter and the glasses. "Odd," I said as I held the lenses up to the light. "These look like bifocals, so I can't imagine he would have been able to see much on the layout without them."

"He might be able to see something by getting close-up," Norm offered. "My grandfather used to take his bifocals off in order to tie his fishing lures."

"Hmm," I murmured. "So, he was at the counter? And went to the layout without his glasses?"

"Maybe he was working with a patron?" Norm asked.

"After hours?" I looked to Heather. "We need a better time of death."

"I know. Lou has her hands full, I think."

"Yeah."

Pointing toward the layout, we followed Heather back to the diorama. In the light of the morning, it was even more impressive, a carefully thought-out miniature version of Windeport that just happened to have a set of tracks winding through it. That we had no regular rail service of any kind for the Village in real life seemed to be beside the point. Once more, my eyes strayed to the slightly off-kilter spire for Saint Catherine's, then traced the tiny version of Route One all the way to the faithfully replicated Brutalist nightmare that was the Public Safety Building. I couldn't help but smile at the set of department SUVs carefully parked in front of the station, for one of them was riddled with bullet holes — a clear reference to an incident from nearly eighteen months earlier.

I wonder why that wasn't updated, I thought. *He's got the new lights along Main Street and the running path to UEM; those both went in after that night in February with Bethesda. Maybe it was an inside joke? I'll have to ask Caitlyn.*

Taking a small Q-tip from her pocket, Heather used it to point at the tiny church. "Surprisingly, we were able to get trace off that. Fibers of some kind that we bagged and will run through our magical equipment in Augusta."

"Someone must have a bit of a snag in their outfit," I said, squinting at the small spire as though I could still see the stray filaments upon it.

"Yes, in a dark blue or black." Pointing to the parking lot in front of the church, she continued. "We nearly missed it, but something was placed here — a coffee cup, maybe, or some kind of mug. It left a ring behind that we swabbed and will try and identify."

I scanned the table. "I don't see any mugs or glasses anywhere."

"You won't," Heather shook her head. "The only items we found were in the kitchen upstairs, in the cabinets or dishwasher that was run recently."

"That's... convenient," I observed.

"Isn't it?" Heather chuckled. "And before you wonder how thorough we were, the trash had been emptied both here in the store and upstairs in the apartment."

"Please tell me the dumpster was still full...?"

"Already pulled and put into the back of our van," she replied. "Don't expect much, though — there were only two bags."

"A guy can hope." I looked at Norm. "Someone was here with Walter? And they cleaned up evidence of their presence?"

"That's my read, too," he nodded.

"This just moved from vaguely suspicious to full on suspicious," I said.

"But wait, there's more," Heather chuckled.

"You sound like one of those late-night infomercials," Norm said as he rolled his eyes.

I glanced at him. "Infomercials?"

He frowned. "You don't have cable, do you?"

"No," I shook my head. "Why would I need it? I can get the Red Sox on the radio."

Norm rolled his eyes again. "I'm starting to understand what Vasily had to deal with," he sighed dramatically.

"He used to do *that,* too," I said, trying to keep the smile from my face as I turned back to Heather. "What else did you find?"

"I'm not entirely certain, actually," Heather replied. Using the same Q-Tip, she pointed to the miniature stretch of Route One that represented what passed for downtown in Windeport; my eyes lingered for a moment once more on the ugly Public Safety Building, but moved on to the tiny two-story brick building the cotton swab was hovering over. "Using contextual clues, I'm relatively certain this is supposed to represent Route One Hobbies."

Leaning down, I nodded. "Damn. I think there is a miniature layout inside that window."

"There is," Heather replied. Shifting the Q-Tip slightly in her gloved hand, she reached down and gently grasped the structure. "And for my next magical trick..." she said as she quickly lifted it up.

My eyes widened as she revealed an intricately detailed interior for the store, right down to the aisles full of tiny supplies. "Holy *shit,*" I breathed. "That had to have taken *years* to do."

"Quite likely," she agreed as she carefully set the exterior shell down on the faux asphalt. "Every structure on this layout has at least this level of detail, though some have quite a bit more." Heather smiled. "There is a Keurig in your office at the police station, for example."

"Clearly Caitlyn was feeding him information," I smiled.

"None of the buildings were glued to the base," she continued, "so I am working under the theory that they were designed to be removed from time to time to showcase the interiors." Heather paused. "More than a few were slightly off their marks, though."

I nodded slowly. "So, either Walter was, what, dusting the interiors? Or someone else just *happened* to be curious about what was underneath them recently?"

"Both hypothesis work," she replied. "Though the dead body might tip me toward the latter. I think someone was looking for something."

"You think Walter hid a secret inside his layout?" Norm asked. "What would be important enough to go to all that trouble?"

"That is a question for the two of you to answer," Heather said with mock seriousness. "I just report the evidence."

"So you do." Squinting at the interior of the store — and chiding myself for leaving my cheaters out in the SUV — I took a longer look at the miniature version of the layout. "This feels a bit like looking at one of those endless mirror reflections," I murmured. "Is that actual *track*?"

Heather nodded. "I'm not up on my model railroad scales, but that's the gauge that would allow a version of Portland to be housed in a briefcase."

I stood and held the plastic bag with the bifocals up. "These feel more than necessary now," I said.

"We found lighted magnifying glasses under the layout," Heather said. "I suspect he would have needed both, plus the insanely small set of jeweler's tools that were also on a shelf down there."

"No kidding."

"I'm glad the layout caught your attention, actually," she continued as she went to the iPad she was holding. Tapping at it, she sorted through some photos before tapping on one to enlarge. Turning it toward me, she explained what I was seeing. "We used the ultra-megapixel digital camera to take shots of the entire layout, and then used a macro lens to get the interiors of the buildings. I thought it would be handy to compare the miniature layout inside the miniature Route One Hobbies to the life-size one and stumbled onto this."

The photo was an enlargement of the rear of the store, showing the stock room; it was rather impressive to see that the boxes of various sizes stacked neatly against the walls were all labelled. "Cork roadbed, paint, balsa wood," I read before looking up at Heather. "This detail is extraordinary."

"Keep reading."

Arching an eyebrow, I did as instructed. "White glue, stretched canvas, garden shovels, sandpaper, plastic—hang on, *shovels*?" I looked up at the wider hobby store. "I didn't know they sold garden supplies here."

"They don't," Heather replied. "We've been through every aisle and all the backstock. This is truly just a hobby concern; save for a few scale nuts and bolts, it doesn't even come close to being a hardware store, let alone a garden center."

I looked down at the small box on the photo. "This seems like an odd thing to represent then," I frowned, "given how hyper-accurate everything else is."

"That's why I flagged it," she nodded. "It may be nothing. But it felt otherwise to me."

Norm shrugged when I turned to him. "If it's a clue of some sort, it's not the strangest one I've ever had."

I smiled. "Yeah, isn't that the truth. Okay, write it up; I'll be seeing Caitlyn later, maybe she can shed some light on this."

"It could be an inside joke," Norm offered.

My eyes went to the bullet-ridden SUV. "If it is, we seem to be missing the punchline."

"I'll have everything into the case system by this afternoon, assuming you find time to create the file for me," Heather said as we started toward the front door. The tech had proceeded us out of the shop and was waiting for her by the van. "Lou should be able to schedule your PM ahead of the panel meeting tomorrow, I would think; expect her call a bit later with the details."

"I look forward to it," I replied. "And the file will be ready and waiting."

Heather nodded, then paused. "Did I tell you she plays handball with the head of Professional Standards?"

"I didn't know her network was that diverse. Or that she played handball."

"We all need a way to decompress after work, Sean. And not all of us are dolphins," she chuckled.

I twisted as if looking for something on the small of my back. "Are my gills showing again?" I asked innocently. "I keep intending to get a longer shirt to cover them."

"Your split ends tell the tale far better," Norm deadpanned.

I whirled on him. "*Et tu*, Norm?"

"I only speak the truth," he laughed. "Why do you think I keep my hair so short?"

Eying his somewhat stereotypical police officer crewcut, I replied: "I suppose it would have its advantages. Far less hair product, for sure."

"And much cooler in this mid-July heat."

"Indeed." I turned back to Heather. "Thanks as always for your hard work. I hope that thing down in South China is not as bad as it sounds."

"Floaters are *always* as bad as they sound," she sighed. "Especially for the Coroner."

"Yeah," I smiled ruefully, "I suppose so."

We watched Heather climb into the van, then waved to the crew as they made the difficult merge into the burgeoning morning traffic along Main Street. Sipping at my now tepid coffee, I took a moment to contemplate where the traffic hid during the overnight hours; while I'd gotten a respectable grade for an athlete in my college calculus class, I'd never quite mastered the math behind the classic *two trains leave a station* word problem. If I had, I might have been better equipped to understand how early the day trippers were leaving from Portland, Bangor or even Boston to get to Windeport in time to snarl traffic by nine. Since my watch was claiming it to be barely eight, things were shaping up to be busy in our fair village.

"I'm going to head home so I can shower and don attire more appropriate for my court appearance later today," I said to Norm as we watched the traffic slowly creep past the store.

"I still think that civil case is bullshit," he replied. "And it's pretty shitty the Village isn't paying for your defense."

I shrugged a bit fatalistically. "I seem to have a love-hate relationship with our employer," I replied before looking at him sideways. "This doesn't have you thinking of jumping ship, does it? I mean, I wouldn't blame you if you wanted to be well out of the blast radius if this thing explodes."

"Hell no," Norm said with a vengeance. "It's bullshit. I came here to work with you, and I won't be driven away by some shortsighted politician. Besides, I've already closed on my house."

"I forgot about that," I smiled. "I can't believe you bought that cottage Alejandro had been renting."

"How could I not? The bank had a fire sale price on it after the liquidation of Donohue, Inc.," he smiled, referring to the late developer Vasily had found murdered in his Mercedes the prior summer. "I meant to ask," he continued, his face shading a bit pink, "could I, uh, take Friday off? I know you like a bit more notice, and the timing is shit, what with us working a case— "

"Sure," I nodded. "I figured Raphael would be appearing sooner or later to help you get settled in your new digs."

Norm's face flushed deeper. "How did you—?"

I shrugged again. "The two of you made quite a connection when we were in Las Vegas," I said delicately, and tried not to smile when my young number two's face began to burn a deep, dark red. I figured it was probably wise not to remind him that in his drunken exuberance, he'd told everyone on our flight back to Maine that he'd found his soulmate. "Vasily also clued me in that Raphael was in Boston this week for some sort of regional meeting."

"It wraps tomorrow, and he's going to fly to Bangor first thing Thursday morning. He's, uh, looking at a position that just opened in Bar Harbor."

This time, I did smile. "You're apparently not the only one smitten," I observed sagely.

For just a moment, Norm wore the same uncomfortable look Vasily often got when I struck a bit close to home. "Yeah," he replied simply.

I squeezed his impressive bicep. "I'm glad you've found someone," I said with a smile. "Especially after how things ended with that jerk in South Windham. I've got the PM tomorrow; whatever comes out of that will take some time to dig through. Why don't you pick him up in Bangor and then go with him to Bar Harbor? If you take your laptop, you can do some of that work while you wait for him." I paused. "I have a feeling he might appreciate the company."

Norm's eyes lit up. "Would that be okay? It would save on the car rental."

"Totally," I smiled wider. "I'll see you at the station in a bit."

He nodded. "Thanks, Chief."

"Of course," I replied as I drained the last of my cold coffee and tossed it into a trashcan on the curb.

It took me a few minutes to find a break in traffic large enough to sneak my SUV into; to my dismay, I had to drive nearly to the Village limit before I was able to make a legal U-turn so I could go in the *actual* direction I wanted. As tempted as I was to flip on the lights and blare my siren, I knew it would only serve to panic the tourists even more and, consequently, make it twice as hard to get where I needed to go. That, and I'd seen one of the Village Council members coming out of the IGA about when my finger had been hovering over the appropriate switches; I figured I already had a hard enough day ahead of me without enduring an unexpected visit from a concerned member of our community's leadership.

Turning onto the Sea Road felt like a welcome sigh of relief, tempered slightly by the slight unease I always felt when I passed the stacks of lobster traps that were slowly decomposing in the July sunshine. We'd lost two more from the ranks of those who had still plied the seas beyond Windeport harbor for the crustacean, underscoring how poorly that portion of our economy was still performing. The houses behind the traps were looking similarly dilapidated, with their whitewashed siding slowly flaking away. Every year there seemed to be a different explanation for why we were losing ground, from Canadian lobsters flooding the market to massive foreign factory ships scooping up everything as they hovered just outside the twelve-mile-limit. At the end of the day, all I could do was mourn the passing of what had once been a uniquely Maine industry — or, perhaps more accurately, one that had been unique to our corner of the Atlantic Ocean.

I passed a Volkswagen New Beetle with its top down and couldn't help immediately thinking of Alejandro Ortega-Cortez, Vasily's boyfriend. *Fiancé,* I immediately corrected myself, for Vasily had told me a few days after I'd seen him in Las Vegas that he'd popped the question. That reminded me of the mischief I was currently plotting with Alex; glancing at the clock on my dashboard, I did the math and hoped that the Career Counselor at California State University, Irvine, was already up and at work given the time difference. Turning onto Ocean View Lane, I hit the Bluetooth speed dial and hoped for the best.

Alejandro picked up on the second ring. "*Hola*, Sean," he said cheerfully. "I was wondering if I was going to hear from you today."

"Apologies," I replied as I pulled into my carport and parked. "Between this stupid civil case and the State's investigation into my actions, I've spent most of my spare time pouring over paperwork and prepping like I'm taking a college final — one that I need to pass in order to keep my scholarship."

"*Caramba*," he breathed. "Vas mentioned it was getting bad."

"Yeah. Naturally, I picked up a case today, too."

"When it rains, it pours," he laughed.

"That it does. The good news is, I took a break from all of that and made a few calls yesterday. It seems that you heard Vasily right: there *is* something called the *Fairytale Weddings* department at Walt Disney World, and they cater to just about any whim. I'm not sure what you had in mind, but from what the person I spoke to said, it sounds like the sky is pretty much the limit — depending, of course, on what your budget might be."

"I imagine exchanging vows on the steps of the castle is out of our price range," Alex mused.

"Probably," I replied. "There is some sort of pavilion on a lake, though, that has a nice view of the castle. That could be an option; when I talked to Suzanne about it, though, she liked several of the packages that held the ceremony at one of their themed hotels."

"That's an intriguing idea," Alex said. "Send what you found to my school account — I don't want to risk *mi amor* stumbling across our plotting. I've got practice tonight, but I can call you afterwards; Vas is working his own case, so I should have the condo to myself."

"Hopefully I'll still be awake," I chuckled. "I've been up since two."

"Yikes. I'll do my best to catch you before you nod off, then."

"Until later then," I said as we hung up.

Grabbing my swim backpack from the rear of the SUV, I entered my bungalow through the carport and found Caitlyn Romero sitting at the small kitchen table reading that day's *Bangor Daily News* over a cup of coffee. She looked up at my appearance and smiled. "I hope you don't mind my making myself at home. The paper was in the driveway when I got back from my walk."

"Not at all," I replied. "Smells like you found the good coffee, though."

"It wasn't hard; someone left the K-Cups on the counter."

"Really?" I asked innocently. "I wonder who did that?"

She just shook her head. "You look like you went to the pool."

"And now need a shower," I nodded. "I've got to be in court at lunchtime, so I've got to transform into the professional everyone is expecting."

"Ah," she chuckled.

"Why are you awake? I assumed you'd sleep until this afternoon."

Caitlyn shrugged. "My internal clock is a bit wonky today. I did get some rest right after Suzanne showed me to your spare room but woke up when the sun rose. I've got way too much on my mind; it won't turn off."

"I can understand that." Pausing for a moment, I smiled slightly. "I don't want you to think we're getting rid of you, but I spoke with Charlie earlier. She's invited you and the kids to stay with her for as long as you need to." I waved at the bungalow. "You are totally welcome to stay here, too, but I'd need to run down to the hardware store and get some inflatable mattresses for my den in order to accommodate the young ones."

She smiled. "Charlie does have the extra bedrooms. I appreciate the offer — and I'll probably take her up on it. I just need to swing by the apartment to pack a few days' worth of clothing for everyone."

"When do you get the kids back?"

"Thursday. We make the swap in the parking lot of the IGA; it feels a bit like a drug deal the way we do it."

"That sounds awful!" I exclaimed.

"But it captures the emotions pretty well," she sighed. "Did Heather clear the scene already?"

"Yeah," I nodded again. "I might need you to look through the photos they took later; of all people, you'd be the one that could tell me if anything looks odd or is missing."

"Sure," she replied. "I'd appreciate doing something — anything, I think."

"Actually, I am putting you on paid leave for a few days," I said. "I don't want you doing anything more than tending to your family until next week."

Caitlyn's eyes went wide. "Chief—!" she started to object.

I waved at her. "We have a pretty good bereavement policy, Cait; I *also* know you want to be part of the action. I'll pull you in when I can, but I want you to take the time you need here."

She nodded. "All right."

I smiled slightly. "At the risk of completely negating what I just said... did your father often have people in the shop after hours?" I asked.

Caitlyn grinned. "Yes, almost *every* night. And I think there was some sort of informal club that met there on Thursdays — they had these little cards and ran the trains around the layout like they were a real railroad on a schedule."

"Do you know who was in the club? Or who would be likely to pop in unannounced on a random Tuesday?"

Caitlyn looked at me, cocking her head with enough force that some of her brown hair fell over an eye. "Someone was there last night, right?"

I nodded. "We think so, yes. But don't have a lot to back that up — yet."

"Then I'll go back to the store later and get Dad's Rolodex. He was old school — landline only."

"That seems totally right, somehow."

"It does, doesn't it?" she laughed sadly. "Damn. I miss him already."

"Yeah," I said, thinking of the ache in my own heart for my mother. "I wish I could say it gets better, but all these years later, I still grieve over my mother."

"I'm not sure we're supposed to truly get over people," Caitlyn replied. "Not really."

"I think you are right," I said softly. "One last thing before I head to the shower, though. Did you know that the buildings on the layout lifted off?"

"Oh yes," she nodded. "Dad *loved* to show off those interiors. My grandfather started that, actually; Dad used to badger people in the Village to get a look inside their homes or offices so he could re-create them on the layout. He's even got Charlie's circulation desk blackened in the spot where that candle burned the counter at Halloween."

"You have to admire his dedication to the craft," I said. "Tell me this — did the hobby store ever sell shovels?"

"Shovels?" Caitlyn repeated to me blankly. "Like, snow shovels?"

"No, more of the garden variety — to dig in the soil."

"No," she shook her head. "Never. That sounds like something for the hardware store. Why?"

"Well, we were looking at the interior of the hobby store miniature, and it had all sorts of small boxes labelled with what you'd expect would be found in a hobby store," I replied. "Plus, one box clearly labelled for shovels."

She frowned. "That's odd — and unlike Dad."

"I thought so too. Does it mean anything to you?"

"Not a clue," she sighed. "You?"

"It's out of place," I said. "And as a consequence, it bothers me."

"If I can get the POS system online, I can check the inventory history," Caitlyn offered. "Maybe that would shed some light on everything."

"Cait—"

"I need to go through the store to settle out the estate anyway," she interrupted me. "Working on the POS system would just be another component of that."

"Are you sure?" I asked, seeing how Caitlyn had cleverly found a loophole to run through.

"Yes."

"Then I'll take whatever I can get," I said, sighing.

"No pressure," Caitlyn laughed.

Four

One shower and three cups of coffee later, I was behind my battleship of a desk in the Public Safety Building, staring at the various stacks of paper containing what I hoped would be enough supporting material that I might still be Chief of Police by the end of the week. Piled up behind them were multiple blue three-ring binders full of my work over the decade-plus I had in the position; I'd been physically going over the case files in the most manual way possible to ensure nearly every detail was fresh in anticipation that the lawyers in the civil suit had done the same. They would be looking for evidence there was a nefarious pattern in my investigations; I had an eye toward trying to fend them off if that was, indeed, what they were planning. Having spent quite a bit of time in various courtrooms, I knew exactly how it was likely to go and desperately wanted to be prepared for any eventuality. Leaning back in my chair, I closed my eyes and rubbed at the throbbing above my right eye, wondering if I might have overdone it ever so slightly. That it might also be a caffeine headache was an option I chose to ignore.

Closing my eyes for a moment, I found I wanted to desperately escape to the mountains in Vermont and the long weekend getaway

Suzanne had planned for us in the immediate aftermath of the Brogan case; the sudden appearance of both investigations into my conduct had shelved those plans indefinitely. As much as I loved my job, I hated having to go through my own history with a fine-tooth comb attempting to look for whatever it was I had missed; part of the stress I could feel just beneath my breastbone was the sense that *anything* looked at with the benefit of hindsight always came up short of expectations. Cracking open an eye to look at the files, I knew that even I had begun to question my own judgement — despite my decisions still looking reasonable and sound years later. I wasn't perfect — no police officer worth their salt would ever admit otherwise — but I had never put anyone behind bars that the evidence hadn't indicated should be there. And the evidence had always been collected by the book, which is why, ultimately, Shelly West was free.

One little Miranda warning and none of this would have happened, I sighed as I turned my chair away from the desk. *Those words that were beaten into me at the Academy — the very essence of the American Justice System — failed me that day in the icehouse. And I've never understood why.*

I could see through my window that kids were playing frisbee in the athletic fields behind the station; the high school on the hill above them looked sad in the filtered light of what had become a partly cloudy day, almost as though it were lonely and looking forward to its halls being full in September. The Brogan case had sent me right back to when I'd been a teenager roaming those hallways, which might lend a partial explanation for my mistake. Teenagers in love make horrible life choices; it appeared their older selves could as well.

A gentle knock at the door to my office had me spinning the chair back around. "Is this a bad time?" asked a modestly tall woman who, despite the insane mugginess of the day, was wearing a perfectly pressed power suit.

"Not at all, Arabella," I replied as I stood. "I didn't realize how late it had become."

Arabella Steinman smiled as she crossed the distance to my desk and took one of my guest chairs. "Good lawyering 101: be in the courtroom early," she said. "We don't have to be there quite yet; besides, I wanted to take your pulse and see how my client is holding up."

Gesturing at the mess that was my desk, I sighed. "I think I am over prepared. Is that even possible?"

"Quite," she nodded as I sagged back into my chair. "From what I can see, though, it's how you've always operated. That's a point in our favor."

"It is?" I asked. "I'm glad we have at least one."

The partner from Steinman, Steinman and Sorentino laughed, hard enough that the sunglasses she'd nestled into her mountain of curly brown hair shifted slightly. "Jimmy told me you had a dry wit," she said as she crossed her legs.

"Did he?" I asked, arching an eyebrow. Maine State Police Captain James Roberts was a good friend and mentor; he'd been the one to recommend hiring Arabella when my legal woes began to pile up. "I hadn't realized he'd noticed."

"He had," she chuckled. Arabella's eyes drifted to the window over my shoulder. "That's Windeport Regional High School back there?"

"The one and only."

"Has it changed much since you were a student there?"

"Not especially," I said, turning slightly to look out the window myself. "A few coats of paint, maybe. I think my graduating class was the last big one; this end of the county is experiencing something of population implosion." Turning back, I smiled at my lawyer. "I imagine the student to teacher ratio is far better now."

"As long as they aren't eliminating them. The teachers, that is; not the students."

I shrugged. "I don't have any kids, so I have no idea. I'll have to ask my cousin, Charlie; her twins are still a few years out from high school but knowing her, she's probably already aware of the situation, warts and all."

Arabella nodded before pulling up her sleeve to look at her watch. "Looks like it's time. Ready?"

"As I'll ever be," I said as I stood. Pausing with my hands on the back of my chair, I looked at Arabella. "I have to admit, I expected some set of dramatic instructions from you."

"Like what to say? Or *not* to say?" she asked before chuckling. "That's not my style. Besides, in the time I've spent working with you these past few weeks, it's become quite clear to me you know what the boundaries are anyway. In my view, giving you advice at this point would only make my job more difficult."

That eyebrow arched again. "Was that supposed to be some sort of pep talk?"

"Yes," she laughed. "Did it work?"

"Hardly," I chuckled. "Let's get this over with."

I guided Arabella through the somewhat busy squad room, and then out past the intake desk currently staffed by Caitlyn's backup. Since I'd formally put Caitlyn on bereavement leave, I had to do some schedule juggling to cover her absence — an exercise that reminded me just how integral she was to my operation. Typically, such work would have been done by Norm as he managed personnel matters for me in his capacity of Assistant Chief, but I'd felt a level of responsibility for having tossed a hand grenade into the middle of his carefully plotted out matrix covering the next fourteen days. After a lot of erasing — and a liberal dose of overtime promises — the desk had been completely covered through when I thought Caitlyn would return.

Pushing out into the sweltering midday heat, I slid my sunglasses on and started across our parking lot to the sidewalk along Route One. Arabella fell into step beside me, somehow able to keep up with my longer strides despite being in heels and a few inches shorter. I felt the sweat immediately begin to bead up along my forehead, but my lawyer looked as cool as a cucumber making me wonder if she had one of those water-cooled air conditioning vests on beneath her blazer. As we pushed onward through the dense humidity, I glanced at the gathering clouds above us and the coming thunderstorms they portended — and what little respite might come with them.

Seeming to sense my thoughts, my companion nodded. "Hopefully it will hold off until we have adjourned."

"Feels like it's been one never-ending weather event after another around here," I chuckled. "Starting with that once-in-a-century snowstorm this past Christmas. Our Public Works folks have been pushed to the limit this year."

"I wonder," she replied with a trace of irony, "when they stop being once-in-a-century events and just something we become accustomed to?"

I glanced at her. "Much like the proverbial frog in a vat of water, I think we'll know that answer a tad too late."

"No kidding."

We continued down the sidewalk in companionable silence, pausing only at the parking lot entrance for the Windeport Public Library for a postal truck to pull out into the stop-and-go traffic on Route One. Standing with equally grand elegance beside the library was the county courthouse, a stately building in granite very much in the Federal style. As we went up the broad steps to the entrance, the sun suddenly disappeared behind the clouds, plunging us into an odd patch of semi-darkness on the cusp of noon. The Doric columns to either side of the double doors somehow felt more ominous in shadow, looming over us as I reached for the handle. Shrugging off the weight of the moment, I held the door for Arabella, then took up position behind her in the brightly lit lobby so we could pass through the metal detectors. The space was quiet enough that the gentle *clink* from placing my badge and gun into the plastic tray for the X-Ray machine reverberated with a vengeance; my blood pressure went up a bit more when the security guard was forced to wand me after the detector went off, triggered by the sunglasses I'd left in my hair.

The courtrooms — all two of them — were on the second floor, accessed via the granite-tiled staircase in the center of the lobby. Our steps echoed as we climbed past oil paintings of past jurists dating back to the founding of Windeport; for the first time, I felt a bit like they were judging us, much like the portraits of my predecessors often did back at the station. Turning left at the top of the staircase, we went down a short hall and then into the wood-paneled space that had windows overlooking Main Street and the ocean beyond. I wasn't surprised that the courtroom itself was pretty much empty, for even on the busiest of days they tended to only host the parties that had specific business before the judge and the odd retiree with an interest in judicial proceedings. Still, my heart lifted somewhat when I recognized the head of raven hair that turned in our direction as we entered; Suzanne was sitting on the aisle in the row behind the half-wall separating the gallery from the court proper and rose to greet me.

Giving her a quick kiss, I smiled at her. "I didn't know you'd be here," I said, my voice hushed in respect to the space. "How did you get away from your practice?"

"I worked a little magic on my appointments," she answered, equally as quiet. "I wanted to be here for you."

Holding her hand, I squeezed it slightly. "Thank you." I turned slightly. "Suzanne, this is my lawyer, Arabella Steinman. Arabella, meet Dr. Suzanne Kellerman, my much-more-than-significant other."

The two women shook, although it was also clear they were sizing each other up. "A pleasure," Arabella said.

"Same," Suzanne replied before narrowing her eyes. "You're going to get him out of this mess, aren't you?" she asked. The way she did so — less a question, more like a statement — had me raising my eyebrows.

"I am indeed," Arabella smiled. "Sit tight and enjoy the show." She looked to me. "Come on, let's settle in."

"I'll join you in a second," I replied.

"Okay."

I waited for Arabella to move through the small swinging gate before leaning close to Suzanne; lowering my voice so she would be the only one to hear, I felt the wall crumbling that had been holding back my fears. "I have some doubts," I said softly.

"Who wouldn't?" she replied as she reached up and brushed back a curl from my forehead. "Have faith and know I will be here, by your side, no matter how it goes."

"The two of us, against the world?" I asked, thinking back to an episode of *Miraculous* we had recently watched together.

"Always."

"Furever?" I asked suddenly, surprising myself by putting voice to something that had been in the back of my head for weeks now.

Suzanne smiled. "Is that a proposal, kitty?" she asked in return, correctly reading my heart.

"Purrhaps, Milady," I smiled back, staying in character. "Though this is not the proper forum for such things."

"When I am with you," she whispered, "wherever that might be, it's *always* the perfect forum."

I didn't know what to say, though the lift in my heart spoke volumes. Smiling, I simply leaned down and kissed her with enough emphasis to let her know there would be much more later. Pulling back, I could see from the twinkle in her eye that she'd received the message; the subtle nod as she sat simply confirmed it. The gate was just a few steps away; my seat beside Arabella, just a few more. I was just pulling out the uncomfortable looking wooden chair when the door to the hallway behind us swung open with a creak; turning, I watched as a tall gentleman with salt-and-pepper hair wearing an expensively tailored three-piece suit appeared. Behind him was the figure of Shelly West, similarly dressed in an expensive but conservative pantsuit; her eyes met mine and were just as coldly calculating as they'd been the morning I'd interviewed her at the station. That look had been my first indication my case against her was going to be rough, though I'd had no idea just *how* rough until the phone call from Captain Roberts.

The lawyer came through the small gate first and paused to shake hands with my lawyer. "Arabella."

"Clint," she nodded before releasing his hand.

"They told me you were working this case," he said as Shelly quietly moved around him and sat at the opposing counsel's table. "Isn't this a little bit beneath you?"

I felt my pulse pound at what appeared to have been an insult leveled at Arabella. My eyes moved to Arabella, who didn't appear phased in the least as she responded. "I'm always interested in righting miscarriages of justice, Clint. You of all people should know that."

Clint smiled, but also looked like he'd been slapped across the face, too. "I suppose so," he replied weakly before bowing. "Good luck."

Arabella reached out and grabbed his arm before he could turn away. "It's not too late for us to talk this out," she said quietly. "I'm not sure you truly want this to go to trial."

"Unless you are offering up your client's immediate resignation and sufficient financial remuneration for my client's pain and suffering, there's not much to talk about."

"I thought you might say that," she replied before turning toward the table and the small briefcase she'd stashed in her chair. Giving me a quick smile, Arabella unzipped the satchel and dug around until she retrieved a small manilla envelope. Turning back to Clint the lawyer, she held it up. "This is just a courtesy, from one professional to another," she said as she handed it to him.

Flipping the envelope over in his hands, his eyes widened at the logo for the Maine State Crime lab on the exterior. "Do you want to explain what this is?"

"Not really," Arabella said. "I wouldn't want to spoil the surprise." Her eyes went to the door that led to the judge's chambers. "If I were you, though, I might want to scan it before we start."

Looking at Arabella askance, Clint nodded and withdrew to his table; Arabella waited a moment before sitting down beside me. "What was that all about?" I whispered.

"My ace in the hole," she replied softly. "It came through this morning."

I looked at her. "*What* ace?"

Keeping half an eye on Clint, she lowered her voice even more. "I called in a favor and had the Crime Lab go back through the evidence you collected at the icehouse," she whispered.

My eyes widened. "They found something?" I asked, incredulous.

Arabella nodded. "An extremely tiny bloodstain *inside* the rubber outfit the victim had been wearing."

I thought back to the evidence we'd collected from the Mustang that Shelly had — allegedly — pushed into the river after killing the girl who'd stolen her former boyfriend. "TJ was asphyxiated," I whispered back. "Unless our thinking about the crime was wrong."

"It wasn't," she replied as we both watched Clint open the envelope and pull out a standard lab report. "The sample came from someone else, likely when they were attempting to wrestle that very tight rubber outfit off of a cadaver in full rigor."

"A scratch? Or an injury sustained from the attack on Lizzie?"

"Probably the latter — a wound large enough that a few drops of blood fell inside the suit." She turned toward me. "The way the rubber had been folded created an airtight pocket around the sample, preserving it."

"Why didn't this come up sooner?" I asked incredulously.

Arabella nodded toward Clint, whose face had gone ashen. "My esteemed colleague over there short circuited everything when he made a mountain out of your molehill of a Miranda violation," she whispered. "The Crime Lab did a hard stop and put the evidence on ice, assuming correctly that the case was going nowhere."

I looked at my lawyer. "I had extensive conversations with the District Attorney about continuing the forensics," I said. "He thought I was nuts. Why did he listen to you?"

Arabella smiled. "I can be persuasive when needed," she replied.

My eyes widened again. "I'm glad you're on my side," I said as I looked over to the other table. Judging from the rapid conversation going on between Shelly and Clint, a bit of panic had crept into their situation.

"I don't like to lose," she whispered. "Besides, I promised Suzanne you'd be okay."

The Bailiff chose that moment to announce the arrival of the judge, and we all stood as the door to the chamber opened; not having spent much time in civil court, I didn't recognize who was presiding over my case, but the slight smile on Arabella's face told me she *did*. "Please, be seated," the judge said before turning his attention to the two lawyers still standing. "Arabella! What a pleasant surprise."

"Your Honor, it pleases me to see you again, though I wish it were under other circumstances."

"Agreed," he nodded before turning to Clint. "I'm afraid I don't know you, sir, otherwise I would extend you the same warm welcome."

"Clifton White," he said. "Of White and Kelsey."

The pleasant smile on the judge's face became forced. "Ah," he nodded. "The firm that sued Camden over the removal of that Confederate-era monument."

Clint colored slightly. "That would have been my partner, Your Honor. She has a... special interest in such cases."

"Does she, now?" the judge said with enough weight that we instantly knew how he felt about it. "This is a preliminary hearing in *West v Colbeth* with the intent of deciding if there is enough to go to trial. Mr. White—"

"If we may approach the bench, Your Honor?" Clint interrupted.

"Approach," the judge nodded.

Arabella stood and followed Clint forward; the ensuing conversation was low enough I couldn't make out more than a word here or there, but the succession of facial expressions on the judge spoke volumes. Maybe ninety seconds later, Arabella returned to our table looking quite satisfied; from what I could see at the other table, though, the opinion wasn't entirely the same. Shelly's dark look in my direction telegraphed her displeasure as the judge struck his gavel to the counter.

"I understand the plaintiffs now wish to dismiss this case?" the judge said.

Clint stood. "Yes, Your Honor. Considering recent evidence presented to her, my client has no wish to pursue this action at this time." Looking at Arabella uncomfortably, he continued. "We formally wish to dismiss this case with prejudice."

The judge looked at Arabella. "I presume you have no objection?"

Arabella stood. "Your Honor, we do not."

"Then so ordered," the judge said as he gaveled again.

We all stood as he withdrew back into his chambers; Clint simply nodded at Arabella as he slipped the envelope into his briefcase and quietly moved back down the aisle toward the exit. Shelly waited a moment before standing, then stared at me for a long moment; the cold look had disappeared from her eyes, replaced with one of grudging admiration. Turning, she followed her lawyer out at a deliberate pace as I looked to Arabella.

"I guess I did over prepare," I chuckled.

"Quite," Arabella laughed.

"All the same, it was an impressive rabbit you pulled out of your hat."

"That?" she chuckled. "All in a day's work. The real magic comes tomorrow with the Professional Standards panel."

I felt some of my jubilation ease. "Won't the results of this civil case help our cause?"

"One can hope," she smiled. "Honestly, you never know how these panel reviews will go; while they are bound by guidelines — and this case, professional standards — they aren't as cut and dry as the law."

My eyebrows went up. "Which means there is room for interpretation?"

"Exactly." Reaching into her briefcase, she withdrew a second envelope bearing the logo for the State Crime Lab and handed it to me. "I thought you might want a copy of those results yourself. The tech I spoke with assured me that the Brogan case file would be updated by the end of the day as well."

I held the envelope for a moment, then glanced at the doors to the courtroom. "You must have been reading my mind."

"It's what I get paid to do," she laughed as she picked up her briefcase. "I'll see you in Augusta tomorrow. Wear your Class A uniform, please."

"Yes, ma'am," I replied as I followed her through the swinging gate.

Suzanne was waiting for me on the other side and looped her arm inside of mine. "I hope you keep Arabella on retainer," she said as she leaned her head into my shoulder. "I like how she operates."

"I'm not sure I could afford that," I sighed. "Nor do I like the prospect of having to keep someone like her *on* retainer."

"Understood," she said as we reached the doors to the courtroom. Glancing meaningfully at her watch, she looked back at me. "I still have the balance of the time I blocked," Suzanne said as we pushed through. "Would you care to join me for lunch at Millie's?"

"It depends. Will you allow me a cup of coffee?" I asked.

"I might have to perform a physical exam later to ensure you don't have any heart palpitations as a result," she replied with that glorious twinkle to her beautiful blue eyes.

"I would happily consent to such an exam," I said softly as I leaned down to kiss her. "Provided it's thorough. I wouldn't want you to overlook any conditions I might have."

"I thought you might," she replied as she returned my kiss.

I lingered on her lips for a moment, then smiled wolfishly. "We could do the exam sooner."

That twinkle in Suzanne's eyes became more pronounced. "Someone's feeling frisky."

"Can you blame me?" I smiled wider as we exited the courtroom. "Your presence is intoxicating."

"Then we'd better get takeout from Millie's," she chuckled. "Because there's no food back at the apartment."

"I think we can do that," as we headed for the staircase.

The lobby of the courthouse held an unpleasant surprise, for Shelly West was waiting impatiently at the base of the steps as the two of us descended. I'd expected she'd want to confront me at some point given what had happened in the courtroom — from working the Brogan case, I'd come to understand just how poorly she took personal losses — but had assumed she'd pick her moment a bit more judiciously. Then again, the anger that was coming off her in waves spoke to an urgent need for vindication. As I reached the bottom step and paused, I wondered if she realized she might be on the wrong side of that equation.

"This isn't over," Shelly said without preamble.

"The judge dismissed it with prejudice," I reminded her. "You've already had a bite at *that* apple; I'd have to wrongly arrest you for a *new* murder if you want to go for a second round."

"I'll find a forensic specialist. They'll toss whatever it is that the lab thinks they found."

I nodded. "That's your prerogative," I agreed. "I can recommend a few places if you'd like."

Shelly stared at me. "Why would you do that?"

"I like to ensure suspects get a fair chance to prove their innocence," I replied.

"I'm not a suspect," Shelly pounced. "As you said, the case was dismissed. You can't have it both ways."

"The *civil* case was dismissed," I agreed as I watched Officer Smart appear through the main entrance. It was hard not to smile; Arabella was nothing if not thorough. "Your lawyer made sure the criminal case never went to court; as far as the judicial system is concerned, I've not even begun."

Shelly arched an eyebrow and couldn't help the snarky smile. "You're not honestly thinking of arresting me again, are you? Because that didn't go so well for you the last time."

"We tried it once your way, Shelly," I smiled pleasantly. "Are you game for a rematch?"

It was fascinating watching Shelly's expression as it shifted from snark to one of dawning realization. "You're actually serious, aren't you?"

I waved to Lydia. "You catch on fast, Shelly. Oh, and before I forget: you have the right to remain silent..."

Five

When the lobster rolls we'd picked up from Millie's went straight into the apartment's fridge — and Suzanne began to tug me toward her bedroom — it became clear that eating hadn't truly been on the agenda. Within seconds of closing the door behind us, clothing began to come off and litter the floor; for whatever reason, the stuffiness of the apartment seemed to amplify the moment and heighten each sensation. Carefully pulling me to the bed, I pressed my body to hers and felt how our skin had already grown slick at our mutual perspiration; pushing her down, I knelt between her legs and began to nibble at some of her more sensitive spots, eliciting a slight shiver each time I hit one. The saltiness of her sweat was on my tongue when I leaned up and kissed an exposed breast; sliding against her, I reached her neck, running my tongue along her now-throbbing carotid artery. I realized I was going too slow when I felt her hand grip me, then deliberately guide me into her; I quickly adjusted and began again in earnest. I wasn't surprised to feel her suddenly tense and then shudder against me; a moment later, I felt my own control evaporate, leaving me a quivering mess on top of her heaving chest.

Once our mutual breathing went back to something close to normal, we shifted so we were lying side-by-side facing each other; Suzanne had wrapped a leg around me, making it impossible for me to withdraw. I smiled slightly, for it was something she often did as a non-verbal indication that she wasn't quite through with me; as always, the prospect for further shenanigans kept me at attention, shall we say. It didn't hurt that she'd begun to slowly grind against me, too.

"We still need to eat lunch," I said as I kissed the tip of her nose. "And probably take a shower, though not necessarily in that order."

"True," she breathed as she slowly increased her tempo.

"I—" I started before any further objection was stymied by her flipping me onto my back.

Having seen this movie many times before, I simply reached up and ran my hands along her back, content to let her continue at her own pace. The fact that it began to drive me a bit crazy after a few minutes was hard to hide from her, but I held out as long as I could before the more animalistic urges kicked in. I scissored up from the comforter and pressed my lips to hers a few seconds before the two of us grunted in unison and fell back to the mattress in a tangled mass of spasms. When my world came back to me a second time, Suzanne was peeling a curl that had become plastered to my forehead away from the skin and wearing a satisfied smile.

"How do you feel?" she asked.

"Like it might be hard to walk out of here," I chuckled.

The smile widened. "Did I wear you out, my love?"

"Quite possibly," I sighed pleasantly. "Shower? Or food?"

"Shower," she said. "I'll use the guest one, you jump into mine."

"Solo?" I asked dejectedly. "I might need some help in my weakened state."

"While I empathize," Suzanne chuckled, "society is going to be looking for both of us pretty quickly." She leaned in and kissed me one last time. "Especially if Shelly West is cooling her heels in your holding cell."

"I'm okay with Shelly having plenty of time to consider her life choices."

"True," she laughed again as she rather erotically ran a finger along my nose. "But you should still make an appearance."

It was hard for me to tear my attention away from that finger, but with great reluctance, I did. "Fine. If I'm lucky, though, she's bailed herself out and won't even be there."

"Wishful thinking," she chuckled as she rolled off the bed. Suzanne slid open a drawer to her dresser and pulled out an oversized UEM t-shirt that she quickly shrugged into, then gathered up her portion of the garments we'd rather haphazardly strewn from the door to the bed. "Be quick," she advised as she disappeared out into the apartment proper.

"Yes, Milady," I intoned as she closed the door behind her.

Sliding off the bed, I bent down to retrieve my clothes before moving into the master bath. It always felt weird using the space now that the apartment was no longer mine; even weirder when I considered that I had once shared it with another woman. Still, the well-appointed bathroom hadn't significantly changed since the apartment had been mine save for the unique touches from Suzanne that marked it as her own. There was a small container of Kleenex on the back of the toilet tank, sharing the ceramic with a scented candle whose purpose seemed self-evident, though matches were in short supply. The set of vibrantly green potted plants sitting upon the sill of the long rectangular window above the shower emphasized Suzanne's abilities tending to the needs of all living things. Dumping my clothes on top of the toilet, I stepped into the shower and quickly went through my routine; not quite five minutes later, I wandered out into the kitchen to find Suzanne already waiting for me by the small breakfast bar.

"Good thing I skipped shaving," I said, arching an eyebrow.

Noticing my expression, she chuckled. "I wanted to maximize our lunchtime — what's left of it," she said as she tied back her damp raven hair with a casual knot. "Can you blame me?"

"Not in the least," I replied.

Suzanne had already placed our food out on two plates with a cheerful pattern along the edge; a modest bowl sat between them holding the freshly made potato chips that had come with our order. Sliding one roll toward me, she came around the bar and sat down beside me, then considered her roll. “I think they padded mine with lettuce,” she sighed.

Picking at the lobster meat in mine, I nodded. “I guess we should have asked for the Locals’ Special,” I sighed.

“What’s that?” my girlfriend asked as she fished a piece from the top of her role and dipped it into the small container of drawn butter.

“What they normally serve between Labor Day and Memorial Day,” I chuckled.

“Ah,” she laughed.

Despite the portions being somewhat skimpy, the lobster rolls were as marvelous as ever; within minutes, I found myself sadly licking the last of the homemade mayo Millie used from my fingers and eyeing the last of the chips in the depleted bowl. “What a day,” I said as I stood and took my plate over to the sink for a rinse.

“And it’s not quite over, is it?” Suzanne reminded me as she crunched on a chip.

“Don’t remind me,” I sighed. “Do you want this in the dishwasher?”

“No, I’ll wash everything up by hand before I go back downstairs,” she said as she stood and joined me in the kitchen. “I wasn’t planning on returning here anytime soon, so might as well put them back clean.”

I looked at Suzanne for a moment. “Where *are* we going to live?” I asked. “We keep bouncing back and forth between here and the bungalow; maybe it’s time for us to make a decision.”

“You seem to be making an assumption, kitty,” Suzanne smiled.

I felt my eyes widen in surprise, and for a long, terrible moment, I thought I had misread, well, *everything*. “I didn’t mean to be presumptive,” I said cautiously. “It... it felt like we were trending in a... certain direction.”

"You're not wrong," Suzanne replied.

The response, while delivered with her usual amazing smile, didn't quite disguise her rising level of discomfort with our discussion. Somewhat foolishly, I chose to ignore the growing pit in my stomach and pressed her a bit more. "Don't you want to move in with me?"

"Sean," she said, a clear note of warning in her voice, "maybe we could table this discussion for later? We both need to get to work."

My eyebrows went up, and though I was tempted to continue the point, the fear I might say something that could lead to my losing the best thing that had ever happened to me was great enough that I forced a smile and a quick nod. "Of course. Do you have a heavy caseload this afternoon?"

"Yes," she replied, visibly relieved at the change of subject. "I'll be ready to go at five-thirty, though."

"I invited Caitlyn to our little soiree, so I'll swing by the bungalow and pick her up first," I nodded. "I can pick you up here unless you're running back ho—back there yourself," I added, hastily correcting myself.

"Here is fine," she nodded. "That will give me time to wrap up the last of my paperwork."

"Okay," I said.

Despite having been intimate with Suzanne not thirty minutes earlier, it felt as though I were standing next to a total stranger there in the kitchen. I cursed inwardly at having blown past the obvious warning signs when she deliberately looked down into the sink and the dishes I'd placed there and quietly continued. "You can drop me back here tonight, anyway; come to think of it, I have a whole series of early appointments tomorrow, and it will just be easier than having to drive back from the bungalow in the morning."

The yawning pit in my stomach forced me to rethink my first response, namely that it was less than five minutes from the bungalow to the old pharmacy building. Or the second response, that being I could drop her off on my way to swim practice at 4:30. Or the third response, the one where I dropped to my knees, apologized for whatever I had just done and begged her not to leave me.

Dear sweet Jesus, I pleaded silently. *Please don't leave me.*

Instead, I managed my best retail smile, and a quick nod. "Of course. Do you want me to grab anything for you?"

"No," she smiled back at me, but it was her version of the retail smile. "I think I have enough here for a few days."

I tried not to look like she'd slapped me and was sure I had failed. Deciding it might be wise to leave before I did any further damage to life, the universe, or my relationship with Suzanne, I leaned over and gave her a quick kiss on the cheek. "Thanks for lunch."

"See you tonight," Suzanne said before deliberately turning away from me and beginning to hand wash the dishes.

I stood there for a moment, frozen, then turned and walked out of the apartment; at the bottom of the staircase, I paused, unusually unsure of what my next move should be. Given how my world suddenly felt like it had been inverted, I wasn't sure heading to the office and trying to act like it was still a normal Tuesday was truly the best course of action. The clouds had thickened appreciably since leaving the courthouse, plunging the day into a somewhat appropriate early twilight that reflected my mood perfectly; shoving my hands into the pockets of my khakis, I trudged down the side street to Route One then turned toward the spires of St. Catherine's By-The-Sea. Tourists on the concrete sidewalk parted around me as I walked, almost as though my angst was palpable enough to form a snowplow wedge in front of me. Crossing the intersection by Calista's Bakery, I went up the steps to the cathedral and found the door was unlocked as always; pulling it open, I paused again just inside, letting the pneumatic hinge gently close the massive wooden portal behind me, cutting off the noise from the busy street. The relative silence of the vestibule washed over me as it always did, momentarily inserting some calm into my turbulent thoughts.

The ornate doors to the sanctuary had been propped open in muted invitation, and I wandered slowly inside. A smile came to my face, unbidden, at the twin smells of candle wax and Murphy's Oil Soap; pausing at the last row of pews, I took a deep breath and looked to the soaring arches of the ceiling, the heights of which were partially hidden in the now semi-darkness of the day. Flickering light from the candles at the front of the church was strangely inviting, and I made my way down to the first row of pews and settled in, eyes watching the flames as they danced in the unseen currents of the room. Church policy for as long as I could remember had kept the sanctuary open to all at any time, day or night; Catholic credentials were not required to enjoy a few moments away from the hustle and bustle of life to commune with whatever higher power you subscribed to. Pressing my hands together in my lap, I found the peace I normally enjoyed in that space elusive; closing my eyes, all I could see was a rapid-fire replay of my conversation with Suzanne in her kitchen, and a commensurate roil of acid in my stomach.

I pushed again, didn't I? I thought as my eyes blinked back open. *I was so certain I knew what I had done wrong with Deidre — and was so afraid to repeat it, I overcorrected.*

Sighing, I looked at the small sign delineating the hymns for the next mass — or maybe from the last one; not having attended formal services at St. Catherine's, I had no idea what the schedule might be. Given how the congregation continued to shrink, it was quite likely they met in the small parish hall next door instead.

Actually, it's worse, my thoughts continued as my eyes turned to the rounded stained-glass windows. Their colors were muted, but in an odd way, seemed to pop more than normal in the half light trickling in. *I didn't misread the situation so much as ignore little signs from Suzanne. We spend all our time together, but every now and then, she has a reason why she's got to return to her apartment for a bit. I've been writing it off as part of being a doctor; maybe there's something more there. Something I wasn't willing to see.*

My stomach flipped again. *Something I was afraid of seeing?*

Looking up at the giant crucifix just behind the raised pulpit, I wondered. The just-concluded Brogan case had been an unexpected vehicle to review all my past relationships through the eyes of an adult, one who had finally realized just how much shrapnel his heart had taken on in the process — shrapnel that had only recently been removed by Suzanne. Contemplating the hardwood floor beneath my shoes for a moment it occurred to me that while my girlfriend was more than up-to-speed on the travails of my love life, aside from knowing she'd divorced a jerk of a husband shortly after we met, I had no clue what sort of wringer *she'd* been through. And what seemed infinitely worse was my stunning lack of interest in finding out.

Holy shit, I breathed as I leaned my face into my hands, *she was there for me when I needed her. And I blithely assumed her life had turned a corner without thinking — without realizing — there were lingering issues there. What the* Hell *kind of boyfriend am I...?*

Not for the first time I wondered if having spent my formative years submerged in chlorine had burned away my ability to be a fully socialized member of society; sure, I'd won a gold medal or two, and had even become Police Chief. But I also seemed to leave a trail of shattered relationships in my wake, hurting those I purported to have loved the most.

Dad.

Deidre.

Vasily.

And now Suzanne?

No, I said to myself forcefully. *Not Suzanne. Not this time. Maybe it's an improvement that I know what I've done — and what I need to do to right this ship.*

I looked up at the list of hymns again and suddenly realized one of them was numbered 1-4-3. I had no idea what the song itself was but had heard somewhere along the line that for fans of numerology, those three numbers represented the phrase *I love you*. Not especially looking for signs from above — and somewhat ambivalent about whether there was a higher power willing to hand them out from time to time — I nonetheless allowed myself to accept it as such and smiled slightly.

"A little faith can go a long way, can't it?" I whispered to the space.

The cathedral wisely chose to remain silent, although as I stood to go, I supposed it had spoken rather loudly in the end.

Six

I broke down on my walk back to the station and swung through Calista's for an extra-large cup of their special roast, and then weakened further and added a freshly made Boston Creme doughnut to the order. I tried to justify the empty carbs by reminding myself I'd not had a proper breakfast after swim practice; a man can only go so far on a blueberry muffin, right? It was similarly easy to use the underwhelming size of the tourist lobster roll as the reason for selecting one thickly slathered with chocolate glaze over the plain version. Honestly, I was rather surprised my blood sugar levels hadn't completely crashed, considering how long I'd been up — and how active I'd been; sipping at my hot coffee as I pushed into the Public Safety building and wandered past the intake desk, I realized caffeine could hide a ton of sins, not the least of which was the fatigue I could feel just at the edges of my consciousness.

Tapping my ID on the reader beside the door leading to the squad room, I turned for a moment to consider the semicircular desk and the person who normally was omnipresent behind it. Caitlyn had been with me long enough that I couldn't imagine anyone else in that role, helping our village citizens through crises both big and small. Not seeing her there was a visual reminder I'd not been as aware as I could have been of what had gone on in her personal life; sometimes the worst part of being a manager was figuring out where the line was between being the boss and a caring friend. Sighing, I turned and entered the short hallway that led to the cubicles, ignoring the portraits of the Chiefs who had come before me as I walked. There were times when I felt like they judged my every move, their eyes seemingly narrowing in displeasure at whatever damage my presence as the leader of the organization was causing to the reputation of my department. I was introspective enough to realize it was my own self-doubt bubbling up — and that most of them were long dead, and therefore unable to provide an *actual* opinion on the matter — but I nonetheless averted my eyes as though not seeing them would make them go away.

Fat chance, I sighed again as I entered the broader space of the squad room.

Glancing across to the interview rooms and the door beside them that led out to the holding cells, I shifted directions and headed toward that end of the station. I had assumed Shelly West would have been sprung by that point in the day, considering how long it had been since I'd arrested her for the second time; I was quickly disabused of that notion as I came through the door into the area and found her seated in one of the three cells, arms crossed, and face reddened with anger. My shock must have been obvious as I paused in the short hallway and looked at her.

"You're still here," was the best I could do.

"No thanks to you," was the curt reply.

"It's a bit like that line in *Hotel California*," I said, thinking of a tune that Suzanne liked and had played for me on more than a few occasions. "My staff are programmed to receive; it's up to your lawyer to get you out of here."

Shelly glared at me. "Which he would do if he could get here," she snapped. "Which he can't, since he's in court. In Bangor."

"I apologize for not warning you in advance," I replied dryly. "Have you had lunch?"

"I'm not hungry."

"That's too bad," I said as I leaned on the wall opposite and took a sip from my coffee. "The cafeteria was serving pizza today, too."

"The hell it is," she snorted before looking away.

"You know," I said affably, "if you don't want to wait for your lawyer, we could always relocate to one of my interview rooms and discuss what happened twenty years ago. Depending on how that goes, I might be able to upgrade your accommodations. I hear the cells at County are bigger, though you do have to share a toilet with someone."

"Go fuck yourself," she replied coldly.

Why do people say that? I asked myself. *I understand the sentiment, of course, but from a practical perspective...*

"Well," I said aloud as I pushed from the wall to leave, "if you change your mind, let the guard know. I'm usually here until five," I added as I paused with a hand on the door, "which is when this offer expires."

From the middle finger she held up, I presumed her mind wasn't *quite* ready to change.

The squad room was its typical muted hubbub, pierced randomly by the electronic ringing of a phone. I'd lost track of where we were on the cruise ship calendar, but presumed based on how quiet it was, we were not currently experiencing the normal deluge that resulted when the tourists invaded. Sipping my coffee, I moved to the side walkway that ran past Norm's office and then onward to mine in the rear corner of the space; as his door looked open, I poked my head in only to find nothing but his laptop in attendance. Figuring he was likely in the building somewhere, I made a mental note to check back later and went down to my office, flipped the lights on and closed the door behind me.

All the material I'd been reviewing as preparation for both Shelly's civil case and the Professional Standards board meeting were still spread across my large desk, and I suddenly didn't want to have to deal with any of it. Settling down in one of my guest chairs, I pulled out the doughnut I'd been carrying with me and carefully held the bag beneath it as I gleefully devoured the delightful pastry. I figured the sugar rush would likely not last long, so I crushed the bag up between my hands and then set about clearing my desk before the inevitable crash came. For a moment, I had a mental image of Norm finding me in a coma behind my chair, another victim of poor nutritional decisions; the smile from the image happened to be on my face when there was a knock at the door and the man himself appeared.

"You're back," he said as he entered.

"Yes," I nodded as I waved him to a chair. "I stopped by your office, but you were out."

"Uh, yeah," he said as he sat down. "I had an appointment with Dr. Kellerman."

His level of discomfort immediately put me on alert. "Okay," I said slowly. "Should I be worried?"

"Not yet," he sighed as he ran a hand along his crew cut. Glancing to my door, he stood up and went to it, closed it, then returned to his chair. "My ex called this morning."

I nodded. I'd met Norm's former boyfriend while I'd been working the Davies double murder case; at the time, I'd thought the Real Estate agent was nice enough, but had learned later he'd been a controlling, manipulating personality. Norm had parted ways with him after a particularly egregious incident that had, among other things, included his being tied naked to a post for an entire weekend in the basement of the home they had shared. Love could be blind, but apparently it also had its limits.

"What did he want?" I asked. "If you don't mind my asking."

Norm shook his head. "I don't, as long as you're okay knowing the gory details of my personal life."

I thought for a moment of how selective I'd apparently been on that front with people I felt close to. "Always."

Blowing out another lungful of air, Norm stood again and began to pace, an activity that was so unlike him that I began to get nervous myself. “He… he told me he tested positive for HIV.”

My heart stopped. “Well, *shit*.”

Norm continued to pace. “You could say that again. I don’t entirely trust him, of course; it could just be another in a long line of things he’s done over the years to mess with me. But if he’s *not* lying…”

“Suzanne gave you the test?”

“More or less,” he nodded. “She had one of those rapid pharmacy kits on hand, but the results were inconclusive. So, she’s sending my sample out to her lab to get a better diagnostic. We’ll get the results back in a day or two.”

“You’re assuming he contracted it while you were still a couple?” I asked.

“Yes,” Norm nodded. “I suspected he was seeing someone else but tolerated it because he always came back to me. At least, that’s what I told myself.” He ran his hands through his short hair again. “I was so careful, too; save for a handful of times when the moment carried me away.” Norm sighed again. “Damn.”

“We don’t know anything yet,” I said. “Let’s take this one day at a time.”

“Yeah, I suppose you’re right,” Norm said before he turned to me, his eyes wide. “Sean… if I have it…”

I didn’t need him to finish the sentence to get a sense of where the panic was coming from. “Have you spoken to Raphael yet?”

“No,” he shook his head as he pulled his phone out of his khakis. “I’ve tried to dial him four times now and I keep cancelling the call. I think I’m afraid to tell him I was a stupid twenty-something who assumed he could never contract HIV.”

Standing from my chair — and for the first time in my professional career, feeling more like a father figure than a trusted friend — I came around and put a hand on his shoulder. “From what Vasily tells me, Raphael is as solid as they come. Call him, tell him what you know — and what you don’t; be honest, and go from there.” I smiled gently. “I suspect he will be shocked, but if he loves you as much as I think he does, you'll be going through this side-by-side."

"And if he doesn't?"

"Love you?" I asked. "Then it's better to know that now, don't you think?"

Norm looked awful for a moment. "Yeah, I suppose so."

"Either way," I continued, "I'm here for you. I'm sure Suzanne is, too. Whatever happens next, you won't be alone."

A shadow of a smile appeared. "Thanks."

"Of course." Realizing my coffee cup was empty, I moved over to my Keurig and fired it up. "Want some?"

"Only if you have Bailey's in that cupboard."

I turned and was going to make a joke about drinking while on duty when I realized just how terrified Norm was. *And why shouldn't he be?* I thought. *Decent antivirals have only been widely available for a few years now, but there's still no actual cure for it. Being HIV positive doesn't carry the same stigma it once did, but if he* is *positive, his life is going to change irrevocably.*

"I do," I said simply. "It's actually in my fridge over there."

"Fridge?" he asked, startled. "You keep Irish cream in the fridge?"

"It's a trick I picked up from my ex-fiancé," I said as he retrieved the bottle and I put a new K-cup into the machine. "You can store it at room temperature, of course, but the shelf life is extended when it's refrigerated."

"I had no idea."

"Live and learn, grasshopper," I laughed.

"By the way," Norm said as we watched my cherished machine chug through a cycle, "Heather's data has already been pushed into the case system, including the amazing gigabytes of photos they took of the layout. I think the photographer might have been a model railroader."

"Checking through the file was next on my list," I nodded as I slid the mug toward Norm. I tried not to comment when he put a sizable quantity of the brownish liquor into the coffee. "Were you able to track down the informal group that met at the store?"

"I did," he nodded after taking a sip. "Mmm, that is what I needed."

"Please don't let it get out that your boss let you drink," I smiled.

"It will be our little secret," he laughed, a genuine smile finally on his face for the first time that afternoon. "Anyway, Caitlyn took a photo of the Rolodex card her father had for the group in question and emailed it to me just before I went to lunch. While Walter was the official leader, I was able to reach out to the guy serving as his number two. He told me the group had a standing meeting in Millie's banquet room on Tuesdays; they'll all be there at four-thirty if we want to talk."

"That will work," I said, groaning inwardly at how close that was to when I needed to pick up Suzanne for our dinner at Charlie's that same evening. "How many people are in this group?"

"Seventeen," Norm said.

"Seriously?" I whistled. "I figured two or three; maybe five, max."

"It takes a village?" he observed.

"Apparently."

"I also took the initiative and began the process of requesting the financials for Walter and his business," Norm continued. "Caitlyn has made it easier — and faster — by providing the appropriate permissions to do so, but I suspect it will still be late morning tomorrow before everything comes in."

"Good." I pulled my own mug from the Keurig and then eyed the Bailey's. *Damn*, I thought as I poured a splash in. "We need to talk to Nick, too."

"Nick Romero?" Norm replied. "That could be tricky. I checked with his office after we parted ways this morning, and he's out of town on business."

My eyebrows went up. "That's rather convenient."

"Isn't it?"

"Where is he, exactly?" I asked. "And I thought he had the kids!"

"He's in New Hampshire with them. Caitlyn was just as surprised,"

Norm continued. "Especially since Nick can't take the kids across state lines without first talking to her per the custody agreement."

"New Hampshire?"

"Yeah. Camping in the White Mountains."

"Let me guess: no cell coverage?"

"None," Norm replied. "I reached out to a LEO there and they referred me to the National Park Police. Someone may be in touch with me later unless you want me to drive out and start scouring the mountains for him."

"We happen to know someone in the National Park Police," I said, smiling slightly. "That's not a bad way to start a difficult conversation."

"I thought about that, too," Norm replied. "Then again, I'm slightly worried that he thinks I'm trading favors for— "

"Probably best that you don't finish that sentence," I interrupted with a laugh. "Without knowing where he is, exactly, we don't know what the round-trip drive time is, either."

"Yeah," Norm nodded.

"I still want to talk to him," I said.

"I figured," he said. "I'll call Raphael and see if he can pull any strings."

"Tell him I pay in lobsters," I said. "At current prices, though, that might run a pretty penny."

"No kidding."

"Anything else?" I asked as I moved back to my desk.

"Not yet," he smiled as he headed for the door. "But the day is still young."

Pulling out my chair, I took a seat behind my desk again and stared at the laptop in front of me. My plan had been to log into the case system and begin to peruse the information Heather had collected, but I also knew I had to call Suzanne and warn her I might be late to pick her up. My hand hesitated over the phone, though, which was a first for me and a clear indication that I was still quite worried over how we had left things at lunch. Swallowing, I picked up the handset and dialed her direct line, then felt my heart rate tick up with each ring at the other end. I was on the verge of hanging up when her wonderful voice filled my ear.

"Hey Sean," she said simply. "You caught me between appointments. What's up?"

"I—" I started, then suddenly found myself unable to speak.

"Actually," Suzanne continued, clearly having not heard my monosyllabic response, "I'm glad you called. I've been summoned to Portland; one of the other doctors in our rotation had an unexpected appendectomy. It's been a bear cancelling appointments through the weekend, but there's no way around it. I'm going to drive down tonight."

My eyebrows went up. In the year plus we'd been together, I could count on one hand how often Maine Medical pulled her in for emergency coverage; her peers were well aware of how vital her practice was to our corner of the county. That they would *happen* to do so a few hours after what had gone down in her kitchen felt more than suspect – and uncomfortably similar to when she'd fled to Portland after I'd asked her to spend Christmas with me. Suzanne had later confessed that her feelings for me at that point in our relationship had terrified her enough to want to put some distance between us; I feared past had suddenly become prologue and tried to tamp back the gnawing dread in the pit of my stomach.

"That's terrible," I managed to say. "How long will you be there?"

"I'll drive back on Sunday night."

"If this case goes well, I can join you Friday evening," I started. "I know it's not our weekend for the Children's Ward, but I can bring my costume—"

"Don't bother," Suzanne said quickly, cutting me off. "I'm going to stay with a colleague, anyway. She's got a small pullout couch."

I could feel my pulse starting to pound. "Ah, makes sense. It's so last minute, reservations are probably nuts at the Marriott."

"Exactly." There was a long pause. "What was it you wanted to talk about?"

There are a bunch of answers to that, I thought morosely, *and not nearly enough time to go through them.* "I... spoke with Norm," I said, shifting gears. "He seems pretty worried."

"With reason," Suzanne sighed. "The good news is that it's possible to control HIV to a point where it's undetectable, but if his test comes back positive, it's going to change his life. I've put him on a reasonably good post-exposure protocol just in case."

"Yeah," I said. "Helluva thing for someone his age to deal with."

"Thankfully it's not like it was," she reminded me. There was another pause. "Look, I've got to go. My next appointment is here."

"Call me when you get to Portland?" I asked.

"If I can," was the reply. "I have to go straight in when I arrive."

"Then hugs and kisses and I'll see you Sunday."

"Ditto," was her curt response before the line went dead.

I'm not sure how long I held the handset to my face after the line went dead; it was long enough that the strange double-beeping alert began warning me the line was being held open. I'd just slowly replaced it when the phone rang. Picking it up, I answered: "Chief Colbeth."

"Sean, it's Lou. Got a moment?"

"I always have time for the Chief Medical Examiner," I replied, trying for humor. Instead, to my ear it sounded sarcastic.

Lou picked up on it, but to my relief chuckled. "Bad day?"

I sighed. "You could say that. Long, if nothing else."

"We've both had our fair share of those, haven't we?"

"Yes. Yes, we have. Are you calling about my postmortem?"

"I am," she replied. "You've got that stupid Professional Standards thing tomorrow afternoon, right?"

"I do. Just after lunch."

"All right," she said. I could hear her typing on a keyboard. "How about 11, then? Will that give you enough time to change for the kangaroo court?"

I smiled. "You don't want me to wear my Class As into the exam room?"

"I'd be honored," she chuckled, "but I suspect the panel wouldn't appreciate how aromatic you would be if you did."

"Maybe that's my secret weapon tomorrow."

"If that is the best you have," Lou replied, "then you might want to dust off that resume of yours."

"Excellent point," I conceded.

There was a long pause. "How are you doing?" Lou asked. "This can't be much fun to go through."

"It's not," I answered, shrugging. "I suppose sooner or later we all have a moment like this, right?"

"I think most of us prefer to skip over that, actually," Lou chuckled. "Look, why don't you come at ten, and then we'll go to lunch afterward."

Despite myself, I felt a smile form. "You expect me to *eat* after attending your postmortem?"

"I do," she chuckled. "See you at ten."

Seven

Norm met me in front of the Public Safety Building and together we walked the short distance from there to Millie's on the Wharf. Despite it being barely four-thirty, the line to get a table had already burst through the double doors and spilled out onto the sidewalk running along Route One, making it look more like a concert venue than the venerable food establishment it was. Since we weren't there to eat (unfortunately), I stepped around the line and worked my way toward the host stand at the end of the short corridor leading to the main dining room. Norm was right behind me, and followed my lead when I cut between two couples arguing about whether the lobster being served were from the harbor or flown in from Canada (really?) so I could reach the banquet room that was just opposite. I'd not actually been inside that space since the night Vasily and I had been working the Pelletier case nearly two years earlier, but as I entered, I realized it hadn't changed one bit. Fish nets were still tacked to the walls, accompanied by lobster traps that were hanging upside from the ceiling. In what was the only nod to the space being used regularly for group meetings, one wall featured a pulldown screen, and a LED projector was tucked between two of the lobster traps. That particular evening, the tables had been arranged into a giant U with the open end facing the screen; a dozen or so men, mostly at the retirement end of the age spectrum, were seated around the U, and judging from the numerous beer bottles and wineglasses, had already begun the meeting with the happy hour portion of the program.

One white-haired man with round rimless glasses saw our entry and stood from the table, then met us in the corner. "Chief Colbeth," he said as he shook my hand. "I'm Aaron Wildwood, more or less head of the Windeport Model Railroad Society."

"Nice to meet you, Mr. Wildwood," I said, then cocked my head. "Hang on — didn't I have you for A.P. Biology?"

Wildwood smiled. "That you did," he chuckled. "I wasn't sure you'd remember me."

"Your fetal pig lab made quite an impression," I smiled. "I can't say it's what drove me into police work, exactly, but I *would* be remiss if I didn't tell you much of what I learned in that class has been put to practical use."

"We don't hear that very often," Wildwood said.

"Are you still teaching?"

"No," he shook his head. "I retired last year after forty years."

"Congratulations, then," I said. "This is Assistant Chief Norm Thomas."

"We spoke on the phone earlier," Norm said as he shook. "Thanks for letting us crash your meeting."

Wildwood looked over his shoulder. "It's a bit more like a wake tonight," he said quietly. "Most of us had known Walter for decades; he really *was* this group. I'm not sure how we'll move forward without him."

"Not easily, I would guess," I replied.

"Come on in, let me introduce you — though I suspect you probably know everyone already."

Wildwood led us over to the table and then quickly did introductions. Having lived in Windeport for as long as I had, it was a set of familiar faces I was seeing; while I didn't know all of them on a personal level, in a village as small as ours you couldn't help but run into people repeatedly. Bob and Carl were the main landscapers in town, mowing from Memorial Day to Labor Day, then plowing the remainder of the year. Jeff was head of personal accounts at First Bank of Windeport; Max, Heath and David were professors at UEM and swam with me most mornings at the pool. Frank and George also worked at UEM, though what they did exactly was a bit unclear beyond aiding various researchers. Phil and Bernie were still teaching at Windeport Regional, in Math and Social Studies (respectively). Larry headed up the deli at the IGA, and his best friend, Sam, ran the bakery; Vicktor was a transplant from overseas and had been with Windeport Fire for as long as I could remember. Ernie was one of the more recent members of the group, a semi-retired columnist for the *Bangor Daily News* who lived close to where Norm had his new place; I'd been an avid reader of his work for years but had noticed they'd become far shorter and much less interesting as of late. Still, I'd been excited to hear he'd moved to the Village. Thomas was married to Ernie and was a retired dentist; without any evidence at all, I'd assumed that was how the couple had afforded the Davies "cottage" when it became available earlier in the summer. One member was missing at the moment — Jack — as he was up county taking care of his grandkids while the parents were away.

I couldn't help but be amazed by the eclectic makeup of the group as I took up position in the empty space at the front of the room. I wasn't entirely surprised that the group was all male, but I didn't know enough about model railroading as a hobby to draw the conclusion that it didn't appeal to women. I felt like my own mother would have loved the intricacies of a layout such as the one Walter had spent his life working on; she'd been pretty good in the electronics department, too, being the one that my father had relied on to keep various portions of our POS and pharmacy systems operational. The image of Mom huddled over a small train car with a soldering iron in hand popped into my head and made me smile.

Scanning the faces that were expectantly facing me, I considered how to start the more difficult part of the conversation. "I know Walter was a big part of this group," I began. "I only knew him through his daughter and the stories she would tell me about what was going on down at the shop. It's to my everlasting regret that I didn't visit the spot more."

There were some nods around the table and a few murmurs of assent.

"I don't really have a hobby *per se*," I continued. "Unless you count my chlorine obsession that has me in the pool twice a day," I added with a smile and knowing nod at my fellow swimmers. "How did this group form?"

"Walter always invited anyone who was interested to stop by the shop after hours to work on the layout," Wildwood said. "I think I got recruited when I was in purchasing some track for my layout."

My eyebrows went up. "You have your own layout?"

"Most of us do," Vicktor said as though it would be self-evident.

"Much to the chagrin of our wives," Max chuckled. "When I'm not doing research, I'm down in the basement."

"Or the attic," Phil interjected. "Not all of us have a nice basement like you, Max."

"Perks of building a custom home," Max laughed. "It was the only way to make sure the steps to the basement were in the center of the house."

"Why would that be important?" I asked, intrigued by the discussion.

Carl looked at me like I had failed some sort of test. Glancing at Bob, he smiled slightly. "That way, you can run your layout around the perimeter of the basement," he explained patiently.

Still feeling like I was missing something, I looked at Norm with a question on my face. "Remember how we had to duck beneath Walter's layout?" he asked.

Unbidden, I began to rub at the small of my back where I had smacked a two-by-four by trying to stand up before clearing the edge of the layout. "Ah," I smiled wanly at Carl. "I can see the benefits."

"Exactly," he chuckled. "Walter didn't have that option in the store, of course."

"Or his basement, come to think of it," Thomas piped in. "I think the stairs ran against the back wall."

"They do," Ernie nodded. I wasn't entirely sure how old he was, but his full head of dark hair made him look far younger than the rest of the attendees. I couldn't tell if the color was natural, though. "And it's one of those old-fashioned dirt basements, so trying to get anything level down there would have been hell."

I nodded. "I think our pharmacy had the same thing, actually," I added. "My grandfather spent a lot of money getting a smooth concrete surface so he could store product down there."

"I'll bet he did," Ernie laughed.

"So, if you all have your own layouts, why get together with Walter?"

"All sorts of reasons," Phil said. "Not the least of which is getting out and catching up with friends."

"I can see the social aspects," I grinned, nodding toward the beer bottles.

"We didn't drink during the operating sessions, actually," Phil continued. "Just coffee and maybe a dessert that someone brought."

"Operating session?" I asked. "As in running the trains?"

"Exactly," Frank stepped in. Of the group, he was the only one wearing a striped hat that made him look like an engineer I'd seen in a book that Charlie had read to the twins. "Walter would place rolling stock all over the layout—"

"Rolling stock?" I interrupted, frowning. "You mean the little trains?"

Frank rolled his eyes. "Yes," he replied. "'Rolling stock' is a term we use for everything that's not an engine — boxcars for freight, tank cars for moving liquid items, flatbeds and the like."

"Those *pull* the rolling stock," Norm added with a sly grin.

I glared at him but returned my attention to Frank. "So, Walter would set things up, and then the group would come and, what, simulate moving the rolling stock from one point to another?"

Frank nodded. "Exactly," he said. "The version of Windeport on that layout is pretty accurate to Windeport as it stands today, but for operational interest, we make some creative adjustments to justify running a train in and out of the Village."

"I noticed there were tracks embedded in his version of Main Street," I said. "I presume that was for boxcars that took product from the canneries that used to be along the wharf?"

"Yes," Max said. "We also have them down the pier, too."

"I must have missed those," I replied. "I'll have to look closer."

"Oh, you totally do," David laughed. "There are so many tiny, *tiny* details built into that layout."

"I saw a few," I nodded. "We lifted off the building for Route One Hobbies and discovered the interior."

"Every structure has an interior," George added. "Walter built several of them, as did his father. Some of us helped with the later additions, especially when he started adding the portion for UEM and Snowden Notch."

"*Every* structure?" I asked.

"Everything," George nodded. "They are all lit, too. At least one has a working television. Did you find that one?"

"Not yet," I shook my head, somewhat amazed at what I was hearing. I wondered if any of the sensitive electronics had been damaged in the short that killed Walter; more than anything, I suddenly wanted to see the layout in all its glory. Something else occurred to me, though. "Which one of you is responsible for the bullet-ridden SUV in the parking lot of the Public Safety Building?"

Heath raised his hand and smiled sheepishly. "I saw it in the parking lot shortly after — well, what happened," he said. "I couldn't help it."

"You all seem to have quite the eye for detail," I laughed. "I do miss that SUV. The new one is nice, but I liked the old one."

"We can get attached to things," Wildwood observed.

"Now that I know I've been missing stuff, are there any other secrets on that layout I should know about?" I asked with a smile. While my question had been jovial in nature, the sudden silence and darting looks among those present started that tiny little buzz I often got when something significant was accidentally uncovered.

Sam ultimately was the one who spoke up and broke the awkward moment. "Walter tinkered with that thing every spare moment," he said. "And most nights he spent a few hours on it after the store closed. I think he once told me there was a list of every detail put into the layout, including stuff that most people wouldn't notice. Or," Sam added after a moment, "stuff that people *should* notice but didn't."

I felt an eyebrow arch; the buzz became something more. "Are you saying it was like an inside joke that only a few people would get? Or something else?"

"Maybe a bit of both," Wildwood replied. "There were plenty of inside jokes that all of us were in on, of course, but I can think of a few unusual details that Walter never really explained."

"Like what?"

Wildwood frowned. "Well, for example, the layout has a statue out in front of the library; there isn't one in real life."

"Or the egg farm on the western side of the Village," Phil added. "It's right next to UEM, but of course, there isn't one physically out there."

"What was the story behind those?" I asked.

"The statue, I think, was of Walter's father," Wildwood said. "I think the story was that his dad always wanted to be a librarian. Or had donated for the expansion that took place back in the 1970s? I'm not sure I remember."

"And the egg farm?" I asked. "Was that some sort of connection to his father, too?"

"Walter was always pretty coy about that," Thomas replied. "Honestly, I always thought he just liked the excuse to run livestock deliveries. The Thompkins place was the last dairy farm in Windeport, so there isn't much in the way of agriculture left these days that we can model."

I nodded. "Has anyone seen Walter's list of secrets?" I asked, purposefully shifting the language.

There were nearly in unison shaking their heads. "We all know it exists, but it was never something Walter shared with us," Ernie said. "Lord knows we asked him enough times."

"Not all of us," Larry said. "Some of us were *insanely* interested in that list," he added, pointedly looking at Ernie.

He waved his hands. "I apologized for that ages ago," he sighed before looking at me. "I made the mistake of writing a column about the group," he explained. "Part of that included delineating all the little touches on the layout we had built; I had a lot of them, but wanted to cross-check what I knew against the master list. Walter was reluctant to share."

"I don't remember that column," I said. "And I read the paper daily."

"I never published it," Ernie sighed again. "It became a *thing,* and it was just easier to drop it."

"You didn't drop it," Thomas said quietly. "You kept at him until you left for Bangor, remember?"

Something washed across Ernie's face before he smiled slightly. "That's right. I worked on him until the very last moment, though."

"And then I started up again as soon we returned, right?" Thomas prompted.

"I suppose I did, didn't I?" Ernie chuckled. "I might be retired, but there's still room for one more big story."

"Why didn't he want to show you the list?" I asked, feeling like I had stumbled onto something, though just *what* was a little unclear.

"Now that is the question of the hour," Ernie said as he grabbed his beer bottle and took a swig. "If I knew the answer, I would have published my column."

Waitresses from the restaurant took that moment to appear bearing trays overflowing with food; they paused briefly when they saw me, then continued to set them down on portable stands so they could serve. Getting the message that my time with the group was running short, I smiled again. "Well, I don't want to get between you and your seafood platters," I said. "One last thing, though. On the nights when the group wasn't there, did Walter host guests?"

"All the time," Bob said. "Anyone was welcome to drop in any evening he was there."

"Whether they were part of the group or not?" Norm asked.

"Yes," Bob nodded. "By everyone, I mean *everyone*."

"That sounds like it could be hard to manage," I observed carefully. "Between the operating sessions and ad hoc guests. Did Walter keep some sort of schedule?"

"Yes," Carl said. "He had a calendar from *Model Railroader* that hung behind the checkout counter. If there was a square free, you could sign up and come."

My eyes went to Norm, who subtly shook his head, confirming my own recollection that nothing like that had been behind the counter when we'd done the search. I made a note to nonetheless review the logs from Heather's team in case we had just missed it in the semi-darkness. "Okay," I smiled as I stepped back to allow the waitresses to begin to serve. "Thank you everyone for your time; enjoy your dinner."

"One second, Chief," Wildwood said as he stood; Norm and I paused at the door to wait for him. Looking back at the table, he lowered his voice before speaking again. "We've been hearing rumors that Walter's death is suspicious. Is that true?"

I kept my voice down as well. "It's normal for us to do a little digging when someone is found in unexpected circumstances," I replied carefully before nodding back to the assembled. "Meetings like this can give us context to understand what was going on."

"That makes sense" Wildwood said, though he still looked puzzled. "Well, if you need to know anything else about Walter or model railroading, feel free to reach out again."

"Will do," I smiled as I shook his hand. "Thanks again."

Norm and I waded out through the crowd in the reception area that seemed to have only grown thicker since our entrance; reaching the muggy air outside felt like more relief than it properly should have been. Pausing off to the side of the line that extended well down Main Street now, I looked at Norm. "What do you think?"

"I think we need another look at that layout," he said as we started toward the Public Safety building. "And maybe need to sift through what is left at the store for that calendar and the mysterious list of details Walter had."

I nodded. "The calendar feels especially important," I said. "If it truly had what visitors were there on what nights, it might give us a better sense of who the *last* visitor was."

"You think they took it?" Norm asked.

"Or destroyed it," I frowned. "I'm hoping they just took it." We waited for a break in the traffic to cross the street. "That list of secrets," I mused as we began walking again. "I can't shake the feeling it's important."

"Why?"

"That's a fair question," I smiled. "A hunch, I guess? It's either that or we tear apart the layout trying to decide what sort of hidden message Walter built into it."

"I'd prefer not to do that. It's almost a work of art."

"I agree," I nodded.

"You really think he was hiding something on the layout?" Norm asked.

"Possibly," I nodded again.

"Something someone was willing to kill him over?"

"Definitely," I nodded a third time.

"Well, *shit*," Norm breathed. "This is one interesting little village."

"That it is," I chuckled as I glanced at my watch. "I'm going to call it a day."

"You'll be in Augusta tomorrow?"

"Yeah," I said. "I'm going to head out after practice for the post-mortem, and then I have that... thing... afterward."

"Good luck," he said as he put his hand on the door. "With both of them."

"Thanks," I sighed as I turned toward my SUV. "I'm going to need it, I think."

Eight

The text message from Caitlyn had arrived while I was at Millie's, letting me know that she'd driven herself out to Charlie's after she'd tried to get the POS system up and running at the hobby store. I gathered from the frowning face she had appended to the message that it hadn't gone particularly well and made a note to ask further details over dinner. It felt odd not picking up Suzanne on my way past the old pharmacy building; I thought about calling her to see if she'd gotten to Portland safely but decided against it, worried about how it might look. Continuing down Route One toward the turnoff for Charlie's farmhouse, I found myself considering some desperate measures to get back into my girlfriend's good graces. *That* made me frown, though, for I wasn't entirely certain that I'd fallen out in quite that way. I *was* certain I had crossed some sort of line inadvertently, a line that I'd not know was there until I'd stumbled over it in spectacular fashion.

A sudden thought about how I could begin to repair things sprung into my head and made me smile; I'd need to do a bit of research to ensure that I was remembering something I had watched online, but if I was right, it could be a clever way for me to apologize while also encouraging her to explain to me what, exactly, I had done to cause it in the first place. By the time my SUV rumbled to a stop behind Caitlyn's vehicle, the first vestiges of a plan had come together. Seeing my face in the rearview mirror, I nodded as I silently made a promise to myself to fix what I had broken.

As I came up the steps to the farmhouse, I paused beneath the overhang, suddenly aware of how quiet it was in the yard. Considering how long our evenings were in the summer, I wondered why the twins weren't scampering about on the rolling front yard, fighting unseen monsters while they brandished their magic wands or light sabers or whatever imaginary items they'd conjured for the moment. Wondering what was up, I knocked at the big wooden door and was immediately greeted by Charlie.

"Right on time," she smiled as she stepped away to let me in.

I paused just inside the door. "Where is everyone?" I asked when it was apparent the twins were similarly not inside the period farmhouse.

"Caitlyn took them to the icehouse," she shrugged. "They wanted to go swimming, and that little pond out there is close at hand."

"That's a bit of a hike for a swim," I said as she closed the door behind me.

The icehouse had been the scene of the crime, as it were, for the Brogan case; it was also the last remaining reminder of a time when massive blocks of ice were once cut from the St. Mark's River during the winter and then stored to be used the rest of the year in the refrigerators of the day. Charlie wasn't wrong, for despite it being a healthy five kilometer walk from the farmhouse, the small pond that had been created beside the river also made for a rather impressive swimming hole. It was probably wise, though, that the kids were young enough not to appreciate how a double murder had taken place out there.

"Which means the kids will sleep soundly tonight," Charlie chuckled. "Want some wine while we wait for their return?"

"Please," I said as I followed her toward the kitchen.

A bottle sat uncorked in the sideboard, alongside four wineglasses.

Taking up the bottle, she began pouring into one of the glasses. "Where's Suzanne?" she asked casually.

"Portland," I said, adding before I could stop myself: "I think."

The tone of my voice caused Charlie to stop pouring and turn fully toward me. "You *think*?"

I felt my face heating up. "Yeah," I nodded, before looking away. "There was some sort of emergency coverage issue at Maine Medical, so she had to take off."

The bottle plunked down on the tile of the counter with a *tinkle-tink* that had me worried the bottle had cracked. "On a Tuesday?"

I nodded, still scrutinizing the tiny shelf holding various spices. "All part of the glamorous life of a physician, I guess."

Charlie's hand to my shoulder forced me to turn back toward her. "What happened?" she asked, her face a mix of worry and concern.

Grabbing the half-filled glass of wine from the counter, I smiled slightly. "I'll need more if you want the full story."

Arching an eyebrow, Charlie moved back to the counter and filled my glass to the rim, then poured out a second portion for herself. "Let's go out to the porch," she said as she led me toward the front door. "With the slight breeze coming up from the river, it's the most tolerable spot in the entire house right now."

"I've been sleeping on my back porch for the same reason," I said as we settled into the Adirondack recliners. "This feels like the hottest July yet."

"It may well be," she nodded. Taking a sip, she eyed me. "Talk, cousin."

Taking a deep breath, I went through my day, highlighting how Suzanne had surprised me at the courthouse to the tense ending in the kitchen a few hours later. I tactfully left out the main reason we'd wound up at the apartment but could tell Charlie had made the connection all the same; her knowing smile had me flushing a bit but didn't prevent me from outlining where I thought things had gone off the rails. "It seemed like a good question to ask," I said as I wrapped up my overview, "but the moment I put voice to it, I knew something was wrong." I took a long sip from the crisp red wine Charlie had provided. "Then I went and made things worse by prodding her further."

"You're an investigator," she reminded me. "To mix my metaphors, you tend to want to dig where others would fear to tread."

"Even when I should know better," I sighed. "I've been thinking about it all afternoon and realized there were a million little signs I'd been ignoring."

Charlie chuckled. "We've gone over that particular shortcoming of yours before," she reminded me.

"Yeah," I nodded. "That we have. For a detective, I sometimes have trouble seeing what's right beneath my nose."

"Only in your personal life," Charlie pointed out. "Though not like before," she added as she leaned forward and reached for my arm. Tapping it, she smiled. "The version of you that lost Deidre would *never* have taken the time to understand what set Suzanne off; the fact that you are openly asking yourself questions — and looking for answers — is pretty damn positive."

I looked at Charlie. "I don't want to lose Suzanne," I said softly. "I'm not sure I was willing to admit it to myself that I've been living in fear from the moment we got together that I might. And then this happens." I swirled the last of the wine in my glass for a moment. "It's a helluva place to operate from."

"Nothing has happened yet," Charlie assured me as she leaned back. "I would also like to remind you that Suzanne is not Deidre — not even in the slightest way. That doesn't mean she's not every bit as complicated of a person — hell, who isn't — but using what happened between you and your ex-fiancé as a guide is not going to work."

I nodded slightly. "I think my heart understands that," I said. "But my heart is also not capable of straight thoughts when it comes to Suzanne, either."

Charlie smiled. "That, my cousin, is the very essence of love."

"So I hear," I chuckled.

"What are you going to do?"

I drained the last of my wine. "I'm going to drive to Portland on Friday."

"You just told me she didn't want you to do that — that she *expressly* told you not to."

"She did."

There was a long pause. "Are you sure it's a good idea? That seems like a pretty clear 'stop' sign to me."

"No," I replied honestly. "I don't. But it also feels like the only play I have."

"Dear Lord," Charlie sighed. "You do have a penchant for drama, don't you?"

"Actually," I frowned, "I don't. I think it's the other way around."

"That drama seeks you out?" Charlie asked. "You know what, I think I could buy that."

"I thought you might," I chuckled. "Is there any more wine?"

"Only if you are planning on staying over tonight," she answered. "I'm not sure you should drive if you have more."

"Yeah, good point," I said as I stood. "Look, I think I'm going to bow out of tonight's s'mores festivities."

"Are you sure?" she asked as she stood, too. "I don't know if you should be alone tonight."

"I'll be fine," I replied.

"I have my chili on the stove," Charlie pressed. "You usually don't turn that down."

"True," I smiled as I handed her my empty wineglass. "I'm not going to be good company tonight; besides, I have a ton of data to shift through on this case, anyway."

"You're also worried about tomorrow, aren't you?"

"I can't deny it's weighing on my thoughts," I sighed. "Which reminds me, I've got to dig out my formal uniform and make sure it's pressed properly."

Charlie eyed me. "When was the last time you ironed *anything*?"

"When I took the job as Police Chief," I chuckled as I started down the steps to the SUV. "We're pretty informal around here."

"That we are," she chuckled. "At least let me send you home with some dinner."

"I—"

Charlie disappeared into the house before I could tell her I wasn't hungry, despite what little true food I had eaten all day. I'd assumed my slight headache had been from the stress of the case combined with my worries over Suzanne, but as I stood there on the covered porch, watching the first flashes of lightning course through the thick clouds overhead, I realized the throbbing between my eyes was more a sign it was well past time to replenish the calories I'd burned. Almost as if she had planned on sending me home with a care package, barely a minute later Charlie returned with a canvas tote bag bearing the classic L.L. Bean logo, which she handed to me.

"It's already warm, of course, so you could eat it as soon as you get home," Charlie instructed, "or you can warm it up in the microwave. I've also included the rest of the wine we started as well ingredients to make two s'mores."

Arching an eyebrow, I smiled. "And how do I make a s'more without a campfire?"

"You'll figure it out," she chuckled. "I'll tell the kids when they get back you couldn't stay but send your love."

"That I do." I looked at her for a moment. "Thanks for listening."

"I've always been there for you, cousin," she smiled warmly. "I think you know that."

"Yeah," I nodded. "I haven't always been smart enough to make use of that, though."

"No," she chuckled. "Definitely not."

Getting back into the SUV, I waved at Charlie before starting it up and pulling around Caitlyn's vehicle; halfway down the dirt driveway, my iPhone rang. Toggling the Bluetooth function, I answered. "Chief Colbeth."

"Chief, it's Norm," came the voice of my number two. "Just got off the phone with Raphael's contact at the White Mountains National Forest. They located Nick and the kids at a campground not far from the ranger station."

"That was fast," I said.

"Yeah," Norm said. "Nick is on his way back to Windeport now; as soon as he heard about Walter's death, he piled everything back into his truck and took off."

"Really?" I asked, surprised. "That's not what I expected at all."

"He seemed quite concerned about Caitlyn, according to the ranger I spoke to."

"Wild," I said, wondering even more about why the two had broken up in the first place.

"He'll get in late tonight, given the distance. How do you want to handle it?"

"I most definitely want to speak with him," I replied as I turned out onto Route One. The thick thunderclouds were momentarily backlit dramatically by the setting sun, then disappeared just as quickly, a stark reminder that the weather was nearly upon us. "I don't see any reason to corner him at his house when he pulls up, though."

"Isn't he a suspect?" Norm asked.

"In what? I don't even have a formal ruling of a suspicious death yet," I reminded Norm. "Not until Lou gets done."

"True, but he did the electrical—"

"And we will want to ask him questions about it," I said. "Right now, *all* we are doing is asking questions."

There was a long pause. "Right. Sorry, Chief."

"Don't apologize," I smiled at the air. "It's always good to think a step or two ahead; tell you what, why don't you pay him a visit while I'm Augusta. See if you can get him to talk you through the work he did for Walter. Then we'll compare that with what the electrical inspector from the State tells us."

"Speaking of, Heather left a note in the file confirming they would be here on Friday."

"I was hoping for sooner," I said. "Well, it's worth waiting for Irving in order to get his experience."

"Indeed."

"How did it go with Raphael?"

There was a long pause. "Not quite as well as I had hoped," Norm replied dejectedly. "Admittedly, we were both a bit drunk the first time we—well, the first time we were together," he continued. "And not thinking terribly straight. Mistakes are often made in those sorts of situations."

"Ah," was all I could think to say.

"Raphael was going to swing through one of those minute clinics and see if he could get a test done just for peace of mind." There was another long pause. "The thing that sucks the most is that I have no idea how long I've had it. If my ex had told me sooner, there are some damn good prophylactic treatments to counteract exposure."

"*If* you have it," I reminded him. "Let's not get ahead of the evidence."

Norm chuckled slightly. "I suppose not."

"Can't you get them now?" I asked. "Those antivirals?"

"No," Norm replied. "They must be taken within a few days of exposure. Suzanne put me on post-exposure meds, but it's fifty-fifty if they'd do anything at this point."

"You left your ex months ago," I said softly. "Shit."

"Exactly." He paused again. "And I found out too late to help Raphael."

"Shit. *Shit*."

"Yeah."

"Is he... still coming up?" I asked delicately.

"Yes," Norm replied. "Though this certainly changes the tone for the visit."

"No kidding." I happened to be passing the old pharmacy building at that moment and had a thought. "If Suzanne gets back from Maine Medical Center while he's visiting, Raphael should touch base with her, too. It can't hurt for him to have a solid medical opinion — especially if, well, you both come up positive."

"That's a great idea," Norm said. "He'd like Suzanne."

"Everyone does," I smiled, then felt a pang of regret as I did. The Sea Road appeared on my left, but as I started to flick on the turn signal, I realized I wasn't ready to face an empty house. I'd wanted to revisit the hobby store anyway, so I willingly leaned on work as an excuse as I continued down Route One. "I'm going to take another look at the layout tonight, and then head home."

"Didn't you already tell me you'd clocked out?" Norm chided.

"I lied," I chuckled. "See you tomorrow."

"Roger that. And Sean," he added, "good luck in Augusta."

"Thanks."

Crawling my way down the busy Route One, I finally was able to pull off and around to the small parking lot behind Route One Hobbies. Walter's sedan was still parked in one of the open slots, and I took the other; turning off the SUV, I dug through my pockets to come up with the spare key Caitlyn had provided for the building, then dug out a pair of latex gloves from the glove compartment, along with my trusty flashlight. I rubbed my thumb along the abrasion where a bullet from Bethesda Thompkins had grazed it — one of many errant shots that had gone through portions of my old SUV but had thankfully missed the human who'd been huddling inside it at the time. Sliding out of the driver's seat, I crossed the parking lot to the rear door and unlocked it, then slipped under the crime scene tape ostensibly protecting the scene within.

The space was as dark as before, if not darker given the impending storm that was brewing overhead. Snapping on my flashlight, I found the main panel for the store and flipped on the breakers for the overhead lights; it didn't improve the situation in the stock room much, nor, I found, did it do anything for the storefront proper beyond the same flickering florescent bulb over the rear of the space. Flashes of lightning were becoming more frequent, momentarily overexposing everything in the most dramatic manner possible, making me feel like I was in the middle of one of those bad horror movies Suzanne loved to watch. Quickly moving down the aisles toward the windows, I detoured over to the checkout counter and snapped on my flashlight; waving the bright white beam against the wall, I located a small nail at about the right height to have hosted a standard twelve-month calendar, though a second search of the shelves beneath the cash register didn't turn up one. I *did* find several flyers for a train show in Massachusetts that had taken place three months earlier, though, and smiled to think that people would actually drive several hours to see a ballroom full of miniature railroad materials. Then again, the portable displays touted on the back of the flyer were nearly enough to induce me to go if the event were ever held again; after spending time with Walter's layout, some of the photos made them look as equally as dramatic and had the same hallmarks of craftsmanship.

Actually, I thought as I put the flyers back into a drawer, *after meeting with those train enthusiasts earlier, I think I could understand why folks would go to something like this. I suppose in many ways it's not unlike Vas and his comic book conventions. Or,* I smiled, *me and my regional swim meets...*

Scanning the countertop, I could see the CPUs for the point-of-sale system had been removed; I knew Caitlyn was attempting to recover what was on them and had likely taken them back to the station as part of that process — despite, of course, her supposedly being on leave. The touchscreen monitors seemed rather lonely without their companions; the handheld barcode scanners emphasized that feeling with their cables unplugged and strewn across the counter. The flashlight reflected off the metal for the two cash drawers mounted beneath the counter, one beneath each of the missing POS stations. They looked fairly similar to ones my father had used in our pharmacy, so playing a hunch, I held the flashlight in my mouth as I ran my hands along the edges of one of the drawers. The manual release button was about where I expected it to be; triggering it caused the drawer to pop open with a slight *cha-ching* noise from an unseen bell. To my surprise, the till appeared to be full; opening the drawer beside it showed the same eye-popping amount of cash. Digging through them took a few minutes, but in the end, there was about three thousand dollars between the two, give or take, plus a handful of checks beneath the large bills. Pulling the till upward and out of the physical drawer, I discovered another stash of credit card receipts, all of which appeared to have been processed within the past week. Sorting through them in the beam of my flashlight, I could see each receipt had the name of a cardholder on them, as well as a date and time stamp for the transaction in question. I was a little surprised Heather's team hadn't bagged and tagged the contents, then reminded myself she'd planned on returning Friday to wrap up processing the scene. Staring at the blank screens, I mused that the POS system could provide far more detail, but if it was truly toasted, the checks and credit cards might be our best lead in determining what might have gone on during Walter's final day.

Dashing back out to my SUV and between the massive drops of rain that had begun to splatter against the pavement, I popped open the trunk and pulled out my backpack, then returned to the counter. It took me a few minutes to take photos of everything with my iPhone, and then a few minutes more to carefully place the contents of the two drawers into evidence bags. Once sealed, I held them in one hand while I waved the flashlight over the counter a final time; not seeing anything else out of the ordinary, I stuffed the bags into my backpack and then slung it over my shoulder before moving across the room to the layout.

The flashlight was admittedly not the best device for getting at the finer details of the layout, but I nonetheless started shining it against the simulated rolling hills around Windeport, trying to get my bearings. From where I was standing, I was looking at the back of Main Street as though I were coming into the village from the west; using that as my base, I ran the light along the tiny road and then caught the intersection by the miniature version of Calista's Bakery, searching for the egg farm that had spurred such a lively discussion at the banquet hall earlier. Sure enough, a small complex of industrial looking barns appeared beneath the white light, with a set of rails running into a small yard beside it; there was even a tiny, framed sign at the entrance to the facility with the name *Levant* printed in bold, corporate lettering. I wasn't sure why I'd missed it earlier, but now that I was looking for it, I could see how odd its location was just a short distance from the campus for the University of Eastern Maine. Even allowing for some creative liberties to include such an industry where none existed, it had been plopped into what was in real life a large, empty field; though I couldn't be entirely sure, I was reasonably certain it was right about where the farm had been that had resulted in the quirky boundary between Windeport and the unincorporated county — that same oddball boundary that had dropped the Donohue case into my lap the prior summer.

Flicking the beam toward the insanely accurate buildings dotting the university campus, I located the arched roofline for the aquatic center and smiled at the small details even that had, including the little glass windows in the roof we often kept open to alleviate some of the humidity from the indoor pool. The parking lot was full of vehicles, and I wondered as I shined my light on them if the license plates would match any real vehicles in the Village. Turning back to the egg farm, I held the flashlight in my mouth for a moment so I could reach over and lift the building upward; unsurprisingly, there was a fully detailed interior, though to my dismay it accurately depicted what life was like for a chicken living in such conditions. Small cages held even smaller chickens and had been arranged in long lines in front of a conveyor belt littered with ovoid objects meant to represent eggs. One portion of the massive barn had a realistic looking pile of manure, including tiny feathers sticking out here and there. Setting that building down, I picked up another and found my eyes widen in surprise, for this one appeared to depict in gory detail the activities necessary in turning chickens into those styrofoam-and-plastic wrapped containers of meat I could buy at the IGA. While I didn't know the exact process, there were enough context clues to assume the chickens were being electrocuted at one end before being bled, de-feathered and ultimately deboned at the other. The scenes were nearly enough to make me a vegetarian on the spot.

Setting down the building, I was somewhat anxious about peering beneath the smaller structure sitting between the two barns. Grasping it carefully, I lifted it up to find a three-story diorama depicting some sort of business office, complete with what looked like a CEO suite taking up almost the entire third floor. The corporate aesthetic had been cleverly captured, right down to a cubicle farm on the first floor and a small break room with presumably employment law posters over the water cooler. Glancing back at all the structures that represented actual places in Windeport — places that Walter could have visited in person to get their details accurate — I wondered where the inspiration for the fictitious egg farm had come from. Replacing the corporate building on its foundation, I searched for any memory of such a business coming to Windeport and came up empty; knowing someone who might have a better sense, I dug my iPhone out of my khakis and called Charlie.

"Hey Sean," she said after picking up on the first ring. "I'm glad you called — I completely forgot to give you the photos you asked for from our archives."

"The ones of Walter's layout?" I asked.

"Yes," she said. "I pulled quite a few newspaper articles dating back to the early 1950s, mostly from the *Bangor Daily News*. We also had a trove of photos from a local photographer that were donated in the late 1970s; most of them are of Windeport itself, but I had about two dozen of the layout that you can compare to the newspapers."

"That's great," I said. "Can you drop them off at the station on your way in tomorrow?"

"Sure, I have to go right past it anyway." She paused. "I imagine that's not why you're calling."

"No," I said as I flashed my light on the egg farm. "Can you dig through the Village archives for me again?"

"I'm starting to feel like your research assistant," she chuckled. "You know librarians *teach* people such as yourself to do these things, right?"

"I do, but I also know you can put your hands on material far faster than I can."

"That is true," she sighed. "It's a busy day tomorrow, but I can give it a shot. What are you looking for this time?"

"Any information about a possible egg or chicken farm that was to be built out toward UEM."

"An egg farm?" Charlie said thoughtfully. "Off the cuff, I don't recall anything like that, but I'll look. About when do you think it was built? Or would have been built?"

I looked at the layout and had a sudden burst of inspiration. "Between 1970 and 1990," I said.

"That's an unusual window. Are you sure about it?"

"Yeah," I nodded to myself. "I think I am."

"Okay, I'll let you know what I find."

"You're the best, Charlie."

"That I know," she chuckled as she hung up.

Nine

I left for Augusta directly after swim practice the following morning; knowing I was going to shower after the postmortem, I channeled my latent freshman student-athlete and tossed shorts and t-shirt on over my still-damp swimsuit for the drive to the morgue. It was early enough that I hit very little traffic on the way to the interstate; as it was only Wednesday, tourists had yet to descend upon the state, so I was able to cruise relatively unscathed down I-95. While I'd planned on getting to Augusta early, I wound up pulling back off the interstate a full hour ahead of schedule; the fact that my angst over the Professional Standards inquiry later that afternoon might have contributed to my lead foot was something I tactfully chose to ignore.

Looking for a good contingency plan, I turned into the parking lot of the IHOP close to the Civic Center and the prospect of a better breakfast than I'd had in a few days. Despite how divine Charlie's chili had smelled when I pulled it from the canvas tote bag the prior evening, I'd found my appetite missing in action and had simply turned off the lights and gone to bed shortly after returning to my bungalow. Sleep hadn't come easily though, and while that was partly due to the intense humidity the thunderstorm had failed to alleviate, the true reason had more to do with the empty space on the bed beside me. At one point, I'd rolled over so I could stare at Suzanne's empty pillow, trying to visualize her raven hair cascading over her angelic face while she slumbered. We'd spent so few nights apart since becoming a couple that it felt odd being alone; on the prior occasions, I knew she'd be back in a day or two, but that night, what kept me awake more than anything was the fear this was the beginning of a new normal.

Locking the SUV, I entered the IHOP and found I was at the tail end of the late breakfast crowd. The host sat me in a booth by the window, giving me an unobstructed view of the parking lot and an ugly office building that sat on the lot beyond. Scanning the plastic menu, I thought of the diner that Vasily had fallen in love with out in Rancho Linda and suddenly felt even more alone; it wasn't a pleasant sensation, especially when I pulled out my iPhone and confirmed for the ninety-ninth time Suzanne hadn't replied to my text messages from the day before. I'd tried to write that off as her being busy, for I was well aware of the sorts of emergencies she had to handle while on duty at the hospital. It didn't help, though, when I recalled how she'd normally found any quiet moment she had to call me in the past, if for no other reason than to simply say hello and ensure I'd not had more than my three cups of coffee that day.

Sighing, I shifted screens and texted Vasily to see how life was going in Rancho Linda. With the time difference, I assumed he was probably still in the pool and didn't expect an immediate response... although I did hold it in my hands for an extra few moments expecting one that didn't come. Sighing again, I set it aside when my waitress appeared and placed an order for scrambled eggs, sausage, and whole wheat toast with a side of chocolate chip pancakes.

The waitress looked at me as she scribbled down my order. "Anything else, hon?" she asked pleasantly.

"Coffee," I said with passion. "And lots of it."

"Coming right up," she laughed.

Staring out the window, my focus shifted such that I could see my reflection in the glass. I'd not done anything with my hair, so it was all akimbo with curls everywhere barely held back by my sunglasses. The slight haze of stubble was unusual for me, but I hated shaving before swim practice and hated shaving at the pool's locker rooms *more*. Even in the bright daylight, I could see faint traces of dark smudges beneath my eyes, evidence of how little sleep I'd gotten the past few nights. And where did those slight wrinkles around my eyes come from, anyway? Rubbing at them as though the crow's feet would magically disappear at my touch, I wasn't exactly surprised at the small signs of aging had begun to appear. As Deidre had reminded me just that past February, I was uncomfortably close to forty, so much so that thirty felt like it had decamped to another continent; while the milestone birthday itself didn't truly bother me, like anyone, I supposed the fact it was on the horizon had me assessing everything. It didn't make me feel any better knowing that Vasily was positively freaking out about turning thirty-five; we'd commiserated about age during our last FaceTime call a few days earlier, enough that I realized my best friend appeared to be carrying around some extra baggage as a gay man. It had concerned me enough to have a side conversation with Alex later in the hopes he could smooth out some of his partner's angst.

The food arrived and I fell upon it, suddenly aware that I was famished. I was somewhat amazed that I managed to eat everything I ordered; only when I drained the last of my coffee and signed for the bill did I remember that Lou had planned on taking me to lunch after the postmortem. Eying my now-empty plates, I wondered if I could talk her into something light and almost immediately knew that was likely not going to happen.

In for a pound, I thought with a wry smile as I stood to go.

I pulled into the parking lot behind the Medical Examiner's office with about fifteen minutes to spare, more than enough time for me to stash my Class A uniform in the locker room and change into a pair of nondescript green scrubs for the procedure. Pushing through the metal doors for the exam room, I found Dr. Louise Hamilton standing beside the elevated exam table, tapping her gloved fingers along the edge. Tying off the facemask I'd been putting on, I wandered toward her and smiled as she turned in my direction.

"Good morning," she said. "How are you doing?"

"I've had a good workout and an even better breakfast," I replied. "You could really make my day if you tell me this was an amazing accident."

"Not asking for much, are you?" she chuckled. "As happy as I am to hear you're remaining physically active, I was more interested in your emotional state."

"That, Doctor, is a turbulent mess that we'd probably better not get into."

"At least you're honest," she said. "Shall we start?"

"Let's do it."

Lou moved to her computer and tapped a few keys on the keyboard, then did her standard introduction for the microphones that were recording the session. Moving back to the table, she continued the one-sided conversation. "Subject is a male, approximately sixty to seventy years of age," she said, forcing my eyes to the naked form lying beneath the high-powered spotlights. "Height of 65 inches/1.6 meters, weight 180 pounds/82 kilos. No visual physical issues, though there is evidence of surgery on the lower legs for varicose vein removal."

I stepped a bit closer to the table and took in the form of what had been Walter Guernsey. When life is stripped away from a body, it often feels like something less than it was — almost as though someone had made a full body mold of a person and left it behind for us to poke and prod. The terribly white color of the skin, the sightless eyes and pooled blood in his torso were visual reminders that person I had once known had long since gone; all that was left was this biological exhibit, slowly decaying before us. I hated postmortems; I hated even *more* how it reduced anyone who wound up on that table to more of a science project than the beautifully complex human who had once resided inside that shell. Perhaps that was why I always had a special antipathy for anyone who intentionally put someone on Lou's exam table; as my eyes finally turned to the blackened hands, I hoped we might get some kind of clue to lead me to whoever had done this to Walter. For contrary to what I had said to Lou earlier, I was increasingly certain someone had killed the proprietor of Route One Hobbies, though I didn't yet understand why.

Lou had continued to rattle off facts and figures while I was musing, but her shift in tone returned my attention to the Chief Medical Examiner. "There is clear evidence of electrical burns along the hands of the deceased," she said, more to me than the recording. "The report said he was holding something when he was found?"

"Yes," I nodded. "We believe it was a controller for the model railroad he was working on."

I caught the edge of her arched eyebrow as it disappeared beneath the head covering she had on. "How much voltage went through that thing?" she asked.

"I honestly don't know," I replied. "The base unit was melted pretty badly if that helps. I've not looked at Heather's data yet, but her team may have provided more information on the device. Why do you ask?"

Extending her gloved index finger, she traced the burn marks around one of Walter's hands. "I've had more than my fair share of electrocutions over the years," she said. "This pattern is similar to one I saw from a lineman who'd been working a high-tension line in Sabattus."

"I take it the line was live at the time?"

"Unfortunately," she said. "My point, though, is this presents as far more voltage than any normal consumer electronic device would be allowed to put out. Was there some sort of surge?"

"From the way we found him — and how most of the electrical system in the store was fried — that was our working theory."

Lou put a hand on her hip. "Not to muddle things too much, but this also looks similar to someone hit by lightning," she said before using her other hand to show the singed skin running down Walter's leg, ending at his big toe. "Whatever he touched — and we'll assume it was the controller — connected him to the surge, and the power went to ground here."

"Was it enough to kill him?"

"I'll know that when I open him up," she replied. "No question it *could* have stopped his heart, though. Even a fraction of the voltage I'm seeing here would have caused a fatal arrhythmia."

I felt my eyebrow arch. "I know you'll be able to tell if he had a heart attack, but will you be able to be that specific?"

"It depends," she said. "The vampires have already been here taking samples for the lab; I'll have them run a few of the more exotic tests to see if we can narrow it down." She leaned in and looked at those sightless eyes. "I'm not seeing any sort of petechial hemorrhaging, so that mostly rules out asphyxiation as a COD. My best guess right now is that he was electrocuted, but like I said, I'll know more after we get to the good stuff."

"I was afraid you were going to say that," I sighed as she picked up her scalpel.

The balance of the hour was spent opening Walter and then carefully removing his organs; all were weighed and then placed into small canisters for further review. When the stomach came out, Lou carefully tipped its contents out into a separate container, then peered into the brilliantly colored liquid before taking a sniff. "Coffee for sure," she said as she took a long cotton swab and began to root around in the fluid. "Maybe some sort of snack mix? I see bits of pretzel and what looks like those little cereal squares."

"I'll have to ask his daughter what he might have munched on while working on the layout," I said. "We've been operating under the assumption he'd closed the store and was visiting with an after-hours guest."

"Around the dinner hour?"

I shrugged. "Maybe? As many times as I've been at the scene now, I have no idea what the actual store hours were."

Lou's eyes wrinkled with the smile I couldn't see beneath her mask. "That would be a good thing to know."

"Yeah," I nodded. "I must be a bit off my game."

"Understandable." She turned back to the cadaver. "Aside from the fact that this poor soul is dead, everything looks great. No evidence of any maladies within; I'll take a section of heart tissue for the microscope, of course, but I am inclined to still rule this was a death by electrocution."

"Suspicious?" I asked.

Lou looked at me. "That's more your department, but if you found him the way the file said you did, I'd probably want a few more answers before signing off on it being an accident."

I nodded. "I presumed as much. Any chance you could give me an approximate time of death?"

"Ballpark?" she mused for a moment. "Back of the envelope would probably be between six and ten last night, based on rigor, liver temp and decomposition. The lab tests will narrow it down a bit."

"I can work with that," I said.

"Good," she chuckled. "Happy to help. I'm going to close; why don't you run off and shower, and I'll meet you in the parking lot in fifteen? We should still be early enough to beat the lunch rush."

Having tried to grab lunch in Augusta when the legislature was in session, I knew what she meant — but also suspected in the dead of July, we were likely to have our pick of places. Still, it felt wise not to point that out. "About that," I hedged, my substantial breakfast is still very much in the process of being digested. "Any chance you'd be okay with just coffee?"

"I'm going to need more than that to get through the afternoon," she said. "Did you eat a late breakfast?"

"Guilty as charged," I said, smiling beneath my mask. "Sorry."

"Well now," she sighed, "that is something of a conundrum. Let me consider our options while you get ready for your inquisition."

"Sorry," I said again as I moved to the door. "I wasn't thinking."

"I may yet have the perfect spot," she mused. "Go shower."

"Yes ma'am," I chuckled.

It wasn't hard to hurry through the shower, given how tepid the water always seemed to be; it took longer for me to remember how to tie my tie in a full Windsor than anything else, but on the dot of fifteen minutes I was walking out into the parking lot behind the morgue. Lou was waiting for me on the sidewalk, dressed in dark blue khakis and a white blouse; it took a moment for me to recognize her, since I normally only saw her in scrubs, with her face mostly hidden behind a mask.

"You clean up nicely," I said as I came up beside her.

"I'll take that as a compliment," she smiled. "And you're right on time, as usual. I'm thinking we need to take two cars unless you're willing to make the roundtrip before you must meet with Professional Standards."

"I would love to, but it depends on how long we dawdle at your mystery lunch place."

"Where's the meeting being held?"

"45 Commerce," I replied, referring to the massive building a few clicks west of Interstate 95 that housed the Maine Department of Public Safety.

"Right," Lou frowned. "Of *course* they would haul you into the mothership. On the plus side, it means we can go to Olive Garden."

I smiled slightly. "As long as you don't mind me eating salad, that works for me."

"I don't," she laughed. "See you over there."

Traffic was unusually light as we crossed over the Kennebec River and into downtown Augusta; the city proper was empty, considering the legislature wouldn't be back in session for a few more months. The various agencies running things were, of course, in full swing, but our route out to the Civic Center and the small set of strip malls surrounding it cleverly tacked around the worst traffic choke points the city had to offer. Maybe ten minutes after leaving the Office of the Medical Examiner, I was standing next to Lou on the paved walkway to the faux Italian facade for Vasily's favorite restaurant. Inside, it was clear from how quickly we were seated that the true lunch rush had yet to begin; we had a quiet corner of the main dining room all to ourselves, allowing for a level of privacy I'd not anticipated us having.

The waitress had barely left from taking our orders before Lou leaned in. "I know the head of Professional Standards," she said, her voice low despite it not truly being necessary. Then again, in a political city such as Augusta, perhaps you couldn't be too careful. "I won't breach any confidences by telling you the office is a bit unhappy with the way this action was filed against you."

"You have an interesting business network," I smiled.

"Not as interesting — or as wide ranging — as yours, I would think," she replied. "Either that or you truly don't know the high regard you're held in around here."

"I've heard rumors," I said, thinking to the many times Captain Roberts had said something to that effect. Shrugging, I gave Lou my best *aw shucks* smile. "I just try to do my job competently."

"What you consider 'competency' is more like absolute excellence in other parts of our world," Lou said.

I shrugged again. "A job well done is the best reward."

"Now you sound like one of those recruiting bromides the State Police use."

"It worked on me," I deadpanned.

"Of course it did," she sighed as she rolled her eyes. Growing serious, though, she looked at me for a long moment. "That sort of sentiment — dedication to quality work — is something those idiots in Windeport don't seem to understand."

I started to say something and then paused, the smile frozen on my face. "Holy *shit*," I breathed as the realization hit me. "Someone from the Village Council called this one in. Holy *fucking* shit."

Lou glanced over her shoulder to ensure the waitress was still out of earshot. "As I understand it, someone wants you gone and put a bug in the ear of the State." She paused again. "I thought you would want to know that before you went in there today."

"Forearmed is forewarned," I murmured as my coffee appeared along with the iced tea Lou had ordered.

"Something like that." Her eyes scanned mine. "You know who it was? I tried to pry it out of my friend, but they were rather tight lipped about the whole thing."

"I have a thought or two," I replied. "Windeport is a small village; there are never that many suspects in any crime."

"I'll remember that the next time I'm thinking of murdering someone there," she chuckled.

"I wish more people would," I sighed as I sipped my coffee. "Thanks for the heads up."

"I thought you deserved it," Lou replied. She looked at me for a long moment. "She... she told me what the worst possible outcome might be."

"About the only thing I have going for me is that I'm not an employee of the State," I said. "The Board can't fire me, directly, but I image it's completely within their purview to recommend that to the very people who want me gone."

Lou nodded. "Yeah. Do you have any sort of backup plan?"

"If I get fired?" I smiled slightly. "I'll probably become a beach bum and live off of my girlfriend's salary."

"That doesn't sound like you," Lou replied.

"People can change."

"*Other* people. Not Sean Colbeth. And I suspect Suzanne would get tired of you sleeping on her couch."

I managed to hide the ache of my current situation with Suzanne behind a smile. "Quite likely."

Lou reached over to hold my hand. "I'm serious, Sean. Do you have a backup plan? If not, I'd move heaven and earth to get you into the Coroner's Office. I could use someone with your skills."

I smiled again. "I'm flattered," I said. "And the short answer is, yes, I *am* thinking about what I might do if I suddenly find myself unemployed."

"I can't see you not being an investigator. Somewhere."

"Yeah," I nodded. "Me neither."

"This whole thing stinks to high heaven."

"It's the price we pay for being employed by politicians," I reminded her. "None of us are safe at the end of the day."

"I suppose not," she sighed. "Now that is a damn depressing notion; I'm wishing I'd ordered wine now."

"We're both on duty, Lou," I reminded her.

"We are also in the state capital," she countered. "The one place where every rule is broken. Constantly."

I blinked and then waved down the waitress. "Then I think I'll join you..."

Ten

I couldn't exactly remember when the new Maine Department of Public Safety building had risen from the pine forests ringing the fringes of Augusta, but to my eye, it still exuded that feeling of being fresh scrubbed and recently unwrapped. The seemingly never-ending summer rains had allowed the grass around the parking lot to flourish into a deep, dark green, though it had also grown to such a height the grounds crew would truly earn their keep whenever they got around to mowing. My front yard at the bungalow consisted of one tree and the remnants of a flower garden the previous owner had lovingly tended; I'd tried my hand at keeping it up, but my schedule (and constantly hopping between the bungalow and Suzanne's apartment) had left little time for such niceties. I'd resorted to dumping multiple bags of bark mulch in the space and calling it good; I counted myself lucky that what little grass that *did* grow on my postage-stamp sized front yard was spotty at best and therefore needed little intervention on my part.

Multiple divisions were all housed in the massive structure, including the headquarters for the Maine State Police; I'd been inside on several occasions, visiting with Captain Roberts for one thing or another. While it was all sleek and modern, the endless cubicle farms and spotless corridors connecting them felt a little bit like they could suck the life out of anyone foolish enough to agree to work there. My own Public Safety building in Windeport might be a Brutalist monstrosity, but at least it had character, something the DPS facility was seriously lacking.

Parking in the Visitor lot, I made my way to the entrance and the ubiquitous metal detector just inside; the irony that there would be one guarding a building containing people whose positions required them to be armed as part of their normal duties always seemed rather rich to me. Still, I dutifully removed my Glock, handcuffs, and extra ammo, placing everything into a clear plastic bin for the officer managing the screening; since I didn't often wear my dress uniform, I spaced and forgot to also remove my badge, setting off the alarms and more than a few smiles in the process. Chagrined, I stepped back through and repeated the process sans badge; passing on my second attempt reminded me of the time I'd false started at a major competition that had been televised on *ESPN*. It had helped that I'd ultimately won the heat, but the sting of being the only person to leap into the water ahead of the whistle had been hard to get over.

I found Arabella waiting for me in front of a wall that was a memorial to all who had died in the line of duty. It was such a somber thing to have in the lobby, but also vivid reminder of how dangerous our jobs could be. My lawyer was impeccably dressed once more, attired in a pantsuit of deep blue nearly the color of the State of Maine flag fluttering on the pole outside. I wondered if that was an intentional sartorial choice, given who we would be speaking to momentarily, but thought better than to ask. She smiled at me as I clipped my badge back onto my shirt and stuffed my sidearm back into the holster.

"You cut a rather dashing figure in uniform, Chief Colbeth," Arabella said as she started toward one of the endless corridors that radiated off the lobby.

"Thank you," I smiled as I fell into step beside her. "Truth be told, though, this collar is extremely uncomfortable."

"I've never met an officer who didn't think that," she chuckled. "My husband was a Marine and felt the service intentionally cut collars a half-size smaller than labelled. He was convinced it was a way to keep their attention focused when they were being inspected."

I looked at Arabella. "I didn't realize you were married," I said carefully. "And the past tense makes me concerned."

"You're perceptive," she replied with a sad smile. "He was KIA in Afghanistan three years ago."

"I'm sorry to hear that," I said.

"It was his third tour, actually," she continued. "I miss him everyday, but he died doing what he loved for the country he adored."

"May we all go in a similar fashion," I murmured as we turned a corner and continued down another bland corridor. I could never shake the notion that trailing breadcrumbs behind me as I walked would be wise. "There's no easy segue from that—"

"No," she smiled.

"—but how are we handling this today? Procedure normally dictates that my union representative is with me, though regulations also allow for legal representation."

"Which is why I am here," she nodded.

"Exactly," I concurred. "That, and I don't have a clue who the union rep is for our portion of the county. Or the state, for that matter."

"I'm surprised you are even part of one, given how small Windeport is."

"They deduct the dues from my paycheck every week," I said. "*Someone* is getting my money. That better mean I have representation. Somewhere."

"You might want to make some phone calls," Arabella observed. "I'd want to know where my money is going."

"I'm an investigator," I deadpanned. "I'll follow the evidence and find out who it is."

"Good point," she chuckled. "If you are asking me whether I have another Perry Mason surprise up my sleeve, I'm not sure I can answer that." Arabella paused and pulled me to the side of the corridor before lowering her voice. "All I *can* say is that I think we have a solid argument that this action is invalid. Proving that might require having you go over key aspects of the investigation in detail."

I nodded. "Which is why you had me reviewing the case files again. And again."

"Exactly," she replied. "This isn't a court of law, though, Sean. It would be helpful to remember that; at the end of the day, they might well still throw the proverbial book at you regardless of how well reasoned our points are."

"I have *some* recourse in that event," I reminded her. "And I happen to know a good lawyer who could help me."

"You do," she smiled. "I just wanted to be sure we are on the same page."

"That this is a total crapshoot?" I sighed. "Yeah, we are."

Reaching over, she squeezed my bicep. "Good," she said before nodding her mass of hair toward the nondescript door across the hallway from us. "Conference Room 111-B. Ready?"

"No," I smiled. "But that has never stopped me before."

"That's the spirit," she laughed.

The room we entered looked as though it had been lifted from an office supply catalog; there was the requisite oblong conference table, slightly wider in the middle than the ends, running the length of the space and surrounded by chairs that looked to be of the three-to-four-hundred-dollar variety. Potted plants stood at the four corners of the room, and a white board was fastened to the wall at the far end, presumably doubling as a screen for the expensive looking projector hanging from the ceiling. An American flag sat on the proper side of the white board, slightly higher than the smaller State of Maine flag on the other side, mute sentinels watching over the proceedings. Three uniformed officers sat along the long edge of the table, looking every bit like actors culled from central casting for a military courtroom drama; two of them were men, both in their late fifties and sporting enough ribbons on their Class A uniforms to look like battlefield generals from some overseas war. They were flanking the third member of the panel, a slightly younger woman with her white hair pulled into a severe bun that screamed *police officer*. I knew without reading her bio that at some past point in her career, she had walked the streets of Portland or Lewiston or some other major metropolis during the most dangerous part of the night, and likely had held her own against anything — and anyone — she had come up against

Of the three officers, she was the only one that seemed incredibly familiar to me, though it wasn't clear why until my eyes caught the name embossed on the small plate fastened to her dress uniform. I felt myself stand a little straighter, knowing that I was in the presence of the current head of the Maine State Police. Her bright eyes caught me assessing her and returned the favor; with a slight smile, I saw some measure of mutual respect there and wondered if not all hope had been lost.

"Chief Colbeth," she said pleasantly as the three stood. "Thank you for coming in today."

"My pleasure, Colonel," seemed like the best thing to say, considering it hadn't exactly been my idea to appear in the first place.

"I'm Colonel Judith Rivers," she said as we all sat, more to Arabella than me. "Captain William Douglass is to my right, and Captain Hiram Johnson is to my left."

My eyebrows went up. "I'm... honored to meet you," I said, barely able to hold back my surprise; it was exceptionally rare to have one flag officer at such a panel, let alone *three*.

Arabella was less inclined to keep her feelings to herself. "I'm Arabella Steinman and will be representing Chief Colbeth during these proceedings," she smiled. "Forgive me, but is it not normal for the head of Professional Standards to be leading this discussion?"

"If this were a normal inquiry, Counselor," Rivers replied. "As the person in question is a Chief of Police, this is *not* a normal inquiry. I felt it was best to handle this situation myself."

"I beg to differ," Arabella replied pleasantly, though her smile was cold. "According to the Standards and Practices manual for the State Police, I believe subsection seven specifically stipulates—"

Douglass waved her off. "That section does not apply, as Chief Colbeth is not an employee of the State of Maine."

Arabella held out her hands. "Then this is likely to be an extremely short inquiry, since by extension that would mean the Office of Professional Standards has no jurisdiction over my client."

Rivers looked at me. "I imagine Chief Colbeth has already told you that resources from the State were used in the recent investigation that led to the wrongful arrest of Shelly West," she said carefully. "Chapter six clearly spells out that the State has oversight in *any* case where taxpayer dollars were used as part of the investigation."

"We were aware of that section," Arabella said before glancing at me. I nodded slightly for we had expected this line of attack. "My client is willing to stipulate to the limited oversight that section gives the State."

"Limited?" Johnson asked. "In what way?"

Leaning over, Arabella flipped open her briefcase and dug around until she located a folder which she placed on the table. Tapping it with a finger, she looked at Captain Johnson. "We've itemized the expenses incurred by the State while assisting Windeport during the Brogan case," she said. "If we understand the logic of the panel's reasoning, these would provide a roadmap for what is to be reviewed, correct?"

"I believe that is exactly the position we outlined," Johnson nodded.

"Then even using this standard for intervention, we would again argue the State has no standing."

I saw a slight smile flash across Rivers' face. "Explain."

"This file contains all of the evidence collected by the team from the State Crime Lab — evidence collected prior to the arrest of Shelly West," she said. "While it is extremely impressive and in its own way makes a compelling case to charge her with murder, it's not what Chief Colbeth based his decision to arrest Ms. West."

"It's not?" Douglass exclaimed. "Then what the hell *did* he base it on?"

Arabella went back to her briefcase and dug out a small portable audio player. "This is the recording of Shelly West voluntarily admitting to the crime," she said. "If you'll permit me to play it—"

"That is not admissible in court," Douglass interrupted.

"This is not a courtroom," Arabella reminded him patiently. I saw that smile ghost across Rivers' face again as my lawyer continued. "And you *did* ask me to explain how Chief Colbeth came to his conclusion."

Rivers chuckled slightly. "She's got you there, Bill."

Douglass frowned; I could have sworn I heard him mutter *damn lawyers* as he took a moment to study his fingernails. I kept my face as impassive as I could, thankful nonetheless that Arabella had decided to take my case. Maybe – just *maybe* – there was a chance to extricate myself from the mess I'd inadvertently created weeks earlier.

Tapping the recorder, Arabella looked at each one of the panelists. "The way I see it, either this panel has no jurisdiction here, or it does; if it *does*, then it is compelled to hear *all* the evidence collected by my client." She paused again. "Evidence that proves he was correct in his assessment; whether or not a court of law actually confirmed it is beyond the scope of this inquiry."

Rivers took a moment to consider Arabella. "The complaint filed against Chief Colbeth is based on that recording, Counselor," she said. "Specifically, how it was obtained illegally and then used to illegally arrest a citizen of the State."

Arabella tapped the folder with the receipts inside. "Returning to my original point, Colonel, the recording was made after the team from the crime lab had finished working the scene. We've also determined that the device used to make the recording was not purchased using State dollars; and, as I pointed out earlier, Chief Colbeth's salary comes from the taxpayers in Windeport, not the State." She smiled slightly. "Again, using your definition — not mine — this panel is clearly only able to provide oversight for evidence and leads developed while using the State's resources. My client *did* have access to those items, and while they may have contributed to his view of the investigation, the charging decision was based wholly on this confession."

"Which you are saying we have no jurisdiction over," Rivers nodded slowly. Leaning back in her chair, she pressed her hands together to form a steeple. "Whether or not we *do*, you're also saying we'd have to consider what's on that tape as exculpatory evidence. Interesting argument, Counselor."

"I think it's always important to keep the wider picture in focus, Colonel," Arabella smiled. "Something my client has repeatedly demonstrated over his near-two-decade career."

Rivers looked to each of her panel mates. "I think we need a moment," she said as they stood. "Would you mind waiting in the corridor for a bit?"

"Not at all," Arabella replied as she packed up her briefcase.

I stood with her and nodded to the panel, somewhat in awe that I'd not had to utter a word. Rivers' pleasant smile as we moved out of the conference room was essentially inscrutable; the looks on the others, though, were a bit clearer, for both Captains were frowning with distaste. Whether that was over Arabella having pinned them in a corner or a statement on my conduct in the Brogan case remained an open question.

Taking up position on the wall opposite from the conference room, I looked at Arabella. "What's your read?"

"I've got Rivers," she said confidently. "Whether that is enough to sway the other two is hard to say."

My eyebrows went up. "You think they are already deciding?"

"Yes," she nodded. "As soon as I saw who was leading the panel, it was apparent to me it wouldn't be a traditional hearing. Colonel Rivers isn't wrong — you're too high in the food chain for the normal process, but that also means whatever they do to you would have to similarly be appropriate to your station."

"They can't fire me," I said. "They can't even suspend me."

"They can make those recommendations to the Village Council, though," Arabella reminded me. "And they can sanction your department, preventing access to any State resources moving forward."

"Which would be the same as suspending me or firing me," I sighed. "We rely on quite a bit from them. Thank God I kept our data center, though. I can't imagine losing access to our case system and the historical files."

"Exactly."

"I'm glad we didn't talk through the downside ahead of time," I chuckled ruefully.

"I find it's not productive to worry about what might not happen," Arabella replied. She glanced back at the door, then back to me. "I suspect it will be a moment. If you'll excuse me, I'm going to grab a quick cigarette."

My eyebrows went up again. "I didn't peg you as a smoker."

She shrugged and smiled sheepishly. "I picked it up from my husband," she replied. "I can't tell you how many times I've tried to quit, but it was something we did together. It became even harder after he died, for now it feels like the last connection I still have to him."

I nodded slowly; I could easily relate, for I had doggedly maintained my curly mop-top just as my mother had liked it for nearly the same reason. "I'll be right here when you get back," I smiled as I ran a hand through my curls.

"Text me if they want us back sooner."

"Will do."

I watched her deliberately stride down the hallway, her high heels echoing as she stepped. Thinking of my mother always opened a hole in my heart, for despite how much time had passed since her death, I never really felt like I had gotten over it. That had led to a bit of a falling out between myself and my father, who'd taken her passing just as hard as I had — maybe harder; only over the course of the past few months did it feel like the two of us had regained something of an equilibrium. Enough of one that I suddenly — desperately — wanted to talk to him. Sliding out my iPhone, I dialed his number and hoped I wasn't interrupting a round of golf.

The warm tones of his voice filled my ear almost immediately. "Sean," he said. "Good timing — I just walked off of the eighteenth."

"Isn't it kind of hot to be playing golf down there in Florida?" I asked, smiling in anticipation of his answer.

"You get used to it," he replied, "and honestly, you can't beat the discounted greens fees."

"I trust you've been drinking plenty of liquids?"

There was a long pause before the droll reply. "We did plenty of drinking, yes."

"That's what I thought," I chuckled.

"What's up?"

I was thinking of Mom and missing her and wanted a hug from someone was what jumped into my mind, but since that wasn't how my relationship with my father was structured, I went with work instead. "I'm in between meetings and wanted to hear a friendly voice."

Father chuckled. "I take it you're in Augusta."

"Oh yeah," I replied, eyes flicking to the conference room door.

"For a police officer, you sure spend a lot of time in meetings." I could hear the air moving around Father, telling me he was walking.

"Par for the course."

"Working a case?"

"Always," I chuckled. "Which reminds me — how well did you know Walter Guernsey?"

There was a long pause. "Oh, God, as well as anyone in Windeport," he said. "I served on the Village Council with him back in the mid-1980s."

"You were on the Council?" I asked, incredulous.

"Twice, actually," he replied. "The first time was a few years before I married your mother. I worked with Walter during my second stint."

"I think I was too young to remember that," I said.

"I'm not surprised," Father chuckled. "You were barely out of diapers. Why do you ask?"

"He... passed away yesterday," I answered.

"Oh, damn," he breathed. "That's a hell of a loss. I'm just now thinking about that incredible model railroad layout he had at Route One Hobbies — at least, the one he had when I moved to Florida."

"It's still here," I confirmed. "And you're not kidding about the details. I've had a chance to get to know it."

That pause occurred again. "He's your case?"

"Yeah," I said softly.

"Damn," he breathed. "What the hell is going on up there, anyway? I move out and suddenly there's a wave of murder."

My eyebrows went up. "Who said it was murder?" I asked, choosing to ignore the implied critique on my abilities.

"I suspect you would have assigned the routine passing of a Village resident to an underling. Or the undertaker, for that matter."

Smiling, I nodded. "True enough," I said before being struck by a thought. "Was the egg farm on the layout before you left?"

"It was," Father replied. "Kind of a story behind that, actually."

That frisson in my gut kicked in. "Really? What is it?"

"I don't remember all of it," he said after a moment. "Other than a passing comment Walt made during a Village Council meeting. There was this Bangor car dealer hoping to open a new Ford or Chevrolet franchise just down the street from UEM; after we voted the zoning change down to help preserve the dairy industry, Walter turned to me and said it was the second time he'd blocked someone for using that land."

"When was the first time?"

"I asked that, actually, and he countered by asking me if I'd seen the new addition to his layout."

That frisson became a knot. "The egg farm?"

"Exactly. It was an odd response, but honestly, I never thought anything of it."

Arabella appeared at the far end of the hallway nearly simultaneously with Colonel Rivers poking her head out of the conference room. "Looks like I've got to go back to my meeting," I said. "Thanks for the info."

"You're welcome, I think," Father chuckled. "Talk to you this weekend?"

"Absolutely," I replied before hanging up.

We quickly returned to our positions around the conference table, and after a long moment of staring at each other, Colonel Rivers began to speak. "Chief Colbeth, panel inquiries such as this one are usually opened when there is clear, compelling evidence of professional misconduct by a member of our ranks. As your lawyer has already pointed out," Rivers continued, waving away Arabella as she stood to protest, "you are not *technically* part of this department. However, I think we can all agree that such technicalities can obscure our true intent, which in this case is getting to the truth at the heart of the matter."

Arabella frowned but sat down.

"The complainant alleges that you arrested her under false pretenses," Rivers said, eyeing me. "You don't deny having taken Shelly West into custody?"

"No, Colonel."

"And your contention is the decision to do so was based purely on the confession Ms. West provided to you at the icehouse?" Rivers asked.

That was a question Arabella and I had anticipated as well. "Evidence collected during the Brogan case *did* lead me to believe a contemporary of T.J. had been the one to kill him," I answered. "In hindsight, I can now see how particular items we discovered implicated Shelly, but at the time, and in the moment, evidence produced by the team from the crime lab didn't necessarily point to any one person." I looked at each of the members of the panel in turn. "I won't deny I suspected Shelly, but she was but one of multiple people I thought had the means and possible motive. Did that lead me to make some inspired connections, connections that landed me in the icehouse that fateful evening? Absolutely."

I paused and smiled. "Investigators move from insight to insight, a fact that I suspect all three of you well understand. And while my insights led me to that confrontation in the icehouse, my decision to arrest her was based purely — and entirely — on what Shelly told me." I looked to Arabella. "I own my mistakes on this case," I continued before turning back to the panel. "But I stand by my judgement."

"Judgement that includes *not* providing a Miranda warning?" Rivers asked pointedly.

"It was a gamble," I said without hesitation. "Shelly was in the moment, and it was important for me to keep her talking. In my view, stopping long enough to Mirandize her would have ended her desire to be loquacious."

"That's the entire *point* of the Miranda Warning," Rivers reminded me; I suddenly felt like a cadet getting a bit of a dressing down in front of the entire cadre. "We have a duty to inform a suspect that they can *stop* talking."

"I don't deny that," I allowed.

"You can see, then, how Ms. West would have a reason to want you disciplined," Rivers continued. "On the face of it, it appears that you disregarded longstanding legal precedent, not to mention standards and practices *every* department in this State should adhere to." The Colonel paused. "I believe the illegally obtained audio resulted in the District Attorney passing on prosecuting Ms. West."

Arabella stood. "I feel obliged to point out again that the court did not have the opportunity to weigh in on the admissibility of the evidence," she said. "Considering Ms. West had been willing to sign a statement backing up what was on the audio, it would seem inappropriate to read into the DA's motivations."

Rivers looked at me. "You had a *statement* from her? That's not in the file."

I smiled slightly. "My powers of persuasion are usually pretty good," I added before looking meaningfully at Arabella. "Unless they come up against an even better lawyer, which is what happened in this case. Otherwise, I am certain Shelly would have signed her statement."

"That's a pretty big gamble to have made," Rivers said.

"Ayuh," I sighed. "Usually, the odds are in my favor, but you can't outrun statistics forever, can you?"

Rivers looked to Arabella. "I'm reasonably certain I don't need to ask you if you have affidavits backing this up?"

"No," she smiled. "For the record, though, the Assistant Chief was in the interview room at the time, and an officer was watching from behind the two-way mirror. We also have the standard audio recordings from the interview as well."

"Was the DA aware of any of that?"

"Yes," I nodded. "All of it."

Rivers considered me for a moment, then looked to each of her fellow panelists. I could see from the way they exchanged looks a decision had likely been reached, one that had been confirmed by the last few minutes of conversation. My heart began to sink, for I wasn't entirely certain that was a point in my favor; then again, the strange slight smile on Rivers' face when she turned her attention back to me seemed to counter that negativity.

"I was rather surprised when this complaint was filed with Professional Standards," she began, speaking in deliberate tones that underscored we'd reached the moment. "Someone with such impeccable credentials and a reputation for professionalism seldom appears on the docket, which is why I took a personal interest in the proceedings." Pausing, she considered her next words before speaking again. "And yet, there are some very obvious issues with how you handled this case — serious problems that led to a lost conviction."

That feeling of being dressed down by a superior grew stronger; the heat on my face underscored the feeling of being a rookie who should have known better. For once, I felt a little bit like Vasily and wanted to jump back into the fray to wage a vigorous defense of my actions; it took quite a bit for me to keep it under control. Instead, I nodded tightly and braced myself for what was likely to come.

"We agree that there are mitigating circumstances, however, not the least of which is the entire jurisdictional issue your council has so appropriately brought to our attention," Rivers continued with a smile at Arabella. "Or the fact that new evidence has been unearthed that ultimately supported your original decision to arrest the suspect." Looking at me, she paused. "That being said, this panel is unanimous in forwarding a recommendation to the Windeport Village Council for a two-month suspension with pay effective immediately."

"The council is not obligated to honor the recommendation," Arabella said. Her frown reflected how likely we both thought it would be that they would ignore the communication, though.

"Which is why we are additionally ordering the recommendation be added to Chief Colbeth's professional packet," Rivers said, referring to the master database of law enforcement professionals the State kept. Rivers looked at me. "I suspect Chief Colbeth knows the Village Council will likely support our request, however."

"With respect," I said, "I would request that the recommendation be amended to allow me to complete the current case I am working." Glancing at Arabella who nodded, I looked back at Rivers. "While I have full faith in my Assistant Chief, I'm not willing to leave him in the middle of an active investigation. I'd like to see it through."

"So noted," Rivers nodded. "Chief Colbeth, we're not blind to the fact that there is a level of personal vengeance underscoring this complaint," she said carefully. "I think we can all agree that it would therefore be appropriate for appearance's sake that we allow this to play out."

"Colonel, you should know that the new evidence—" Arabella started before I caught her arm. Her eyes widened when she saw me subtly shake my head, then raised an eyebrow to confirm what I was essentially telling her.

"Counselor?" Rivers prompted.

"My apologies," Arabella said as she sat down. "I have nothing further to add."

"Then we are done here," Rivers said as we stood. "Thank you for your service, Chief Colbeth. I hope to hell I never see you here again."

"That makes two of us," I replied, forcing a smile.

Eleven

The drive back from Augusta felt longer than normal, allowing me to replay in excruciating detail the events of the day repeatedly as I churned my way up the turnpike toward home. I wasn't usually one to succumb to foul moods, but it had been hard to sidestep one after the panel's ruling had been handed down; it felt like I had one of those cartoonish thunderclouds over my head, one that periodically erupted with a bolt of lightning each time I pondered what effect the so-called recommendation from Professional Standards might have on my career. Those same clouds had darkened considerably after the short hallway conversation I'd had with Arabella as we'd exited the conference room; she'd been understandably annoyed that I'd not let her argue the point further regarding the late breaking changes in the case against Shelly West and had disagreed vehemently with me when I'd explained my reasoning. It hadn't been an accident that the head of the Maine State Police had taken an interest in my case; that I'd managed to get through it with just a recommended suspension spoke to my lawyer's ability to argue the facts, though at the end of the day those facts had run up against the cold political calculus of the situation. I'd known even before my phone had pinged with an email notification that the Village Council would wholeheartedly agree with the panel's recommendation; I'd pretty much been on thin ice with them since the Thompkins death more than a year earlier and knew that despite the clever maneuverings from my cousin and others in the community, it was just a matter of time before my contract wasn't renewed.

I'd had high hopes that the prior fall's elections would shift a few seats on the Council in my favor, but the grim reality had demonstrated I'd also never been very good at anticipating which direction the political winds were blowing. Lacking that skillset pretty much explained why I was constantly being hauled to a Council meeting to explain myself. Repeatedly. Guessing the moves of the last Village Council had been well beyond me; about the only thing I could divine from the latest iteration was their open hostility to both me and the department I represented. It had therefore seemed prudent to begin fine-tuning my resume on the off chance I found myself unemployed next summer. As I turned off the turnpike and onto Route 203, I found myself smiling at the idea the Professional Standards Board had given me a two-month head start — with pay — to begin looking for a place to land. I'd dusted off my list of contacts in the industry once before; no reason not to make a few discreet inquiries while I had time on my hands.

With the pine trees whisking past me as I drove slightly faster than was technically legal, I squashed yet another impulse to call Suzanne; while ostensibly it would have been to find out how it was going in Portland, I knew myself well enough to know that I was looking for a friendly ear to which I could vent. I *had* called Vasily already, knowing he was likely to commiserate with my situation; his phone had gone straight to voicemail, though, telling me he was knee deep in something himself. I decided not to leave him a message and had instead pressed the accelerator a little harder, intent on putting as much distance between me and Augusta as quickly as possible in the vain hope it would ease the creeping feeling of doom that was threatening to overwhelm me.

Time dilated in that weird way it always does when you didn't want it to; the familiar outlines of Route 203 became less so as the sun grew lower on the horizon behind me, making the road ahead seem to stretch out much further than it should. For once, there was little traffic to contend with, enhancing a monotony that even the dulcet tones of Joe Castiglione calling the early evening Red Sox game did little to alleviate. It was nearly a physical relief when I saw the edge of the UEM campus appear off to my left; glancing at the clock, I decided I could still make the evening workout and turned into the small parking lot beside the aquatics center. Finding a space proved to be difficult, but at length I snuck the departmental SUV in between a minivan and a hatchback, then killed the engine.

Pulling my iPhone from the holder beside the radio, I stared at the lock screen and the multiple notifications that had piled up upon it while I'd been driving. Scrolling through them, it didn't take long to locate the email from the current Chair of the Village Council, Violet Kepler. Sighing, I tapped the message and began to read.

To: Chief Sean Colbeth, Windeport Police Department

From: Chair Violet Kepler, Windeport Village Council

Dear Chief:

The Council is in receipt of the recommendations from today's Professional Standards meeting in Augusta. In reviewing the documentation included, the Council has voted unanimously to adopt the recommendations in whole. Effective immediately, you are suspended from active duty with pay and benefits for a period of no less than sixty business days. Assistant Chief Norman Thomas will serve as Acting Chief on an interim basis; please surrender all departmental items to his custody by end of business today, including your vehicle, badge and sidearm. Access to the Public Safety Building or any Windeport Police resources is prohibited pending your return. Violation of these terms may result in a lengthened suspension or outright termination for cause, as allowed by the employment terms of your contract.

During this period, the Village Council will undertake its own investigation into the series of events that led to this suspension and the multiple lawsuits filed against the Village and its employees. Under the terms of your contract, should the Council find definitive cause, they are within their purview to decide not to retain you after the suspension concludes.

Should they be needed, counseling services are available to you through the State at (555) 555-9829.

I read the short memo two more times and tried not to laugh at the morbid joke the situation had become. Whether due to outright callousness or a simple rush to judgement, the fact that the Village Council had passed on allowing me to complete work on the Guernsey case was telling; that they had cc'd both my boss, the Village Manager, as well as Captain James Roberts at the State Police told me this was but the opening move in a long-planned chess match. I still had a few pieces left on the board, but it was clear I was in jeopardy of being caught in checkmate unless I altered my own strategy.

Shoving the phone into my uniform pants, I got out of the SUV and then took a moment to shed the most dangerous parts of my wardrobe, locking the gun and ammo into the glovebox safe. Then I grabbed my swim backpack from the rear seat and made my way to the propped open side door for the pool and the waiting locker room beyond. Shucking out of my dress uniform, I balled it up and tossed it onto the top shelf of my locker in protest, knowing it would do little to make the situation better. Rooting around my backpack, I found the shockingly purple Speedo Vasily had loaned me in Las Vegas and smiled slightly; it was most definitely *not* my style and therefore *exactly* what I needed at that moment. Pulling the Spandex garment on, I grabbed my swim cap and goggles, locked up my unit and then made my way out onto the deck.

Just as it had been twelve hours earlier, my lane was wide open and waiting for me at the far end of the pool; Coach had apparently seen me heading into the locker room, for when I knelt to splash some of the cool water against my chest, I noticed he'd propped a small whiteboard against the starting block. Quickly reading it over, I discovered it contained a workout that made running back-to-back marathons in the desert of Death Valley during the heat of July seem easier. Much like the purple Speedo, though, it was *exactly* what I needed, and I immediately dove in. When I finally came up for air nearly ninety minutes later, the deck was empty and the only lights left on were the underwater ones; bobbing at the edge of the pool, I allowed the strange quiet of the massive space to wash over me for a moment before beginning my cooldown.

I hardly ever used the hot tubs that sat on either side of the diving towers, but that evening felt the need to spend a few minutes with the jets turned up as high as they could go. Slinking down into the hot water so my chin was just barely above the surface, I closed my eyes and leaned into the bubbles, trying hard to put aside what had happened that day; I didn't completely succeed, but the knot that had formed in my shoulder had eased quite a bit when the timer for the jets finally clicked off. Still, I sat there with my back pressed to the tile, reluctant to get out and face the remains of the day.

The sound of the timer being reset followed by someone wading into the jacuzzi beside me caused my eyes to open; they widened further when I saw who had joined me. Closing my eyes again, I leaned back into the jets once more. "Are you sure you want to be seen with me, Norm?" I asked. "I appear to be quite radioactive at the moment."

"Since we are the only two here currently, I feel somewhat safe," was the chuckled reply. "But for the record, I've never really cared what people thought about me anyway."

"Duly noted," I smiled. "How did you know where to find me?"

"It's a small Village," he replied before waiting a beat. "And... I may have pinged your iPhone."

"Duly noted," I repeated with a chuckle. "Next time, I'll turn it off." The silence weighed heavily between us for a moment before I decided to acknowledge the elephant in the room. "I take it you've already been informed of your promotion."

"I'm just holding down the fort until you get back," Norm replied, but it was clear he was unhappy. "I have *never* wanted to be the guy in charge."

I cracked open an eye. "There is a real chance I won't be coming back," I said, my voice just loud enough to be heard over the machinery of the jacuzzi. "I wouldn't blame you for wanting to look elsewhere for your career at this point."

"The hell with that," he said. "So, I spoke with Nick Romero while you were having fun in Augusta."

Both eyes opened and I turned slightly so I could see him fully. "Norm, I can't talk to you about this any longer. I'm off the case."

"The *hell* you are," he replied forcefully. "My first act as Chief was to hire a consultant to work the case."

"Consult—?" I started before my eyes went wide. "You didn't."

Norm's smile spoke volumes. "I think if you don't come to the office, we'll get away with it. Now, do you want to hear about Nick or not?"

I smiled slightly and cocked my head. "It won't fool them for long. But I admire your creativity."

"I learned from the best," he said quietly. "Now, Nick?"

"Yes. Go."

Norm stretched his arms out along the tile ringing the jacuzzi and leaned his head back for a moment while he gathered his thoughts. "I caught up with him at the house he used to share with Caitlyn. Nice place just at the edge of town; it seems like he retained it due to his contracting business."

"I wondered how everything had been split between them," I said. "It has a barn, right?"

"And several smaller outbuildings," Norm nodded. "All crammed full of stuff his firm uses." He looked at me for a moment. "The guy seemed nicer than I expected. I assumed anyone who was stupid enough to dump Caitlyn had to have been a Grade A jerk, but it was clear he was very concerned with her and the kids. After we spoke, he went directly to Charlie's farm to check in on his ex."

"I didn't know him very well," I replied honestly. "I also don't know why they split."

Norm smiled slightly. "It was the first thing Nick told me," he said. "Apparently she caught him in bed with his foreman."

"For*man*?" I blinked. "He's... bi?"

"Apparently," Norm nodded. "Which was a bit of a surprise for Caitlyn."

"I can imagine."

"What did he say about the wiring?"

"It was about what you would expect," he continued. "Walter had used Nick's firm many times over the years doing upgrades here and there to both the hobby store and the building proper; the contract for rewiring the store was just the latest in a long line. Nick worked on it personally; according to him, he got along famously with Walter right up until he split from Caitlyn."

I shifted slightly to allow the jets to work on a twinging muscle in my lower back. "What did the work entail?"

"We'll need to run all of this past the electrical inspector when we see him," Norm hedged, "but according to Nick, he replaced the main panel and upgraded all the breakers. He also ran several new lines directly to the layout."

My eyebrows went up. "Really?"

"Yeah. Walter was redoing the electrical on the layout proper and needed more power than what he had already. Nick finished the work back in April, then came back once in June to add another outlet beneath the layout."

"Let me guess," I frowned. "That wouldn't happen to be the outlet the transformer was plugged into?"

"It would be," Norm nodded. "I neglected to mention that to Nick when we were talking."

"Good man," I replied. "Talk about muddying the waters a bit, though."

"Agreed." Norm rolled his neck; it wasn't until I saw the sweat on his brow that I realized just how hot the water was. "Without giving him specifics, I tried to ask him hypotheticals regarding how a short would work with all the new wiring. Surprisingly, he kept telling me it would be impossible, especially with the new breakers he'd added."

"In the circuit box?"

"Not just there," Norm shook his head. "There's a secondary panel just below the layout, accessible from the basement. Nick routed a main to it so the layout would be isolated from the rest of the shop."

I frowned. "Then how did the lights and POS systems get fried?" I asked before the answer hit me. "A second short?"

"It would have to be, given how Nick explained the wiring."

I nodded slowly. "Someone was covering their tracks and hoped we'd not dig too deeply."

"That's my take as well." Norm wiped at his brow. "I think we might want to have him handy when we talk to the electrical inspector."

"Agreed."

"What do we do next?" Norm asked.

I closed my eyes. "Well, as your consultant, I would presume my recommendation would be to verify what we can of Nick's story. I think we need to understand fully what sort of electrical mishap took place in the hobby store." I opened them and looked at Norm, who had slipped down into the water a bit more. "My original assumption about what happened seems to be off. I wonder if there is any way to know the timing of the shorts?"

"Like if the one for the POS systems happened *after* whatever killed Walter?" Norm nodded. "Knowing the order of operations tells us something, doesn't it?"

"It sure does. The crime lab is still working on the box Walter was holding?"

"I believe so. Nothing's appeared in the file. Why?"

"We might have made other assumptions about the source of the short," I mused. "I know not much was left of that gizmo, but if we are really lucky, it, too, might have a story to tell."

"I'll call out there in the morning." He looked at me. "What are you going to do?"

"Disappear," I smiled. "At least for a day. I have an errand to run in Portland; I was going to put it off to the weekend, but now that I'm currently on leave, I can do it sooner. I'll be back on Friday."

I could see Norm's eyebrows go up. "Portland, eh?" he asked. "Isn't that where Suzanne went?"

"Speaking of Dr. Kellerman, did you get your test results back yet?" I asked, shifting the subject slightly.

"No," he shook his head. "The lab she sent it to must have quite a backlog."

"Probably," I replied, though my heart sank a little. I knew from dating a doctor that tests such as the one Norm had taken were turned around very quickly; Suzanne often said the slowest part was informing the patient, especially when the results required some delicacy. Not wanting to dwell on either subject, I smiled as I pushed myself off the small, tiled seat. "I'm going to call it a day, officially," I said as I pulled myself up the small staircase to the deck. "Is there a chance my consulting gig comes with wheels?"

"It can," Norm replied as he exited the jacuzzi behind me. "Why?"

I smiled slightly as we walked toward the bleachers and the towels we'd both draped over the lowest level. "Would you believe I don't own a vehicle?"

Norm looked at me. "Seriously?"

"Seriously," I shrugged. "I've never needed one; the department has always provided me with transportation."

"Then take the SUV," he replied. "I'll need to take your gun, though. And," he added after a long moment, "your badge."

"I figured," I said as I toweled myself off. "I'll have to get creative without the badge," I frowned. "I've gotten quite used to flashing it at people and getting what I need out of them as a result."

"I don't think it was the badge that did it," Norm replied.

"No?" I replied innocently.

"No," he replied quietly before putting a hand to my exposed bicep. "You are far more than just a badge, Chief."

"Well, I guess we're about to find out," I joked as we walked to the locker room. I had to admit I was touched by his observation, though; for the first time that day, I finally felt like I was on solid ground.

Such as it was.

TWELVE

I left for Portland directly after swim practice the next morning, heading into uncharted waters for the first time in quite a while. The lie I was telling myself — that I was headed South to follow up on some leads for the case that I was, technically, no longer a part of — barely covered my unease over possibly repeating my fiasco with Deidre two years earlier. Glancing at my swim backpack in the seat next to me, stuffed to overflowing with everything I'd need for the next few days, it was hard to ignore memories of trying to track down my ex-fiancé at a wedding purported to have taken place at the Boston Harbor Hotel; much like the closet Deidre had cleaned out in the apartment we had shared, there'd been no trace of either her or the wedding. It had been a harsh reality check as to our actual status, one proving just how blind I had been to what had gone wrong between us — both literally *and* figuratively.

With Suzanne, I felt like I understood where our relationship had jumped the rails and was cautiously optimistic that this time was different. Sure, appearing on her doorstep in Portland was a somewhat provocative move — okay, maybe completely, *unequivocally* provocative — but if my idea played out the way I intended it to, with luck, she'd see it more as a desperate move by a guy madly in love with her and hoping beyond hope he'd not ruined everything irrevocably. Glancing at my swim backpack a second time, I couldn't help the nagging sense of self doubt the previous experience with Deidre was creating and took a big gulp of the hot coffee I'd picked up from Calista's before practice. Tapping the petite Thermos sitting in the cupholder next to my mug — gift from Suzanne, ironically — I figured it would take every ounce of what was inside, plus a few refills, to get through the day.

Sleep hadn't come easily, which wasn't much of a surprise given how my brain was trying to deal with multiple crises at the same time. Somewhere around midnight I'd thrown in the towel and pulled out my laptop, then waited until it was *after* midnight to brew my first cup of nirvana; since it had technically been *Thursday* at that point, my caffeine meter had been reset for the new day, another lie that helped me sort through the data files for the case. Heather's team had made a few updates while I'd been embroiled in my Augusta meetings, and Norm had thoughtfully scanned the materials Charlie had dropped off from the Library's archives. There was a lot to go through, so I'd focused mostly on Heather's notes and set the archive data aside; if things went south in Portland, I was likely going to need something to do while I cooled my heels at the Marriott that evening. Considering my new status as a contractor, I wasn't sure it was strictly legal that Norm had allowed me to retain the MacBook and VPN access to the department's servers but was glad he had; much like the SUV I was driving in, I had relied on departmental resources for as long as I could remember. Aside from my iPhone, I didn't own any technology outright, one of many startling realizations while I'd been huddled over the laptop in my den. If the consulting thing became permanent, I was going to need to lay out some cash to join the modern era.

Aside from Heather noting that she and the electrical inspector would be back at the hobby store mid-morning Friday, much of the rest of the additions were results of the hundreds of small lab tests they had conducted on items retrieved from the scene. Several fingerprints collected had been tied back to Caitlyn and Walter, with a few sets still in the unknown category; I'd made a note in the file to get exclusion prints from her kids and the entire informal club that I'd met with earlier in the week. My eyebrows had gone up at the entry noting that there had been two sets of prints on the small box Walter had been holding; one set was his, of course, but the other had yet to be identified — and also matched prints taken from one of the POS screens at the checkout counter. It was enough of a red flag that she'd recommended a more thorough dusting of the area, which I immediately signed off on.

I'd been surprised at a long entry one of Heather's lab nerds had added, tagged to the throttle controller we'd found in the victim's hands. To my untrained eye, it had looked like whatever current had run through the small metallic box had fried it completely, but according to the tech, enough of the internal electronics remained that they'd been able to pull manufacturer specifications for the device — as well as a partial fingerprint that was giving the databases fits. The implication was clear that it seemed as though someone had popped the cover and tampered with the device, but the scorching had obliterated any signs of such an effort; in a similar vein, the molten mass that had been the transformer powering the throttle held nothing of interest save for the fact it was designed *explicitly* to not overload the way it had. In short, the tech was confident one or both devices had been sabotaged, but without an undamaged model for comparison, would be hard to prove.

That assessment had led me down an internet search rabbit hole, looking for any vendors that might sell the product we *thought* we had on our hands; not wanting to be caught walking the scene without my badge hunting for something that might well be in the shelves at Route One Hobbies, I instead discovered a retailer in Brunswick with the completely appropriate name of Whistlestop Shop appeared to have several in stock. Adding the address to my iPhone, I'd decided it was worth swinging through on my way to Portland if for no other reason than to give the entire trip the razor thin veneer of being part of the official investigation. As I turned onto I-295 in Gardner, though, my grand scheme seemed less grand and more like a scheme beneath the harsh glare of the morning sunshine; whatever confidence I'd built up during my early morning hours of research faded more and more as the miles dropped away. It felt like a similarly bad portent when I drained the last of the coffee from the thermos just as I reached the Brunswick exit, or at least enough of an emergency that I swung into the first Dunkin' Donuts I could find to replenish my supply. That a half-dozen donuts also accompanied the refill was more a nod to the fact I'd skipped breakfast completely in my determination to hit the road; hunger got the best of me, though, and forced me to pull into a spot in the parking lot so I could snarf down two of the chocolate-covered raspberry jellies before continuing to the store.

I'd not been to Brunswick in some years. Vasily and I had worked a case involving an illegal puppy mill that had been operating out of a farmhouse on the edge of town, helping to document the squalid conditions the poor creatures had been subjected to. I wasn't particularly religious, but felt strongly that if there *was* a Hell, it had a special place reserved for people such as the ones we had busted on that case; animal cruelty was right up there with murder in my book.

Slowing as the divided highway of the interstate exit became the more familiar four-lane Route One, I slowed further as residential areas began to appear on either side of the road; since it was nearly ten, tourists were in abundance and slowed me enough that it became stop-and-go traffic as I approached the small downtown area. While I waited at the light, I thought again of how the city felt very similar to Windeport, albeit much longer and far more established. Part of that had to do with the fact that Brunswick had been the host of a naval air station for many decades; despite that economic engine having long since shuttered, unlike Windeport, the city appeared to have continued to thrive. It probably didn't hurt that passenger rail had been extended from Portland, making it fairly easy to commute back and forth to Boston.

Finally getting my chance to turn onto Maine Street (I had to look twice to verify the spelling), I kept half an ear on Siri as she counted down to my destination while hunting for some place to park. I saw the whimsical sign for Whistlestop Shop a few heartbeats before Siri announced I'd arrived; with no sign of a free slot along the main drag, I turned onto the first side street that presented itself and managed to parallel park the SUV in front of the final remaining parking meter for as far as the eye could see. Why tourists had descended so early on a Thursday was a mystery that I didn't particularly care to delve into; instead, I locked the up the SUV, slid on my sunglasses and wandered back toward Maine Street.

The crowd along the sidewalk felt comfortably familiar as did the various storefronts offering varied tourist memorabilia; it seemed like some sort of inside joke that Whistlestop was sandwiched between a bookstore and a florist, a joke whose punchline seemed to be eluding me. Pulling the glass door open for the store, I smiled slightly at the cowbell that rang out as I did so, for it seemed completely on brand. Pausing just inside, I took my bearings before locating the checkout counter and the smiling older woman who met my gaze. Heading in her direction, I was impressed as just how different Whistlestop was from Route One Hobbies; I'd expected the same sort of clean retail layout that Walter had favored, but instead found an amazingly haphazard collection of irregularly spaced aisles overflowing with items that appeared to have been randomly placed everywhere. About the only thing that had some semblance of organization was the glass display cabinet behind the register; it contained a wide variety of scale engines and other rolling stock, carefully arranged by size and, if I was reading the price tags correctly, value. The counter also appeared to be a display cabinet, though the light was either off or burned out, making the items within difficult to view.

"Hi there," I said as I stopped at the edge of the counter. "Beautiful morning, isn't it?"

"That it is," she nodded. Closer, I could see she was wearing a denim apron over a nice blouse and matching slacks; her brown hair was cut short in a very feminine style and had a few streaks of gray about the temples. A petite name badge proclaimed she was Helen. "With luck that means we'll be fairly busy today."

I nodded toward the door. "No offense, but I don't see this as being a huge tourist draw."

Helen chuckled. "None taken, and all things being equal, you'd be right. But as it turns out, there are very few hobby stores left these days; we pull in people from out of state quite regularly. We also have a vibrant mail order business." She chuckled again. "Listen to me. No one calls it mail order any longer; we have a *website* that does brisk business."

"How very modern," I laughed, not wanting to bring up I'd used that very website to find them. "I suppose the internet has become the great equalizer."

"Maybe," she nodded. Helen took a moment to look at me thoughtfully. "You seem awfully familiar. Did you go to Bowdoin?"

I shook my head. "No ma'am, but I did swim a meet or two there while in college."

She snapped her fingers. "Damn, you're that Olympian, aren't you? Vasily something-or-other?"

Trying hard not to laugh — I never once thought I'd be mistaken for my best friend — I shook my head again. "Close. I'm the *other* Olympian, Sean Colbeth."

"Oh," she replied, squinting at me. "Yes, of course. I'm sorry."

"Happens all the time," I lied, gentling it with a smile. "The pool at Bowdoin was pretty nice, though. I broke a few records there."

Helen nodded, but I knew it was more for form's sake. "What can I do for you, Mr. Colbeth?" she asked.

"Please, call me Sean," I answered. "And I was wondering if you could help me locate a new transformer for a model railroad."

"Ah," she said as she came around the counter. "We do have a bit of a collection over here," she said as she led me across the store and then between a freestanding shelf and the wall. Boxes and boxes of product were sandwiched together with no eye toward size or shape; I was hard pressed to see how anyone found anything. "What scale?" Helen asked as she scanned the shelves.

"Scale," I repeated, suddenly stumped. "Actually, I don't know. Is that important?"

"Yes," Helen said, turning to look at me. "And no. The larger the engine, the more power is needed to get it to move; there are other considerations, too, ranging from lighting elements on your layout to switches or other automation." Tapping her chin with a finger, she thought for a moment before continuing. "Usually, the scale is selected before deciding on a transformer; you must be pretty new to the hobby."

"You have no idea," I chuckled as I pulled out my iPhone. "I'm actually work—*consulting* on an investigation," I said, quickly correcting myself as I brought up a photo of Walter's layout. "This is the layout I am trying to power."

Helen took a quick look at the photo. "That's Walter Guernsey's layout," she replied, her eyes going back to mine. "And he stocks his own transformers." She paused. "What sort of investigation? Are you a cop?"

"I'm assisting the police, yes," I replied, staying as close to the truth as I could. "Walter died unexpectedly a few days ago, and we're just going through the motions of ensuring it was an accident."

"An... accident?" she asked. "What kind of accident?"

"That's partly what we don't know," I said, trying not to reveal too much. Swapping photos on my phone, I held up the image of the melted transformer. "For example, can this happen?"

Reaching into the pocket of her apron, Helen brought out some reading glasses which she put on before squinting at the image. "That's the TrainPack 27," she murmured as she rotated the photo. "Typically used on HO- and O-scale layouts." Pulling off her glasses, she looked at me again. "To answer, no, that can't happen. Those devices are built to trip when there is an overload of any sort."

"Do you stock this model?"

"Yes," Helen answered, turning back to the shelf. Running her fingers along the boxes, she quickly located one and pulled it out. "This is the base unit," she said as she handed it to me and then returned to the shelf. "Somewhere I have the throttle control... yes, here it is." Pulling a second, smaller box from another shelf, she handed that to me as well. "We usually sell them as a pair."

"Do I want to know how much they go for?"

Helen smiled. "These are top-of-the-line," she said. "Three-fifty for the base unit and two-twenty for the throttle, but it also includes all of the necessary wiring to get you going."

My eyebrows went up. "Is this an expensive hobby?"

"It can be," she chuckled as we moved back to the counter. "As with most things, it depends on the quality the hobbyist wants at the price point they can afford. These units cost a bit more up front, but they are also likely to be the last ones you'll ever need to purchase; I carry others that are made someplace in South Asia and won't last beyond the parking lot."

"'A car for every wallet,'" I paraphrased, thinking about a case study I had done in college on General Motors.

"Exactly," Helen smiled. Tapping at the boxes I'd placed on the counter, she thought for a moment. "May I see that photo again?"

"Sure," I replied as I produced it once more on my iPhone.

Putting her glasses back on, she took a few moments to examine the photo, expanding it a few times to look at details I had no idea were there. At length, she put my phone back on the counter and then started to open the larger of the two boxes to reveal the pristine version of the transformer; unwrapping the plastic bag from around the golden-colored metal, she started to point to the gizmo. "This is where you hook the power lines that go out to the rest of the layout," she said, tapping at some screws that appeared to be color coded. "And this is where you plug the throttle controller."

I leaned closer. "That looks like an old phone connection."

"It uses the same kind of cable, yes," Helen nodded. "All very straightforward technology, easy even for those who have a limited electrical background."

"Like me," I smiled. "This looks like a regular plug," I said, tapping the long cord extending away from the box.

"It is," she nodded. "Just like the one on the back of your toaster. And it uses about the same amount of power, too."

I looked at her. "I suppose you could get quite a shock from your toaster, can't you?" I asked carefully.

"If you are stupid enough to stick a knife in there to get your bread out," she laughed before pointing to the transformer. "This beauty is insulated far better, though. No chance of getting a shock unless you, well, cracked it open and shoved a finger inside at the wrong moment." Helen looked at me. "Even then, though, it might make your hair stand up, but that would be about it."

"I'll keep that in mind," I said. "If someone has questions about using one of these things, do they come to you? Or call the manufacturer?"

"Both," she said. Flipping the transformer over, she tapped a nail against a small sticker on the bottom. "This 800 number goes right to their customer service, and there is also a website with helpful support articles."

I wondered just how helpful those support documents were, and whether they included a complete breakdown of what was inside the transformer; unsure of how to ask that question, though, I simply smiled instead. "Awesome. I'll take it," I said as I pulled out my wallet.

Helen eyed me, and for a long moment, I wondered if she were going to press me on why I'd buy it from her instead of Route One Hobbies. Thankfully, the debit card in my hand attracted more attention. "Would you like a bag?"

"Please," I said. "And thank you for your help."

"Of course," she replied as she rung me up.

I left Whistlestop a few hundred dollars poorer but somewhat more informed; walking back to the SUV in the hot mid-day sun, I thought I had essentially backed into confirmation that either the transformer or the throttle had been tampered with. With luck, the bagful of tech I was hauling back to Windeport would support that hypothesis further, though I wondered for a moment if I'd ever be reimbursed for the purchase. The parking meter showed I had ten minutes to spare when I unlocked the SUV; stepping back as I opened the door allowed me to avoid the rush of superheated air from the interior, another reminder that it was still July and devilishly hot. Looking down at my cargo shorts and sandals, though, I thought perhaps *not* being on official duty had some perks; there was also no question that my casual summer vacation attire helped me to blend in with the crowd in a way that my gun and badge often didn't. Sliding into the hot front seat, I thought again about a conversation I'd had with Vasily about going private the first time I'd visited him in Anaheim; I'd been on the cusp of doing so then only to back away when my situation had resolved itself in Windeport. Staring at potential unemployment for a second time, however, had me revisiting the idea once more, and on the whole, kind of finding it more attractive.

Pulling away from the curb, the one-way streets surrounding the downtown area forced me into an odd U-shaped path that ultimately led me back to Route One; the rumble in my stomach reminded me I still had a handful of donuts left from earlier, though to my dismay, I discovered in the heat of the car, they had melted into a single mass of squishy carbohydrates. It was enough of an excuse to pull into a McDonald's that was along the way to procure a Quarter Pounder with Cheese and a large order of fries; I rounded out my excess with an extra-large coffee, allowing me to stretch what was left in the thermos just a little bit longer. I'd just polished off the burger and was halfway through the fries when my iPhone sang the merry tune I'd assigned to Vasily; rather guiltily, I quickly stuffed what was left of the fries back into the bag and ran the napkin across my mouth before answering.

"Hey, dude," I said merrily. I wasn't sure if my sudden good humor was due to the fact my stomach was full of calories or that my best friend was on the phone. Tossing the bag into the trash as I exited the restaurant, I continued as I wandered back to my parked SUV. "I hope I didn't interrupt something earlier."

"You did," came the delightfully wicked chuckle. "I'd taken a half day and was at the beach with Alex."

Pulling out of the McDonald's, I frowned. "Were you surfing?" I asked, trying to figure out why he'd not answered his phone.

"No," he replied with a chuckle. "I mean, we *had* been surfing, but then we had to shower off all of that salt..."

"Oh," I said, the penny finally dropping. "I... see. You must have been quite... thorough... in your showering."

"We usually are," Vas replied with a slight emphasis on the *we*.

I could see in the rearview mirror my cheeks were flaming slightly. "Shit, Vas," I sighed. "I don't think I needed to hear that."

"We've been friends too long for that to embarrass you, Sean," he laughed. "Though, honestly, it's kind of cute that it still does."

"If you say so," I sighed again.

"How are you doing?" Vas asked. "Did you have your day in court already?"

"I did," I replied. "The good news is, Shelly West is back in custody."

"Really?" he asked incredulously. "I thought the tape wasn't admissible."

"It wasn't," I answered. "Our friends at the crime lab came up with something else, making the tape unnecessary."

"Shit," he breathed. "Well done."

"I wish I could take credit, but it was all my lawyer."

"Keep her on retainer, dude."

"I'd need to have a better paying job for that."

"I hear you." There was a slight pause. "Dare I ask if there is bad news?"

"There is," I replied. "Professional Standards sided with Shelly and handed me a two-month suspension. The ink wasn't even dry on the memo before the Village Council yanked me."

"*Fuck*," Vasily said with emphasis. "Those fucking idiots. You're going to fight it, right?"

"There's not much to fight," I answered. "I have no illusions that this will be the pretext for finally cancelling my contract; the elections last fall brought in a new majority that are, shall we say, anti-Sean Colbeth."

"My offer still stands, then," Vasily said without hesitation. "Come out to California and consult for me until you figure out everything."

"I may take you up on that," I said, then hesitated long enough that Vasily picked up on it.

"There's something else, isn't there?" he asked.

"Suzanne," I said before choking. "Suzanne left," I managed to get out before my vision blurred enough that I had to pull to the side of the interstate. All at once, the emotions I'd been holding in check suddenly burst through; I couldn't keep from sobbing, loud enough that I was sure Vasily could hear my heartache. The shocked silence at the other end spoke volumes. As the traffic whistled past me on the highway, I wondered what my best friend was thinking; it became somewhat apparent when he finally spoke.

"Tell me everything," he said, "and then we can talk about how you're going to fix it."

"Do you have that much time?" I laughed bleakly as I wiped away the tears.

"For you, my friend," Vasily said fondly, "I have all the time in the world and then some."

Thirteen

As it turned out, Vasily didn't think my idea was half bad, though he did recommend a few tweaks to keep it just below out-and-out stalking. Since he had some firsthand experience in that department, I was rather amenable toward any suggestions to keep from inflaming the situation further; the last thing I needed was to be on the receiving end of a restraining order, or worse, wind up spending the weekend in jail should my girlfriend completely misunderstand my intent. I had zero desire to be added to the ranks of police officers who'd misused their position to intentionally hurt the people they purported to have loved, which was partly why I had begun to overthink my brilliant plan just a tiny little bit. Vasily had done an excellent job of refocusing my efforts; in fact, he became so enthusiastic, he figured out a way to insert himself into it. By the time I pulled into the parking lot of the Marriott I favored in South Portland just a bit past three, we'd managed to nail down just about everything. After wishing me luck — and extracting a promise that I would call him later with the results, no matter the hour — I grabbed my gear from the SUV and headed inside to check into my room.

That the Marriott had become her home-away-from home with me had been something of a surprise; after her divorce, Suzanne had spent nearly a year working at Maine Medical and living out of a cute – but extremely small – studio apartment directly across the street from the hospital. While she'd loved the location, as infrequently as she traveled to the city for her rotations, it just wasn't an expense she could continue to justify. I'd found out about her having given up the lease when she'd asked for a hotel recommendation that was both reasonable and within easy driving distance of Maine Medical; the Marriott had been at the top of my list, but I'd only provided it on the condition she allow me to tag along to ensure the property measured up. While she'd easily seen through my ruse, Suzanne had nonetheless happily agreed to my terms; one weekend led to another, and before long, I discovered just how much I enjoyed our irregular getaways. I knew my girlfriend was doing important work when she was on the wards, but for me, the time we still managed to spend together represented a much needed though all-to-brief respite from the drama that was the Windeport Village Council.

So it went without saying I was a familiar face to the staff behind the counter at the recently renovated four-star resort; I'd also accumulated enough nights with the chain that they routinely upgraded me to the concierge level, a benefit that I had come to appreciate. The slightly nicer rooms and dedicated lounge were wonderful perks, as was the ability for me to get into my room early or check out late. It certainly had made traveling more tolerable.

Dropping my bags on the king bed in the room, I took a moment to run through my plan one final time before moving to the phone at the small desk in the corner. As my fingers hovered over the dial pad, I had a moment of panic before putting the call through to Maine Medical Center. A professional voice answered promptly; my heart lifted slightly when it was the one I had hoped to hear.

"Scheduling, this is Velma."

"Hey Velma, it's Sean," I said, trying to put a smile into my voice.

"Sean, honey, how are you?"

The warm reply brought a flame of embarrassment to my cheeks, for

I was feeling slightly guilty at using the secret back door number Suzanne routinely called when setting up her weekends when she was on duty — and scheduling our superhero rounds at the Barbara Bush Children's Wing. Velma was one of the three women on the scheduling desk I had gotten to know quite well over the nearly two years I'd been accompanying Suzanne to Portland; she was a single mother with three kids between thirteen and nineteen who had somehow made ends meet doing three twelves as an RN in the Radiology ward followed by two more twelves on the schedule desk. Velma also happened to be one of Suzanne's closest friends in Portland; I was reasonably certain she might also be who Suzanne was staying with, but making that determination was going to be tricky. Guilt at leaning into Velma's good nature in order to find out made the flame on my cheeks burn deeper.

"It's been a Hell of a week, honestly," I said, which was quite true. "As a matter of fact, I got suspended from my job."

"No *shit*," she fairly hollered into my ear. "What the fuck did those bastards in Windeport do this time?"

A genuine smile hit my lips, for I'd not realized how common knowledge it was that the Village and I didn't exactly see eye to eye. "It's a long story and I don't want to depress you. The good news is, though, it means I can spend more time with Suzanne this weekend."

There was a long silence, confirming another suspicion. "I'm not sure that's a great idea, honey," she said carefully. I could almost see her elegant face frowning.

"I messed up royally," I said, plunging forward. "And I want to rectify things. I have a plan, but I need a little help — and some guidance. If you think I should stay away, I'll head back to Windeport and lick my wounds."

The silence stretched for another long moment. "What are you going to do?" Velma asked finally.

"Listen to her," I replied simply. "*Truly* listen to her."

"You already do that," Velma said unexpectedly. "It's one of the things she loves the most about you."

"Well," I said, slightly taken aback, "maybe it's more that I need to let her know that I will *always* listen. To whatever she says. Or, more importantly, to what she *doesn't*."

"Oh, *shit*," Velma sighed. "You are a one-in-a-million kind of guy, you know that? I wish my ex was half as good as you."

"I'm not feeling that way right now," I replied. "Do you think I can see her? Or should I wait?"

Velma thought for a moment. "No, you should go to her. She's getting off at six and had planned on making dinner for my kids tonight. I'm stuck here until midnight."

"How on earth do you do it, Velma?"

"Easy," she replied. "I just look at my kids each morning. They're all the motivation I need."

"That's brilliant," I said. "By the way, are you allergic to any flowers?"

"No," Velma replied, though I could hear the suspicion in her voice. "Why?"

"No reason," I replied innocently.

There was another long pause. "You know what? I just remembered my mother was going to take the kids tonight. I'll let Suzanne know she'll be alone this evening."

"Velma," I started, "that's not—"

"There goes the other line," Velma interrupted. "I've got to go. See you tomorrow?"

"Quite likely," I replied, "unless Suzanne gives me the boot."

"I doubt that very much," she chuckled. "Good luck."

I replaced the handset on the phone cradle and stared at it for a moment. The call had gone far better than I'd expected; glancing at the clock radio on the nightstand, I moved over to the swim backpack on the bed and unzipped the main compartment. Rooting around, I retrieved the carefully folded Chat Noir costume my cousin Charlie had made for me, then pulled out the rest of the accessories that came with it. Holding the blond wig for a moment, I ran a finger along one of the faux black leather triangular cat-like ears that she'd sewn into it and remembered how the costume had once before helped me make an apology to someone I cared deeply for and had inadvertently hurt; smiling slightly, I thought about the other research I had been doing the past few evenings, namely reviewing the five seasons of *Miraculous* that were now available. Much like the teenaged feline superhero in that show, I'd truly not had much experience in the ways of love — that is, not until Suzanne had arrived in my life. Loosely basing my plan on the antics of that costumed character was a bit of a risk, but Suzanne was worth it; if I were lucky, seeing me in full superhero mode would soften some of her lingering anger. At the very least, it might make it slightly easier to gain a long enough audience for me to fall on my sword.

Or baton, I mentally corrected as I hefted the small metallic tube that was Chat Noir's actual weapon. *Though that might be a tad more painful going through the heart, methinks...*

Laying everything out on the bed, I grabbed my shaving kit and headed for the bathroom to take a quick shower; I'd found over my time impersonating the feline superhero that being freshly scrubbed — and completely shorn of facial hair — made it easier to apply and then later remove both the makeup and domino mask that was part of the costume. Less than twenty minutes later, I was staring at my transformation in the full-length mirror of the closet door, twisting slightly to ensure that the belt had been fastened *just so* to enable it to function as a ludicrously long tail. Picking up one end of it with my gloved hand, I twirled it a few times the way I'd seen Chat do it on the show, then practiced the sly half smile he seemed to use when he was about to take down the villain of the week.

Probably not the best analogy here, I sighed as I shifted to my normal smile. *If anyone is the villain in this situation, it's me.*

Watching my masked green eyes look back at me, I was once more taken with how freeing it was to be hidden behind the domino mask, wig, and full-body costume; no, perhaps *freeing* wasn't quite the right word. Liberating, maybe? In a way that the normal *Police Officer Who Is a Reserved Native Mainer* façade I normally wore could never be. My smile in the mirror turned to one of astonishment when I realized Suzanne had known that from the very beginning; she'd seen *exactly* who I was that night at the Windeport Public Library in a way no one else ever had.

Well, shit, I thought. *Maybe this is a better idea than I thought.*

Returning to the bed, I unzipped the large duffel I'd brought upstairs and poked around the accessories I'd need to pull everything off; satisfied, I zipped it back up, then stared at the side pocket of my swim backpack for a moment. There was one final piece to the plan, one that I still found myself waffling on; pulling on the zipper, I opened the pocket just enough to retrieve a small jewelry box in unrelieved black, then placed it on the palm of my gloved hand. There was a small green feline paw print in the exact center of the top, mirroring the one on the baton; I'd found someone online who had been able to fashion a custom container to any specification, and smiled again at how accurate — and beautiful — it was. Sliding a claw-tipped finger along the edge, I cracked the box open and looked at the engagement ring nestled within the folds of velour inside. The diamond was a custom cut from a jeweler in North Conway Suzanne had often talked about and sparkled in even the gentle light of the hotel room. I'd ordered it months earlier after deciding that I was finally ready to pop the question; I'd originally planned on proposing to her at the comic book convention in Anaheim, but my little fiasco during the Davies investigation had forced me to punt.

Finding out Vasily was engaged had spurred me back into action; it was funny that I'd felt a bit competitive in that area with my best friend. Then again, we'd had a healthy rivalry while in the pool, so I guess it shouldn't have surprised me all that much. In working with Alejandro to scope out possible ideas for their wedding, though, I'd given serious thought as to what Suzanne might want for hers and begun to form the first inklings of an idea. As I closed the box and then tried to decide if it would fit in the rather useless pockets of the costume, I wondered if proposing to Suzanne that evening would be viewed as a desperate measure to win her back. Sliding it into the small storage area Charlie had created in the baton, I decided to play it by ear; if the evening went well, the box might make a reappearance.

If it didn't, I might well be headed to North Conway in the morning, my hopes and dreams dashed.

Grabbing the duffel bag with one gloved hand, I juggled my wallet, keys, and iPhone in the other, then made my way out of the room. The hotel staff had seen me in costume more times than I cared to admit, so I was quite used to the smiles I saw from the concierge as I crossed the lobby to the sliding glass doors of the exit. The same wasn't necessarily true for at least one of the valets as I trotted down the driveway to my SUV in the parking lot; her confused expression brought a wink from me, which made her frown even deeper before whispering something to the colleague just stepping out of a car he had driven up. Despite how late it was in the afternoon, the heat of the day was still intense, for once making me appreciate how thin the fabric of the costume was. Unfortunately, since it was the darkest shade of black imaginable, I was extremely thankful for how quickly the air conditioning of the SUV cooled me down.

Velma's house was on the far side of the city, in a small residential neighborhood that was one of many to have been built during the first renaissance of Portland during the early 1990s. Her subdivision was right on the border between Portland and South Portland and had replaced the last working dairy farm to have still been within city limits. Progress appeared to move apace, it seemed, for even Windeport had succumbed to the same pressures around development; nearly a year after Bethesda Thompkins' death, the condos Brad Donohue had envisioned as an extension of his real estate empire were finally beginning to go up. I still couldn't fathom how timeshares were more valuable than what the elderly widow's working farm had been contributing to the local economy, but then again, I'd only taken the 100-level Finance course in college to satisfy part of my core curriculum requirements.

Siri began to gently count down the distance, and I shifted lanes to make the left turn into a comfortably sized side street. Vehicles were parked end-to-end along the curb in both directions, which seemed to be a default situation in Portland; space truly appeared to be at a premium, though, for the short driveways couldn't hold anything more than the few bicycles and Big Wheels I saw scattered about. The homes themselves were typical three-story city townhouses and appeared to be the same design replicated endlessly down the street. About the only differentiating feature was whether the garage was on the right or the left, leading me to think that the plans had simply been mirrored to keep the planners from getting too bored. I had to admit, I was in love with the wide steps leading up to a classic covered front porch each home sported; more importantly, they all featured a nice, wide banister railing along the risers as well as a matching version along the edge of the porch. As I passed Velma's house, I smiled to see that other than an American flag waving patriotically from its post on the side of the house, her railings were clear of any of the ceramic critters or potted plants that had infected just about every other home on the street.

Two houses down, I found an open spot just barely wide enough to parallel park the SUV. The clock on the dashboard told me I had just enough time to get everything ready before Suzanne appeared; grabbing the duffel bag, I locked up and then hustled back down the street to Velma's. Trotting up the steps, I dumped the duffel on the slats of pressure-treated timber, then unzipped it; the carefully wrapped package of roses came out first, followed by a large bag of rose petals. Both had been purchased at that small florist in Brunswick I'd seen nestled beside the Whistlestop, and the divine smell had permeated the interior of the SUV despite being buried beneath layers of plastic wrap. It took a few moments for me to unwind the roses from their prison, then a few minutes to carefully tie pairs of them to each of the posts holding up the porch. I had just enough left to festoon the base of the staircase as well, then set about sprinkling the fragrant petals along the steps and then up on the porch proper.

The final items to come out of the duffel were a half-dozen of the stout candles Suzanne and I often used to set the mood at either the bungalow or the apartment. Scanning the railings, I selected a few spots and then placed them, then put the remainder on every other step leading up to the porch. Glancing at my iPhone where I had propped it against the railing, I took a deep breath and dug the box of matches out of the duffel, then quickly lit one after the other. Given the neighborhood's position in the city and how tall each of the homes were, the sun at that hour happened to be behind the houses across the street; it placed Velma's into enough of a shadow that the gentle flickering of the candle flames popped ever so slightly against the darker railing. Admiring my handiwork from the sidewalk for a moment — and amazed that no one had come along to question my activities — I hurried back up the steps and slid the duffel bag beneath one of the two rocking chairs taking up the space. Turning back to the railing for the porch, I tested its ability to hold weight before pushing myself up and onto the wide board; fixing a mental image of what the *actual* Chat might do, I shifted to my side and placed my head upon a hand, then made sure my faux tail was within easy reach.

Taking another breath, I began my vigil, resisting yet again the urge to ping Suzanne's location using my iPhone. In the end it wasn't truly necessary, for less than fifteen minutes after I'd taken up position, the recognizable shape of my girlfriend's Subaru Forester appeared at the gentle curve in the street; I watched as it slowed, presumably looking for a place to park, then started that sly Chat smile when it screeched to an abrupt halt in front of Velma's. Grabbing my tail, I started to twirl it behind me, patiently waiting to see what the next move might be.

The driver's side door opened, and the raven head of Suzanne appeared over the roof of her car. Her look of amazement seemed slightly tempered by one of annoyance, which made my heart drop. Still, I continued to smile, hiding my anxiety as best as I could. It helped I was wearing a mask, and that the dark color of my costume was hiding just how badly I was sweating — and not just from the heat.

"*Meow*velous evening, isn't it?" I asked, eyes watching her intently.

Her smile quirked. "How long have you been up there?" Suzanne asked, her eyes straying for a moment to the candles on the steps before returning to mine.

I tried to appear nonchalant and looked to the darkening sky. "A while," I replied. "The sun was *purr*fect on this porch," I added as I sat up a bit so I could make a show of stretching. "It was too hard to resist."

Suzanne rolled her eyes at me. "I see," she replied, before looking at the candles and rose petals again. A look of dawning recognition appeared on her face. "This seems... familiar," she observed.

"Does it?" I smiled as I swung off the railing. Leaning down, I snagged the single rose I'd left on the small table between the rockers before moving to the head of the steps. Holding it in my hands, I cocked my head at her. "I might have borrowed the idea from someone."

Suzanne nodded. In the half darkness of the shaded street, I could just see her brilliant blue eyes as they considered me. "Why are you here?" she asked at length.

I was encouraged that her tone was more curious than accusatory. "I wanted to listen to you," I said as I slowly stepped down the staircase.

Her eyebrows went up. "Listen?" she asked. "Don't you mean *talk*?"

"No," I shook my head as I paused at the bottom of the steps. "I truly mean *listen*." Looking down at the rose, I idly noted that the red color was a bit lighter at the edges of the petal. "I'm not sure I've done enough of that lately." Looking back at her, I smiled sadly. "It also became acutely apparent to me that I might not have made you feel comfortable enough to let me listen to anything you might want to tell me."

Something washed across Suzanne's face — whether it was shock or amazement was hard to tell, given how quickly it passed. "Listening has never been your problem," she said after a long moment.

"Perhaps not in the traditional sense," I nodded as I stepped a bit closer to the sidewalk. "Hearing what *wasn't* there seems to be an issue for me, though. I've only recently discovered I can do something about it."

She eyed me thoughtfully. Nodding at the porch, she smiled slightly. "So that's what this is? Your way of telling me you're ready to listen to whatever I'm *not* saying?"

"Yes."

"Even if it means I might not *tell* you anything?"

"You don't have to say a word," I promised quietly. "My role is to hold you tight and remind you that whatever it is, it doesn't diminish in any way how deeply I love you. To remind you," I continued as I reached the side of her car, "that I love you no matter what. And that I am here to help you through it."

Her smile flickered a bit, and I thought I could see a slight sheen to her eyes. "Even if it means I might hurt you?"

"You could never do that," I said. "Ever."

"I'm not so sure," she whispered.

Seeing the tears begin made my eyes go wide. "Suzanne—"

I didn't have a chance to complete my sentence for in a blur of movement, my girlfriend got back into her car and pulled away from the curb in a virtual cloud of dust. Standing there on the sidewalk, my heart felt as though it were about to pound its way from my chest as I watched the Forester disappear around the corner at the far end of the street. I waited a few minutes to see if she might return, then decided to wait a few minutes more, convinced that what had just happened had not, in fact, just happened. It wasn't until the streetlights came on overhead that I realized just how long I'd been standing out there. I looked down at the rose in my hands and felt acutely the presence of the engagement ring in the baton at the small of my back. Glancing up and down the street one final time, I suddenly felt incredibly silly standing there in the thin spandex of the costume; tossing the rose to the street, I turned back toward the house and began the long process of cleaning up, all the while wondering if I had seen the last of Suzanne.

Fourteen

I'd ignored the shocked stare from the clerk who handed me my Quarter Pounder with Cheese combo at the first McDonald's I passed, though unlike his California counterparts, I suspected the poor teenager had rarely seen characters of *any* kind passing through the drive through. The smell of my greasy dinner quickly filled the SUV, forcing me to roll down all the windows in an attempt to air it out. That it was my second fast food stop of the day wasn't lost on me; more concerning perhaps was my willingness to indulge in more empty calories instead of diverting to the local YMCA and the release an extended workout normally provided. I knew a little of the human psyche — you picked up a thing or two working as a cop — and intrinsically recognized the signs that I was crumbling emotionally. I just didn't know what to do about it any longer.

All I could muster at the moment was to focus on the road and return to the Marriott. The back end of the evening rush hour was still clogging the roads in the city, allowing me to make the most of my aggressive driving techniques from the Academy. I wondered idly how the other commuters felt when they saw a man in a cat costume swiftly navigating around them, and then realized I truly didn't care. I had the same attitude when I finally reached the hotel and made my way back through the lobby to the elevators; the stares from the people in the restaurant barely registered a fraction of a moment before the doors to the carriage closed on my masked face.

I made one detour to the small alcove where the ice machine was housed and dumped what was left of the roses and rose petals into the shared trash bin beside it; the last thing I wanted was the fragrant reminder of a plan gone horribly wrong. Being me, I kept replaying the encounter in my mind, searching and failing to see how I had managed to push Suzanne away a second time; the cold fear that I had misread everything *again* felt like an icy hand squeezing my heart into oblivion. Taking a deep breath made me realize that if I took another, tears were likely to fall; given I was still wearing the eyeblack for my costume, it seemed best to try and stave it off, so I hustled down the hallway to my room. Fumbling the card at the door didn't help matters; pushing the door open as soon as the light on the lock flicked to green, I dropped my duffel in the hallway then leaned my back against the door to close it with a resounding — and refreshing — slam.

Pressing my eyes closed, I slid down the door until I was sitting on the cold tile of the floor, oblivious to how the fabric of the costume was catching in the uneven surface; pulling my knees up to my chin, I sat there until I thought I had some semblance of control. The smell of the likely lukewarm Quarter Pounder ultimately spurred me into action once more, supported by the rumble of a stomach that hadn't had a proper meal in a day or so. Opening the grease-stained paper bag, I retrieved the wrapped burger and the side of fries, placing both on the flattened bag. Only then did I realize I'd left the coffee I'd ordered with the meal back in the SUV.

Figures, I thought darkly. *Fuck it.*

My mood didn't improve appreciably after devouring the cold food, though I was reasonably certain I had never eaten in quite such a depressing location. Scrunching up the wrapper, I stuffed it inside the container for the fries and then put that into the paper bag; sighing, I pushed myself back up and wandered into the bathroom to toss the remnants away. Getting back out of the Chat Noir costume was never easy under the best of circumstances; that evening proved I'd not deviated from the mean terribly much, especially when the bell-topped zipper snagged at the base of my throat. It took every scrap of self-control not to rip the damn thing open in a Superman-esque fashion; instead, I managed to jiggle and verbally cajole the obstinate device into submission, getting it far enough down that I could wriggle out of the tight embrace of the fabric.

Maybe thirty minutes after getting back into the room, I was sitting on the small couch beside the window staring blankly at my laptop. I'd done an impressive job of ignoring the increasingly frantic text messages from Vasily, who had therefore escalated to multiple voicemails. Tapping out a terse reply that I'd talk to him in the morning seemed to put him at ease, though for all the wrong reasons. As desperately as I wanted to talk to someone about Suzanne, I just didn't have it in me to burden my best friend with my latest set of troubles. The laptop had been my attempt to focus on something else, but it had been an unintentional reminder that the professional side of my life was equally as fucked up. So, I sat there, staring, for another forty minutes before I set it aside and dug through the mini bar for a package of trail mix and the smallest bottle of red wine I had ever seen.

Tearing open the trail mix, I fished out an almond before twisting the screw cap from the wine bottle. Not standing on decorum, I took a swig from the bottle and immediately knew I was going to be overcharged for the worst vintage ever bottled. I made a note to mention that on the survey I would likely get after my stay, and then thought better of it; I wasn't any sort of wine connoisseur, so who was I to say that this was a terrible brand to have in the room? Setting it down on the small side table, I dug out a peanut from the trail mix and then returned my attention to the image on my screen.

Staring back at me was the first tranche of photos from the historical archives that Charlie had provided. I'd been looking over the impressive array capturing the day Route One Hobbies had opened back in the 1940s as documented by the *Windeport Observer*; that we'd even had a local newspaper came as quite a surprise, given how I'd only ever known the *Bangor Daily News*. Shifting to my web browser had allowed me to dig up a bit of a history on the paper, including the fact it had once been housed in a since demolished building beside the IGA. Changing demographics in the late 1970s had led to it being purchased by the *Bangor Daily*; the nameplate had been discontinued not long after. Tapping at my keyboard, I marveled at just how little had changed at the hobby store, for even back then, the layout was front-and-center. Several photos from then showed it was about a third smaller than the version I'd seen, though the level of detail was just as impressive.

Setting the photos aside, I began to read the accompanying articles, jotting down notes as I went. Walter's grandfather apparently had the same sort of ad hoc model railroad club even back then, though the size was much larger, with membership topping out in the mid-thirties. Considering the economy was still booming, I wasn't surprised there were more people to draw in; a similar article when Walter's father took over in 1962 mentioned the group had dropped to under twenty, but also noted that an expansion of the layout was underway, one that would feature the portion of the UEM campus that just touched the Village's Eastern border. Flipping ahead to the crime scene photos, I tried to see if I could determine exactly how the new addition had been grafted onto the existing layout, for no photos from the period seemed to have captured it. I thought *maybe* there was a seam along one of the rolling hills between the downtown part of the Village and campus but wasn't entirely sure. I made a note to ask Caitlyn on the off chance she'd been around when it had happened. Flipping back to the items from the early 1980s, something in the article from the *Observer* caught my attention, causing me to backup and re-read the paragraph.

Full disclosure: this journalist has been part of the group since 1967 and plans on continuing well into retirement.

It was such an odd thing to insert into the article that I scrolled back to the top to determine who the author was; that was when my eyebrows shot up at the name appearing there.

Ernest Stables? Holy cow... that's the same Ernie that is semi-retired from the Bangor Daily News, *isn't it?*

I sat back on the couch, thoughts suddenly all over the place.

I never thought to ask any of the members I met how long they had been with the club, but I got the sense most had been there for a good while. Then again, he only rejoined the club when he and his partner moved to Windeport, so in some sense, he might be the one with the least longevity in the group. I'll have to pull his official bio on the paper's website, but if I do the math on my fingers, he must have been in his early twenties when this article was written. That might make him in his teens when he joined the club — wait, how old was Walter?

Using the mouse, I shifted screens again and brought up the Motor Vehicle Division's system and pulled Walter's license. *So, he was 65 when he died*, I thought to myself as I scanned the data. *That means he might be about the same age as Ernie. I wonder how many other teens were part of the group back in the day? And is that even important?*

Something inside me said, resoundingly, *yes*.

Flipping back to the list of people I'd talked to so far, I tracked down the record I'd created for my visit to the current iteration of the model railroad club and scanned the names I'd put into it. Highlighting Ernie, I paused and then highlighted his husband, Thomas, and made a note to follow up with them when I returned to Windeport. At the very least, I was intrigued enough to want to hear the story about how Ernie had returned to his former stomping grounds; if I were lucky, he might remember something about the old layout that could explain some of the changes I was seeing on the new one. Glancing at my watch, I decided there was no time like the present and dialed the number Ernie had provided at the meeting.

He picked up on the second ring. "Hello? This is Ernie Stables."

"Ernie, this is Ch—Sean Colbeth," I said, self-correcting on the fly.

"Sean... Colbeth?" came the puzzled reply.

"We met the other night at Millies?" I prompted, a bit surprised. Normally my more than six-foot frame was quite memorable.

"Chief!" Ernie replied cheerfully. "Of course! What a pleasant surprise."

I opted not to correct him and pushed ahead. "I'm sorry to catch you so late, but I wondered if I could swing by for a chat tomorrow or Saturday?"

"I'm tied up tomorrow morning, but I could do something late in the afternoon or first thing Saturday." He paused. "Is this about the case?"

"Tangentially," I replied. "Our conversation the other night has spurred an interest in all things model railroading for me, and I can't think of anyone better to talk to about it."

"Flattery will get you everywhere," Ernie replied with a chuckle. "How about Saturday morning? Stop in around eight and I'll have coffee and fresh muffins ready."

"That sounds great," I said as I put the entry into my calendar. "Will Thomas be there, too?"

"Probably not," Ernie answered. "He goes to Mass and won't be back until he's drunk every drop of coffee at the fellowship hour afterward. Why? Do you need to talk to both of us?"

"Only if he happens to be around," I hedged.

"It might be hard to pull him away from his own layout, honestly," Ernie said with a slight conspiratorial tone. "But I can do my best."

"Ah," I said. "I would appreciate it. Between the two of you, I might finally begin to understand the attraction of the hobby."

"We both love it. It's not hard to lose yourself in creating little touches on the layout, or watching the trains slowly make their loop. That's one thing Tommy enjoys the most," Ernie said. "I think it fits with him having been a dentist — small items and an attention to detail."

"I could see that. How long has he been retired?"

"Just a few months," Ernie answered. "He hung up his scaler for good back in the spring after thirty years in the business. The insurance system drove him out."

"I can understand that," I said. "My girlfriend says the same thing. She's a doctor."

"Then she knows the struggle is real," he laughed again. "See you on Saturday!"

"Looking forward to it," I replied, and then hung up

Putting my iPhone down on the couch beside me, I polished off the last of the wine and considered the story Ernie had written back in the 1980s once more. Having read his articles for years, I wasn't surprised to see that his early writing had the same flourishes and polished phrasing I had come to enjoy; considering that particular article had been published at a time when every word counted due to the costs of printing, it was even more impressive just how packed full of information it happened to be — as well as being eminently readable. This was no dry delivery of facts, nor a rote recitation of information; the article read as though it had been pulled from one of those long-form magazines, with all the depth that would allow for. I wondered if it had, in fact, run in another publication and jotted that down as a note to ask Ernie on Saturday. Scanning the article one last time, I came back to another section I had flagged on my first read through. I wasn't entirely sure *why* I had, but re-reading it again confirmed that it seemed like an unusual tidbit.

When asked why the layout was in the store and not in the basement, Mr. Guernsey laughed. "Basements are for burying secrets," he said. "Not for model railroads."

Burying secrets? I wondered. *Is he being literal? I seem to recall Norm telling me the basement of the brownstone was dirt. Might be worth a look, I suppose, but I don't know what I'd be looking for in the first place.*

Yawning, I realized that the events of the day were finally catching up with me and began to shut down the case system; as it closed out, my iPhone rang once more. Assuming it was Vasily yet again, my eyebrows went up when I saw the number was not his. Tapping to answer, I tried not to sound surprised. "I'm not sure you should be talking to me, Caitlyn."

"The Village Council doesn't scare me," she replied easily. "I know it's late, but Norm wanted me to pass on an update."

"Aren't you still on leave?" I asked.

"I was," she replied, "until you went and got yourself suspended, leaving us short a person. Thanks to you, I'm now Acting Assistant Chief."

"Congratulations on the promotion."

"It's not the way I want to get it," she replied.

My eyebrows went up. "I didn't realize you were interested in the first place, Cait."

"I'm not, at least not until the kids are in college."

"I will keep that in mind. What do you have?"

"A few things," she said. I heard her rustling paper, which was unusual in our digital age. "Hank had a chance to look at the electrical for us ahead of Heather's expert arriving tomorrow. As a side note, we really need to get him used to using a tablet or something; going through his paper report is giving me flashbacks to high school and an English teacher who required essays to be submitted longhand."

"I think I had that teacher, too," I chuckled.

"I'll transcribe this into the case system later tonight, but the short version is that the recent electrical work from Nick was impeccably done; Hank actually did the final inspection when the job was originally completed."

"So, it wasn't the source of the short that killed Walter?"

"Doesn't seem to be, no. In fact, the new panel Nick added to the store was essentially what prevented the entire building from having an electrical meltdown. Instead, the shorts were isolated to the particular circuits that had been run to the layout and the POS counter as part of the update."

"Interesting," I replied thoughtfully. "So, there were definitively two *different* electrical shorts?"

"There had to be," Caitlyn replied. "There wasn't any way for a short to have jumped from one circuit to the other; the panel would have prevented it, based on the wiring Hank saw — or what was left of it, rather."

"Could he tell the cause of the short?"

"Not entirely. We might have to wait for the state expert on that."

"Sounds like Hank might have had an idea, though," I prompted.

"He did," she replied. "The layout end is clearly the transformer that you already identified, though it's speculation on his part since he hasn't seen the actual device. Most of his speculation is based on the burn pattern beneath the layout, which in his opinion indicates a surge of electricity that the device wasn't capable of handling."

"How would that even be possible?" I wondered aloud. "I don't know as much as Irv, obviously, but given the research I've done so far, the device was built to handle a certain amount of power and no more."

"If it hadn't been altered," Caitlyn replied. "I'll get to that in a moment."

I nodded to myself. "The lab nerds came through, I take it."

"After a fashion," she chuckled. "The POS short was more clearcut; Hank thinks someone plugged an independent power source into the quad outlets below them and forced an overload by feeding the circuit more power than it could handle."

I nodded again. "I feel like I've heard that happening in the past with people who use portable generators when the power goes out; if they plug them directly into the house network without turning off the main, they will have a bit of a surprise when the power comes back on."

"Exactly."

"I can't imagine someone lugged a generator into the store," I said. "If they had, it would have been noticed."

"True, but they didn't have had to," Caitlyn replied. "Walter had one down in the basement."

"Let me guess: right next to a long extension cord?"

Caitlyn chuckled. "Which I've already assigned one of our folks to dust for prints. Nothing yet. I'm also going to ask Heather's team to cross check anything we might find against prints from the circuit box; unless I'm wrong, our suspect would have needed to ensure the generator wasn't feeding the store directly while it was operating."

I frowned. "This is far more methodical than I would have initially suspected. And also speaks to someone who has had access to the store — to the *building* — for enough time to have become familiar with everything in it."

"I agree."

"What did the lab geeks tell you?"

"The report just landed in the case system tonight," she started. "Cutting through the technobabble in it required a call to Heather herself. Per her translation, the transformer in question had been carefully augmented to include a rather sizable capacitor; as the device was used, it stored a fraction of the power it was receiving, much like a battery."

"I'm not an electrical engineer," I reminded Caitlyn. "But I've never died from touching a battery."

"Neither am I," she chuckled. "I'm just repeating what Heather told me. Anyway, from what was left of the circuit board inside the transformer, they were able to determine the damn thing could hold about four hundred percent more power than it was rated to handle."

"Holy *shit*."

"Yeah. But here's the kicker — the way it was wired, this capacitor thingie would only release if there was a specific draw from the throttle."

"Draw?" I asked. "You mean, like how fast Walter might have been driving an engine?"

"Yes," she replied. "Turn the knob over eight and that was that."

I frowned. "The night Walter died couldn't have been the *only* time someone drove a train at that speed."

"That has the lab geeks stumped, too. They have some theories, ranging from solid to fantastical."

"Great," I sighed. "Well, it's a few more pieces to the puzzle for sure. I'll take what we can get."

"Exactly." Caitlyn paused. "I've not had any luck getting the POS systems back online, but I did sort through the credit card receipts you located. All are from the day in question; everyone is local, save for one transaction that I traced to a tourist from Canada."

"Anyone we know?"

"You spoke to three of them," she replied, "if the notes from your chat at Millie's are accurate. Ernie Stables, Phil Washington, and Jeff Duncan. There are more, of course, but the folks from that informal club felt like ones to follow up on."

I nodded, curious that Ernie had popped up again. "Sounds like I need to have a chat with them; I've already set something up with Ernie for Saturday. Did you know he was a member of the group back in the 1980s?"

There was a long pause. "You know, my father used to talk about a fellow teenager from school who came with his dad most weeks. They were close until something drove them apart."

Thinking I might know what that was, I decided to keep quiet; being gay in the late 1970s would have meant hiding in the closet — until someone smoked you out. "He wrote an article about his experiences at Route One Hobbies, back when he worked for the *Windeport Observer*. I ran across it when I reviewed the historical material Charlie dug up for us."

"I'd like to read it," Caitlyn replied. "It's in the case system?"

"Yes. By the way, did you come across a calendar when you were sorting through your father's items in the apartment?"

"Calendar?" she asked. "Not that I can recall, but I wasn't doing a thorough search. Why?"

"We seem to be missing one," I explained. "The club told me Walter had one behind the checkout counter where people could schedule a night to work on the layout with him."

"Oh, *that* calendar," Caitlyn said. "It wasn't on the wall behind the POS system?"

"No."

"That's weird."

"How about the secret list of what's on the layout?"

Caitlyn chuckled. "I've heard of that one, actually," she replied. "Dad never showed it to me. In fact, he went to great pains to ensure I could never find it."

"Any reason why?"

"When I was a kid, I used to cajole him horribly about it," she said. "At the time, he always said I needed to be an adult to understand the reasons behind what had been built. I didn't accept that answer, of course, so I made it my life's mission to hunt it down."

"Sounds like you were a budding investigator."

"Not a very good one," she sighed. "I looked everywhere, including that super-scary basement. At one point, I'd become convinced he'd locked it in a small box and buried it down there, actually." Caitlyn chuckled. "He found me one weekend with half of the dirt turned over."

"I take it you were grounded afterwards."

"Oh yeah," she chuckled again.

"What made you think it was in a box?" I asked. "That's a terribly specific image."

"Funny you should ask," she replied, pausing for a moment. "I have this memory of seeing Dad loading items into one of those small, metal bank boxes at the checkout counter. It wasn't something he did regularly, so I did the standard kid thing and assumed he was hiding something from me in it."

"How old were you?"

"Oh, shit, maybe ten? Grampa hadn't been gone more than a few years by that point," she said before adding. "I think I assumed he'd put it into the basement because my grandfather often said basements were for secrets. It became an irresistible treasure hunt."

My eyebrows went up. Unprompted, Caitlyn had repeated the very phrase in Ernie's article. "Were there any secrets in the basement?" I asked.

"Hell if I know," Caitlyn laughed. "There's certainly enough space to bury a few there, though."

I jotted down a note to text Heather, for I was suddenly very interested in seeing if there *were* any down there. "Indeed. I suppose that also means Walter never shared the list when you became an adult."

"No," she replied. "But that was more due to the fact I had lost interest in it. I had my own life by then and plenty to deal with."

"Don't we all," I sighed. "Anything else?"

"That's about it," Caitlyn replied. "Are you headed back to Windeport tonight?"

I glanced at the empty bottle of wine, then the clock beside the bed. "No, I'll hit the road first thing. I want to dig through the rest of the case file and type up my notes. What time are you expecting Heather?"

"About nine."

"I'll be there," I replied, groaning inwardly at how early I would need to get up.

"See you then," she replied, then paused. "What they did to you is still shitty, Sean."

"Well, the good news is they may not be totally done," I chuckled.

"That is my worst fear," she replied. "If they do fire you, I hope you sue their asses."

"The thought had crossed my mind."

"Good," she said. "See you tomorrow."

Fifteen

Despite what I'd told Caitlyn, I shut down my laptop and shoved it into my backpack, then stripped to my boxer briefs and got ready for bed. The face in the mirror I saw as I brushed my teeth and took out my contact lenses looked infinitely world weary, as if the weight of what I was handling had become manifest. Turning off the lights, I slid between the sheets of the bed, intent on getting some shuteye before having to drive back to Windeport despite the emotional turmoil of my thoughts. I had to have been far more tired than I realized, for it felt as though I had barely closed my eyes when the alarm on my iPhone sang, jarring me back to reality. Sluggishly, I swung off the bed and then stumbled into the bathroom; a hot shower and an iffy cup of coffee from the Keurig in the room helped to make me feel more human, if not completely awake.

The lobby was quiet as I crossed the tile to the exit; out in the parking lot, the cool air of the pre-dawn morning was a blessed relief from the prior day's oppressive humidity. I'd peeked at the long-range forecast for the weekend and hadn't been impressed to see we were locked into a pattern that would continue the high humidity, barely offset by the promise of afternoon thunderstorms. I feared Norm would have little outdoor quality time with Raphael were that to be the case, then realized that might not be as high on his list as other more intimate activities; as I unlocked the door to my SUV, I wondered if the HIV test results had finally come back, and if so, what sort of fallout Norm might be dealing with. Despite my own troubles, my heart ached at the notion his romance with Raphael might be short-lived — or that the rest of his life might look very different than he'd planned.

This has been the week from Hell, I sighed as I started up the SUV. *And not just for me.*

Traffic between the Marriott and the Maine Turnpike was insanely light as befitting the hour; the Turnpike itself was similarly empty save for a few pragmatic tourists trying to get a jump on the logjam guaranteed to occur later in the day as the tide shifted in favor of weekend visitors. I planned to be back in Windeport long before the bumper-to-bumper traffic that was the norm every Friday afternoon between Memorial Day and Labor Day reared its ugly head, barring any sort of unforeseen issues. I made a brief stop at the Gray rest area, procuring a cup of extremely overpriced Starbucks coffee that I paired with a blueberry muffin nowhere near as tasty as anything I had ordered from Calista's Bakery. I considered repeating the mistake when I reached the Gardner rest area but powered through until I saw the first sign for a Dunkin' Donuts and its promise of redemption. My second coffee — an extra-large — washed away my earlier misdeeds in that department, as did the box of two dozen Munchkins. I managed to savor both the coffee and the donut holes all the way to the exit for Route 203 and home; only then did I realize I'd been successful at not thinking about anything beyond food and drink.

I tried to continue that strategy as I drove into the rising sun, but my professional brain clicked in without my consent and began to plot out how the day would go. Heather had responded to my late-night text message and confirmed they would be bringing equipment to help speed up the search in the basement; what I expected to find down there remained a bit fuzzy, though the mysterious box Caitlyn remembered seeing as a kid was a leading contender. Did I think Walter had continued to use it to store the secret list of items from the layout all these years later?

Only if I was very, *very* lucky.

UEM appeared and with it my normal guilt over missing practice; as I drove past, I committed to returning that evening and doing a double to make up for it. A quick glance at the dashboard clock told me I had enough time to swing through Calista's and get a proper cup of coffee; as I returned to the SUV with a freshly brewed takeaway cup, I smiled somewhat sadly when I heard Suzanne's voice in the back of my head gently imploring me to reduce my caffeine intake.

God, I miss her, I thought bleakly as that ache gripped my heart again.

Route One was already hopping when I arrived in front of the hobby store; as there was no on-street parking, I turned off and squeezed the SUV between two of the crime scene vehicles already huddling against the side of the building. Grabbing some exam gloves from my glovebox, I lifted my coffee from the holder and exited the SUV. I could see the door to the rear of the store had been propped open, so I headed in that direction and found Norm leaning against the doorframe. Seeing me, he looked into the building for a moment and then stepped out toward me; to my surprise, the striking form of Raphael Gonzales appeared in the doorway, smiled at me, and then followed Norm.

"Chief," Norm said as we formed a small clutch just behind the loading dock. "I hope you don't mind another set of eyes," he continued with a quick glance at Raphael.

"Not my call any longer," I reminded Norm as I reached for and shook Raphael's hand. "Good to see you again."

"Same," he nodded with a smile.

Dressed in cargo shorts and a t-shirt that had a severe V-neck, the officer with the National Park Police looked far more like a tourist on holiday; it was clear he spent most of his time outdoors, given how deeply tanned his complexion had become. Expensive looking sunglasses had been pressed back into his significant head of dark hair, and though his beard was as impeccable as when I'd seen it last, there was a faint hint of grey around the edges of his mouth that served as a reminder of the age gap between Norm and Raphael. Being in a May to December romance myself, I wasn't as worried as Vasily had been about the park ranger robbing the cradle, as it were; besides, I'd become quite comfortable with the notion that Norm was capable of handling whatever came his way. As I looked at the handsome Latino who appeared to have captured the heart of my number two, I realized I was privately thankful that Raphael had entered Norm's life; after finding out how bad it had been with his ex, I figured Norm deserved a bit of happiness.

"I hear the department is hiring all sorts of consultants these days," I said to Raphael before looking to Norm. "I hope he's paying you what he's paying me."

"I believe there was some sort of in-kind trade going on," Raphael deadpanned, which brought a slight shading to Norm's boyish cheeks.

"Indeed," I smiled, which made Norm look even more uncomfortable.

"I'm sorry to hear what's been going on here," Raphael continued. "I hope it's resolved in your favor, and soon."

"Time will tell," I nodded, not wishing to get into that right at the moment. "I presume he brought you up to speed?"

"Yes," Raphael nodded before looking to the building. "The team from the State is already inside."

"Good," I said and then started toward the door.

Norm grabbed my arm. "Before you go in," he said as I swung toward him, "can I talk to you for a moment?"

The expression on his face brought me up short. "Of course," I said, then looked at Raphael. "Go on in, we'll join you in a moment."

"Okay," he said, then disappeared back through the door of stock room.

I waited a few extra moments to ensure he was out of earshot before looking back at Norm. Whatever control he'd been exerting while around Raphael had finally failed him, though I wasn't entirely surprised to see outright panic on his face; putting my hands to either shoulder, I shook my head, then lowered my voice. "It came back positive."

"Yes," he said, his voice shaking. The agony was hard to hear. "My fucking ex did this to me. And now I've given it to Raphael."

I glanced at the door. "His test came back positive, too?"

"No," Norm replied, "but it was one of those rapid ones. He's going to head to Suzanne's practice and have the doctor covering for her run the same lab panel I took."

"You told him, then?" I asked.

"Yes," Norm managed to get out. "I felt terrible, but he needed to know; the clinic where he took the test put him on a course of prophylactic antivirals. Suzanne left a prescription for me if the test came back —came back—"

In seconds, my stoic number two had dissolved completely into tears, suddenly looking more like a frightened teenager discovering their world had been upended. Feeling a bit like that father figure once more, I pulled him toward me and held his shaking body while the wave passed through him; I wasn't sure how long we stood out there in the early morning July sun, but I was determined to be there for as long as he needed me to be. At length, the sobbing subsided and he pulled away, wiping at his nose with the back of his hand. Red-rimmed eyes looked at me, then darted away as the embarrassment of losing his composure in front of his boss took hold.

Knowing what he was thinking, I put a hand to his arm. "I'm your supervisor; I'd also like to think I've become your friend," I said softly. "Friends help each other and always have each other's back."

He looked at me.

"I've got yours, Norm," I smiled gently. "We'll get through this."

"Raphael has to *hate* me," he said morosely.

"That can't be true," I replied.

"How can you know that?" he demanded, his voice wavering.

"He's here, isn't he?" I asked. "He didn't run from you when you told him, did he?"

The look on Norm's face shifted. "No," he replied after a moment of consideration. "In fact, he asked if he could extend his stay for a few extra days."

I nodded toward the door. "Raphael is in for the long haul, dude," I said softly. "I can't speak for him, of course, but if I am right, what he feels for you is deep enough that he'll move heaven and earth to see you through this."

"He's only known me for a few weeks," Norm said.

"Love can be a mysteriously wonderful thing," I smiled.

"Yeah," he replied after a long look at the empty doorway. "Yeah, I suppose it is."

We stood there for a few moments contemplating life; my own concerns suddenly felt small when stacked next to Norm's. "Do you want to take a bit before we go in?" I asked. "I know I'm only a consultant, but I *have* run a crime scene a time or two."

Norm looked at me and smiled his more familiar half smile I often saw. "No," he said. "Let's do this."

We found Heather and Raphael just inside the store, chatting with a short, balding gentleman wearing thick safety glasses. The conversation paused as we entered, and I extended my hand to the latest addition to our group. "Irv, it's good to see you again."

The stout man smiled and quickly pumped my hand. "Despite the circumstances," he chuckled. "I hear the Village Council is out to get you again."

I glanced at Heather who was studiously examining her nails. "Word gets around quickly."

"It's a small state," Irv chuckled.

"I've driven most of it," I replied. "I would beg to differ."

"All right, then a small law enforcement community," he amended with a wink. "Either way, it sucks. I hope you come out on top."

"The odds are not in my favor this time," I sighed. "Have you had a chance to look around?" I asked, hoping to forestall any further discussion of my future.

"Just about to jump in, actually," he said with a nod toward Heather. "The crime scene techs are already checking out the basement for you, but I wanted to review the panel down there before they got too far."

"Makes sense," I nodded before turning toward Norm. "Why don't you take Irv downstairs and help him get started? I need to chat with Heather for a moment, and then I'll join you."

"Will do," he replied before looking at Raphael. "Do you mind lending a hand?" Norm asked.

"Not at all."

"All right. This way, Irv; we can access the basement though the stockroom."

"I remember," Irv said cheerfully as he bent down to retrieve a small pack brimming with tools I couldn't begin to identify. "Since I was down there earlier..."

I smiled as I watched the strange threesome disappear into the stockroom. "There has to be a joke in there somewhere," I said to Heather.

"Anything that starts with 'a detective, a park ranger and an electrical inspector go into a basement' sounds more like a horror movie to me," she chuckled.

"Yeah," I replied, "you're right." I looked at her for a moment. "Technically, I can't ask you to do anything— "

"Oh, the *Hell* with that," she said forcefully, waving at me. "As far as I'm concerned, I never got the memo you aren't in charge any longer. What do you need?"

I smiled slightly. "Are you sure? I have no idea how large the blast radius will be when they finally take me out."

"Honey," Heather said with a hand on her hip, "the State can't afford to lose me or my team. I'll talk to whom I please. And what's with this fatalism? That's not like you at all."

"It's more like realism," I sighed. "And maybe I'm just tired fighting the good fight."

Heather looked at me and thought about saying something, then thought better of it. "What do you need?"

"I know your team only went through the store and the backroom the first time," I said. "As much as I hate to ask, I need them to go through those spaces again, plus both the apartment and the basement."

"Okay," she frowned. "I'm glad I brought the whole team. Are we looking for something in particular?"

"*Two* somethings," I replied. "A wall calendar and some sort of secret list."

Her eyebrows went up. "Those are *quite* particular."

"Don't I know it."

"The calendar should be obvious when we run across it; what is this list going to be on? Or in? Are we looking for a notebook, or a clipboard, or what?"

"I have no idea," I shrugged. "It could be an old papyrus scroll for all I know."

"You're not being very helpful, Sean," Heather said accusingly.

"Well, whatever it is might be inside a metal box, like one of those old-fashioned fire containers from forty years ago."

"Oh goody," she frowned again. "There's nothing I like better than a scavenger hunt."

"Thee doth protest too much," I chuckled. "You live for this kind of thing."

A tiny smile appeared. "I'll never admit it," she said quietly.

"Your secret is safe with me," I chuckled again, mimicking zipping my lips closed with my fingers.

"Good," she chuckled. "We'll get started, then. I'll meet up with you in a bit."

"Sounds good."

I watched Heather move over to the half-dozen techs that had been loitering by the layout, then followed in the footsteps of Norm and company. Making my way through the rows of carefully arranged boxes in the stockroom, I found the wooden door for the basement already propped open; noise of the activity well underway trickled back up the steps as I paused at the threshold. It wasn't hard to hesitate before starting down the extremely steep staircase; I might have been a decorated police office, but as a human, always felt that vague unease entering such a damp, dark and musty smelling space always triggered. That creeping sense of horror was only enhanced by the earthy smell wafting from the hard packed dirt floor; thoughts of what sorts of unfathomable secrets might literally lay mere inches beneath my feet were hard to ignore. The uneven surface of the dirt seemed at odds with the cheerful fluorescents doing their best to banish the shadows and with them, any fears. An old furnace sat in one corner, connected to a brick chimney that was original to the building; beside it, some sort of hot water heater of a far more modern vintage. Metal shelving had been carefully placed in even rows along the irregular floor and were comfortably filled with boxes of every shape and size imaginable; much like the stockroom above, everything was neatly labelled for easy retrieval, though the filing system in use seemed foreign to my eye. What few gaps existed against the foundation exposed the original stone masonry laid more than a century earlier.

Pipes and electrical conduit ran in the floor joists a few inches above my head, a reminder that this basement had been built when humans were well under six feet in height. I found myself crouching slightly to avoid knocking myself senseless; judging from how one of Heather's techs was rubbing his forehead and quietly cursing, it seemed wise to be cautious. At the front of the space, two small casement windows were wedged between the rocks of the foundation and the floor, providing some natural light and an awkward view of feet as they walked by on the sidewalk. It also appeared that the main utilities came in from the street as represented by a cast iron pipe for the sewer, and a much smaller — and more modern — set of copper pipes for water.

Irv had put his bag down on the dirt just a few feet into one of the ad hoc aisles and appeared to be pointing a flashlight at a bundle of cables just above his head. Norm and Raphael were beyond him and had already donned gloves to begin the process of going through the items in the basement. I pulled my own gloves from where I had stuffed them in the pocket of my shorts and snapped them on, then moved over to the next row to begin the long slog through God knew what. The work turned out to be exactly what I needed, though; I hadn't realized how focused I'd become until Irv tapped me on the shoulder to say he was moving upstairs for the next part of his work.

"I'll finish this stack and then come up," I said, nodding to the final part of the shelf I'd been working on.

"Find what you were looking for yet?" he asked as he hefted his bag.

"Sadly, no," I replied. "But there is more to go through."

Irv chuckled and then hustled off; his steps faded up the wooden stairs as I returned to my task. By the time I rounded the corner and met up with Norm and Raphael, I'd grown an entirely new appreciation for the minutiae of the hobby business; that, and I was likely to go crosseyed if I had to dig through another box of chiffon pipe cleaners. From the expressions on their own faces, it looked like they were on the same wavelength.

"Please tell me you've found something," I implored as I cast a glance at the two remaining rows of boxes.

"No," Raphael said. "However, I now know there are sixteen sizes of plant stems."

"Ah," I sighed. The two techs appeared from where they had been working. "Anything?"

Both shook their head.

"Shit," I sighed, then moved to the final row. "Well, if we each tackle a section it will go faster."

"And if we don't find anything?" Norm asked.

"Then we start digging."

He looked at the dirt beneath his dress shoes. "That wasn't on my Bingo card today."

"Murder rarely is," I chuckled. "Come on, let's get this over with."

I was just reaching for the top box in my section when I heard footsteps on the stairs. "Sean?" came the voice of Heather.

"Over here," I said.

The figure of the head field technician appeared at the end of the row; she was holding a plastic bag. "I might have something you want to see," she replied.

Handing my box to Norm, I moved around Raphael and the two techs and made my way to Heather. "Indeed you might," I said when I was close enough to determine it was a wall calendar in her bag. "Where was it?"

"There's a tiny space between the top of the box holding the cash drawer and where it connects to the cabinet," she replied. "You have to push it in from behind, too, which tells me someone was in a hurry but also knew it wouldn't easily be found."

My eyebrows went up. "I ran my hands over the drawers looking for the manual release," I said. "I didn't find that gap."

"It's not much, but it was just enough. This is a pretty thin calendar," she added as she handed it to me. "I've simply bagged it; I figured you would want to go over the items written on it yourself."

"That I would."

"Irv is also ready to give you his rundown, if you have a moment."

"Sure," I said, then looked at the calendar in my hands. "I kind of want to see who was scheduled for the night of the murder."

"You'll also want to dust for prints first, too," she reminded me. "Come on, Irv's waiting."

"Sadist," I accused.

"I suspect you already know the name you'll find there," she replied as we went up the steep staircase.

"I might," I smiled.

"Then savor the suspense while it lasts."

We found the inspector in the stockroom, his bag already packed and waiting at his feet. "The wiring is pristine," he said without preamble. "I don't see any evidence that the short that caused the death of your victim came from outside the store; in fact, I'm quite certain it was localized to the layout."

I nodded. "That was our working theory."

"It's a good one," he agreed. "I also see evidence of a significant back feed into the point-of-sale system; it's clearly a secondary event not tied to the first one. In my professional opinion, it was designed to fry the electronics on that side of the store."

"Which it did rather effectively," I nodded again.

"I'm not surprised," Irv said. "I must hand it to whoever redid the electrical, though. It's a tidy little job, and everything is nicely isolated. The layout had its own dedicated circuit, which tripped before any further damage could be done to the store."

I glanced at the flickering lights in the store through the door of the stockroom. "Did the POS event do that?"

"Yes," he nodded. "Although it has a dedicated circuit, it happened to also share it with the lighting feed. It's not all that unusual given the power requirements, though I would have preferred an isolated power line; computers can be temperamental when the voltage fluctuates."

"They are temperamental under any circumstances," Heather laughed.

"True," Irv smiled. "I'll write up my results and add them to the case file for you by tonight."

"Thanks," I said as we shook.

"I'm not sure I did much," he replied, arching an eyebrow. "I have a feeling you already knew what I told you."

"Suspected," I corrected. "And you confirmed it."

"Good," he laughed. "Heather."

"Irv. See you back at the farm."

He nodded and waddled out of the stockroom, humming a merry tune. I felt an eyebrow arch. "I can never get over how cheerful that guy is. No matter what."

"He loves his job," she replied.

"Clearly."

"Admit it," Heather said, tapping me on the chest. "You love your job, too."

I frowned. "I used to," I said, surprising myself by verbalizing my thoughts. "I'm not sure any longer."

"I think it's not the job that's the problem," she said softly. "More like the environment."

"I love Windeport!" I protested.

"That isn't the environment I was thinking of," she replied.

Before I had a chance to reply, I was interrupted by a shout from the basement. "Sean? Are you up there?"

Eyes widening, I hustled to the steps and called back down. "Yes! Do you need something?"

"A shovel," Raphael said as he appeared at the base of the steps. "I think we found what we were looking for."

Sixteen

"Norm had told me about the hyper-detailed buildings on the layout upstairs," Raphael explained. "Including the non-sequitur of the garden shovels in the back room for the hobby store."

I nodded. Heather had followed me back down into the basement, and the two of us were standing with Raphael and Norm about a third of the way along one of the informal aisles. "Caitlyn confirmed that the store to her knowledge had never carried anything of the sort. At least, not the the life size versions; I never asked if they carried them in scale."

"They do," Raphael smiled. "That's what caught my attention."

With that many of us crammed into the tight space, the air was feeling a bit heavy. I put a hand to the cool metal of the shelving. "What, exactly, got your attention?"

"This," he said as he pointed to a brown box.

"That looks like every *other* box down here," Heather said.

"Look closer," Norm encouraged. His eyes were dancing with excitement, a welcome change from earlier.

I stepped forward and leaned in; Heather wasn't entirely wrong, for the box seemed incredibly ordinary. Still, I carefully scanned the label and came up short when I saw the small icon of a shovel beside the printed text of the contents. "This says the box holds yarn," I said, glancing up at Norm. "The shovel seems out of place. Is that logo on any other box?"

"None in this row," Raphael confirmed. He seemed as excited as Norm. "I've not checked the other rows, but it feels like a good bet they won't have them either."

"Okay," I said, standing upright. "What's in the box?"

"Tiny shovels," Norm said as he pulled it out and opened the top. Tipping it toward me, I could see he was right; small shovels in several varieties were in small bags, each tagged with a barcode for the store.

"This could be a strange coincidence," I said as I reached in and pulled one of the small bags out. "Damn, these are detailed."

"Yes, they are," Raphael said. "And I don't think it's a coincidence. Check this out." We took a collective step back as he crouched at the base of the shelving. "Can you see these markings in the dirt?"

Despite the brilliance of the fluorescents, I had to squint to see the faint lines Raphael was pointing to. "Looks like some sort of scraping," I said.

Raphael nodded as he stood. "Just like you would get if this shelf moved out from the wall."

My eyes shot to the metal structure. "Holy *shit*. This unit isn't connected to the rest, is it?"

"It's not," Raphael smiled. "Most of the boxes on this shelf also happen to be fairly light."

"Making them easy to remove," Norm added.

I looked at Heather. "Please tell me your van has shovels?"

"It does," she said as she started for the stairs. "Don't touch anything until we get the camera down here."

I won't lie, it was excruciating waiting for Heather to return with a set of shovels and one of her techs who was sporting the fancy digital camera they used at the crime scene these days. We loitered at the far end of the basement impatiently as the young man set about documenting Raphael's discovery; once he'd photographed the shelf as we'd found it, boxes were then removed, and more photos were taken of every square inch exposed. Then and only then did Raphael and Norm take to the sides of the shelf and slowly pull it out from the wall; I was surprised at how easily it moved, an unanticipated side benefit of the hard-packed dirt surface it was on. Shifting positions slightly, the duo pushed the empty shelf up against the aisle behind us, creating an awkward space in an already cramped area.

A few more photos were taken before we were able to crowd around the now-exposed surface of the floor. Eyeing it, I looked at Norm. "If something is buried here, it's been here for a long time. This surface doesn't seem to have been touched in *years*."

"Or it was packed down thoroughly before the shelf went back over it," he offered in return.

"Maybe." I looked at Heather. "This is where you come in, I'm afraid. How do you want to tackle this?"

"Deliberately," she smiled. "If I could have some space?"

We shifted out of the way as best as we could, allowing the ace crime scene tech access, then shifted further when two more of her techs appeared. One was carrying a brilliant blue tarp, the other, a small dirt screen with foldable legs. The pair unfurled the tarp off to one side of where Heather was standing, then carefully placed the screen on the edge closest to the exposed spot. I tried not to frown, for I'd seen this operation before and knew that sifting every shovelful of dirt would take time; I also knew how professional Heather and her team were, and therefore chose to bite my tongue.

A fourth tech materialized out of nowhere carrying a long-handled shovel; with a curt nod from Heather, he stepped carefully into the space we had cleared, then gently tapped the shovel a few times around the perimeter as though he were sounding the depth of the soil. Starting nearly in the exact center of the rectangle, he quickly shoved the edge of the shovel into the dirt, then lifted a sizeable section out to place it into the screen. He repeated the process two more times before one of the other techs began sifting through the soil, slowly allowing dirt to rain down onto the tarp. My patience began to ebb when by the fourth iteration it seemed like all we had accomplished was moving dirt from one pile to another with nothing to show for it.

"This is going to take all day," I sighed, unable to stop myself.

"You don't usually fidget like this," Heather chuckled.

I tried to smile, but the sense of time escaping felt very real to me for some reason. "The longer this goes, the less optimistic I am there is anything to find," I said, nodding to the square hole that was maybe a few inches deep at best.

"Go get some coffee or something," she advised. "I'll call you when we find anything."

"Like I need more of *that* today," I sighed. "I think the caffeine is actually making me more impatient."

"Perhaps, but at this point I'd rather not have all of you under foot. Go. I'll call—"

The metallic *clang* that suddenly rang out through the tiny space had all of us swinging toward the tech who had been digging; he was already on his knees and using his gloved hands to gently slide dirt away from whatever he'd hit. Pushing in closer, we crowded around him and watched as he slowly revealed the edge of a metal container. My mind immediately went to the sort of box that Caitlyn had recalled seeing, which in turn lead to a slight quickening of my pulse, something that always happened when it felt like I was close to a break.

"I need some space, gentlemen," Heather said. "If you please."

I looked at her, chagrined. "Sorry," I said as the three of us stepped back once more.

The tech with the digital camera appeared and did another round of photos, then continued to click away as the tech on his knees slowly dug around the box with a trowel that had materialized out of nowhere. And it did appear to be a box, based on the one edge that had already been exposed; the off-gray metal surface reflected the overhead florescent lights in a rather hazy way, making me think it had either been buried far longer than I'd realized. Or, perhaps, the box itself was quite old, and possibly buried quite recently. Despite the scraping marks I'd noted to the team earlier, it was actually very hard to gauge just how long it had been submerged in the dirt, but as I glanced back at the shelving that had been moved out of the way, something struck me.

"I'm not sure this was something Walter accessed frequently," I said, still looking at the shelving. "It would be a ton of trouble to offload everything, move the shelf, and then dig everything up just because you want to stash your savings bonds in a safe place."

Norm looked at me. "Savings bonds?" he asked. "What are those?"

"You must have taken a Finance class in college," I started to explain before seeing the impish look on his face. "Smart ass. Just for that, your next month of paychecks will be in savings bonds."

"Good thing you're not my boss at the moment, then," he chuckled.

"Through the heart," I sighed. "And how soon they forget."

We returned our attention to the activity in front of us and lapsed into silence. The sounds of scraping, intermixed with the occasional click from the photographer's camera, became the soundtrack for the basement, an appropriate accompaniment to intense earthy odor that had filled the corner of the space. The pace was excruciatingly slow, almost as though I were living inside one of those carefully paced documentaries featuring an archeological dig in some exotic portion of the world. All that was missing was a narrator with a clipped British accent doing play-by-play. In what felt like days (but in reality, had only been a few hours), enough of the dirt was finally removed, exposing a stout metal box with a handle fastened at the exact center of the lid. A small keyhole was below it, another confirmation of it being the lockbox Caitlyn had seen. With a bit of a grunt, the tech who had dug it out lifted the container from the hole in a smooth motion, then walked on his knees over to a clean spot of the tarp before setting it back down.

More photos ensued before Heather knelt and inspected the lock with a lighted magnifying glass. "Something is broken off inside the keyhole," she said, looking up at me. "We're going to have to open it the hard way."

"At least that means we don't need to locate the key," I smiled.

"Thank God for small blessings," she chuckled. "You want to do it here or back at the station?"

I shot a glance at Norm, who nodded. "Here, if you don't mind."

She smiled, then reached down into the toolkit she'd placed on the tarp beside her. I wasn't sure what I'd been expecting, but it certainly wasn't the small battery-operated drill-like device she retrieved. After ensuring the charge was good on the gizmo, she inserted a long bit into the business end then turned it on; the high-pitched whine immediately dropped several octaves as she pressed the tip into the lock. Within moments, she'd efficiently cut through the mechanism; setting her handy device to the side, she gripped the handle, flipped the latch on the edge open, then pulled the top up. The resulting frown on her face didn't instill much confidence in me, though, and I felt the adrenaline that had been surging through me taper off and then dip.

"Mostly paperwork," Heather reported before turning it toward us. "And not much of that, in fact."

I knelt beside her and squinted into the box; without my cheater reading glasses, under certain lighting it was hard to make out details these days. Poking at the paperwork with a gloved finger, I started to call off what I was seeing. "Deed to the building. Last will and testament for Walter. Life insurance on Walter and Caitlyn. Incorporation papers. 1964 New York World's Fair map. Another copy of the deed. A *third* copy of the deed. Caitlyn's High School Diploma." Shifting the paperwork, I raised my eyebrows. "There's also a tidy sum of cash in here, too."

"How much?" Heather asked. "I didn't see that initially."

Picking up the two stacks of wrapped bills, I thumbed through them. "Couple of thousand, easy. And these bills look old," I added, handing a batch to Heather.

She nodded. "1985, actually. I remember my parents joking about this Secretary of the Treasury, since his name was so similar to the President."

I looked over her shoulder. "Donald Regan?"

Heather laughed. "It was pronounced *Re*-ghan, emphasis on the first syllable."

"Ah." I sat back on my haunches. "Well, so much for being the keeper of secrets," I sighed as I looked up at Norm. "I don't see the secret list of what's on the layout in here. Everything else seems on the order of personal items better suited for safety deposit box at the bank."

"Fuck," he replied morosely. "And a damn peculiar place to 'hide' such normal stuff."

"I know," I said, looking back at the box and flipping through the papers a second time. "Although I'm sure Caitlyn will appreciate having a copy of this policy in hand. But the rest of it—"

I wasn't sure how I had missed it the first time around, but the *second* time my eyes scanned the three deeds, it occurred to me that the addresses listed were different. Squinting, I also realized the dates were wildly disparate; the one for the building housing Route One Hobbies was dated April 12, 1940, which fell into the date range of when Walter's grandfather began the business. The August 1972 date on the second deed was far newer; the third, a 1985 date. Both newer deeds listed addresses I didn't immediately recognize.

Until I did.

"Maple Street," I murmured. "That's the actual road name for Route 203."

"Sorry?" Heather said.

I looked at her as I held up the deeds. "These two deeds are for property along Route 203," I said. "Unless I miss my mark, somewhere between the Village and UEM."

"There's nothing out there but empty farmland," Norm said.

"True," I nodded.

"Maybe your victim had a long-term expansion plan," Raphael said. "That's the major east-west route from here to the Interstate, right?"

"It is," I nodded, a slight smile forming on my face. "In fact, it's got to be one of the most desirable commercial sites in the Village. Anything out there would avoid having to deal with traffic on Route One." I paused, my smile growing slightly larger. "If I'm not mistaken, the right-of-way for the old railroad that once served Windeport ends just at the edge of the property, too."

"Railroad?" Norm repeated blankly. "That can't be relevant, right? No railroad serves Windeport now."

"Other than the fictitious one on the layout upstairs," I reminded him.

Norm looked at me, confusion clouding his features. "I'm not sure I'm following you. Or I've missed something significant along the line."

Heather was already shaking her head. "He's solved it."

"Solved *what*?" Norm asked, looking between us. "The case?"

"Yes," Heather chuckled.

"Shit," he breathed, eyes wide.

Heather looked at me. "Want these bagged up?"

"Please. And if you don't mind, I'd like to keep the deeds for a bit."

"That might be a bridge too far, considering your current status," Heather replied softly.

"I'll take it instead," Norm replied, before looking at me. "Solved? *Seriously*?"

I hedged. "I don't want to get ahead of the evidence."

"Like *Hell*," he sighed with exasperation. "Vasily warned me about this, didn't he?"

"Yes, he did," I nodded.

"Are you going to share your observations with the rest of us?" Raphael asked.

"After we drive out to that address," I nodded.

"What are you expecting to find there?" Norm asked as he took the now-bagged deeds from Heather, signing for it in the process.

"Clarity," I responded. "And maybe some measure of closure for all involved."

"Amen to that," Heather chuckled.

Seventeen

Norm and I parted ways on the sidewalk in front of Route One Hobbies; while our intent had been to caravan to the address on Maple Street listed upon the deed, it had grown late enough in the day that he worried whether Raphael would still be able to get his second round of HIV tests at Suzanne's practice. While I was relatively certain the doctor covering for her would sneak them in, I wasn't all that upset at being asked to go on ahead and scope out what might or might not be a significant lead for our case. While every bone in my investigator body knew it to be the former, I also realized I had little to back it up — yet — and hoped a few minutes alone wandering the area might indeed provide the clarity I was seeking.

The lethargic pace leading to our discovery in the basement meant I'd missed lunch; given the traffic flow on Route One as I pulled away from the side street where I'd parked, I solved two problems by turning south. Since I needed to make a U-turn anyway, doing so at the light in front of the IGA was completely logical; ducking inside the grocery store long enough to pick up a sandwich from the deli counter was just a fortuitous plus. Continuing the strange sweet tooth binge I was on, I added one of the bakery department's massive chocolate chip cookies as dessert, then rounded out the whole affair with yet *another* cup of hot coffee. Unsure of just how many I'd had since leaving the Marriott that morning, I quickly took stock of my heart rate and, not finding any palpitations or other cardiac events in progress, decided I could handle one more.

I was just putting the plastic lid on the takeaway mug when I heard a soft chuckle behind me; turning, I found Thomas Levant standing there holding a half-full market basket and wearing an amused expression bordering on a smirk. The small section of white stubble along his chin told me he'd missed a spot while shaving that morning, but otherwise he was impeccably dressed in a button-down and khakis that had clearly been ironed, not exactly reflective of our summer resort style. It struck me that retirement might not be sitting well with the older gentleman; I'd known quite a few people who'd had trouble adjusting from the structured world of their career to the more freedom not working presumably endowed upon them. Having been unexpectedly disconnected from the department had given me a preview of how I might handle my own situation, and I was finding the results somewhat unsettling. In a weird way it helped me understand we were all creatures of habit, no matter the age; humans were attracted to structure, whether imposed or by design.

"And here I was thinking it was just a tired television crime drama trope that police work ran on caffeine."

"Oh, I'm sure that was based on extensive research by the writers," I smiled. "Accuracy is important in these matters."

Unsure if I was being sarcastic, Thomas looked at me for a moment. "I suppose that would be true."

Changing the subject slightly, I nodded at his basket. "Ernie sent you for supplies, I see."

Thomas frowned and then looked down at his haul. "He wants to make fresh blueberry muffins for your visit tomorrow morning," he replied. "Unfortunately, that required fresh blueberries. And flour. And sugar. And all the other baking supplies we were out of."

"Sounds like the pantry was empty," I chuckled. "Not dissimilar to my own, actually."

"Now that seems on-brand for a police officer," Thomas replied without missing a beat.

I felt an eyebrow arch. "That we have empty pantries?" I asked.

"Yes," he nodded. "And empty houses."

That eyebrow went higher. While I knew it was unlikely Thomas was aware of my difficulties with Suzanne, it didn't make the intended barb any less painful. "It's the life," I replied after a moment. "There are days when I can't recall if I chose it, or it chose me."

"I can imagine."

"Forgive me for being frank, but I'm getting the sense I will be intruding tomorrow," I continued, shifting to my retail smile.

"You are," he said. "Ernie should have checked with me before committing us."

Us? I thought. "He seemed to think you'd be at Saturday Mass," I replied with a slight frown. "I didn't intend for it to become a party."

"I've not done Saturday Mass since we left Bangor," Thomas said. "We usually spend the morning together working on the layout."

I shrugged. "Well, I'll try to make it as quick and painless as I can," I said.

"That would be most appreciated. I — *we* — have a lot planned for the day."

My eyebrows went up. "For retired folk, you sure keep a busy schedule."

A half smile appeared. "It's either that or wither away waiting to die."

"That's one Hell of an outlook on life," I said.

"Maybe." He nodded at me. "Until tomorrow, then."

"I look forward to the muffins."

"I'm sure you do," Thomas replied, shaking his head.

I trailed Thomas to the checkout, but despite our proximity, he made a point of chatting with the clerk behind the register and avoided any further eye contact. I'd been in the business long enough to read the nonverbal cues radiating off the older man and wondered for the first time what it might be like living with someone such as him. My brief glimpse told me the early indicators were not good; it didn't take a burst of insight to know I'd likely be getting more of a firsthand view when I dropped by in the morning. It was hard not to roll my eyes at what I now imagined would be a tense standoff over cups of cooling coffee and whatever Ernie was able to make from the ingredients Thomas had procured for him.

Not that the interview would have been easy in the first place.

Traffic out on Route One was just as snarled as it had been when I'd turned into the IGA parking lot; thankfully, the light allowed me to nudge my way into the northbound traffic, but the going was nearly as ponderous as the digging had been in the basement. The chocolate chip cookie had been easier to unwrap and therefore had been reduced to crumbs by the time I finally turned onto Route 203; cars spread out a bit more on the secondary highway, and at least for a few minutes, I enjoyed the relative freedom of driving faster than what our harbor-master putatively referred to as headway speed. Unsure of exactly where I was going to stop — Siri hadn't been able to locate the address when I'd punched it into my phone — I instead drove all the way up to the aquatics center at UEM, then turned around and slowly drove back toward Windeport. I knew the street number for the pool, and what the address was for Calista's back in the Village. Without my normal access to the Village Planner's office, I had to make an educated guess as to where to stop. Slowing further, I pulled off the pavement and onto the dirt verge close to the ditch where Vasily had found Brad Donohue almost a year earlier.

Putting the SUV into park and idling with the AC running, I smiled slightly at the irony of the location. An odd quirk in the boundary between Windeport and the unincorporated county had landed the murder investigation in my hands, and at the time, I'd thought my best friend was healed enough from his assault back in California to take on the case. I'd been wrong, of course, and had nearly wound up losing him for good in the process. My schedule for swim practice meant I drove past the visual reminder of my mistake at least four times a day; that I was now sitting there, possibly looking into something relevant to my current case while on the cusp of losing something else — namely my job — was too rich to ignore.

I made short work of my roast beef sandwich before grabbing my coffee and pushing out into the late afternoon heat. Once more, the sky had the look of approaching thunderstorms with dark clouds billowing upward into the atmosphere. The wind that normally foretold the worst had yet to kick in, so I felt fairly safe walking down the steep slope beside the road and out into the wide, grassy field beyond. The grass was about ankle high, and the patterns indicated that someone had been through recently to collect the bound bales of hay that had been sitting rather forlornly in the field earlier that week. The field itself was fairly flat, though it did begin to slope toward the thick pine forest at the edge and the river I knew to be just beyond; though not as robust as the Saint Mark's behind Charlie's farm, it was wide enough for a canoe or two making it a favorite for those down from Bangor for the day.

Searching my memory as I walked and sipped at the still-hot coffee, I recalled that this particular property had straddled the original boundary that had been surveyed prior to the Village incorporating. The exact reason why the line had gone *through* the property versus *around* it was probably on file somewhere back at the municipal building; for my purposes, all that mattered was that a deal had been made to jag the border just enough to keep the entire property within the Village. I presumed that was to ensure that Village services such as water and sewer would have been made available to it; in the end, of course, it probably wouldn't have mattered, for as soon as UEM broke ground, Windeport fell all over itself to ensure the campus was connected to the

Village infrastructure — but had gone to great pains to ensure the school paid for it, too.

Probably seemed like a good idea at the time, I thought. *Until campus grew. I bet they never annexed it since the University is exempted from property taxes.*

Pausing about two hundred yards from the road, I considered the wide field as I turned in a complete circle. Whatever farmhouse had been there back in the early 1800s had long since been razed; for as long as I could remember, the field had been just that, a *field*. Like everyone else in Windeport, I'd heard the inevitable rumors over the years about the spot being developed, but it had never come to pass. Now I wondered if that was because Walter had owned the property. Nestling my coffee down in the grass, I pulled out my iPhone and brought up the photo I'd taken of the deed, then zoomed in a bit more on the section that described the boundaries. Written in the days before accurate GPS coordinates were used, the language was full of phrases like "starting sixteen steps west-northwest of the running brook" or other colorful locations; eying the property anew, my appreciation grew for whomever had traipsed through the area to delineate it. Scanning further, though, got me the section that had triggered my investigator brain.

From the running brook, turn east for twenty yards to the westernmost terminus of the railroad right-of-way.

Taking my bearings, I picked up my coffee and set off in a general western direction, sort of aware of where the railroad tracks had once lay along that portion of Route 203. There had been a time in the mid-1940s when students had been able to take passenger rail to the UEM campus all the way from Boston; a small Art Deco-styled depot still existed closer to campus, though these days it was essentially rented office space. The trains — and the tracks that had brought them — were removed in the late 1950s when cars began to dominate travel; that, in turn, had made it more difficult for the canneries along Main Street to get their wares to market, signaling the beginning of the end of that industry in the Village. Something of a passenger renaissance had begun in the early 2000s when Portland and Boston were reconnected, but it seemed clear that outposts such as Windeport would never again be part of such service.

The heat of the day had sweat trickling down the small of my back by the time I reached the gentle hump of what had once been the end of the line; after all these years, it wasn't much more than a subtle height differential from the ground around it. Turning, I looked back at the balance of the field, and smiled. Looking down at my iPhone again, I shifted to the photos of the layout I had added, then zoomed in on one featuring the egg farm. I smiled wider when I saw the train tracks leading into the main part of the factory in a manner not unlike what *could* have happened in real life, had such a farm been built on that property.

So, I have one deed from 1972 that says Walter Guernsey owns this bit of land. A nice, convenient property that multiple commercial concerns have wanted to buy over the years. And yet, no sale has happened since he bought it. It can't be a coincidence it's also the one piece of land in the entire Village with the strangest property boundaries ever.

Looking at the land, I frowned.

Why did he buy it? I think I know why he didn't sell it, but why buy it?

A small group of butterflies drifted up from the grass as I started back toward my waiting SUV. I wondered if there was a name for such a thing.

Not to expand his shop. Not out here, I mused, continuing my train of thought. *I'd assume investment, but then again, he never sold it, did he? Even after repeated overtures from interested parties.*

I paused, then turned to look at the right-of-way. It stretched away from me into the distance, generally paralleling the highway a few hundred yards to its side. I was able to trace the path right up to where it disappeared into the thick pine forest at the far western edge of the field. Measuring distance in such spaces was tricky at best, but it felt like maybe a half-mile or so from where I was standing to the edge of that western forest; it seemed like enough land mass to build something, making me wonder even more why Walter's piece had seemed more desirable.

Oh shit, I thought suddenly. *The utilities! I'm standing inside the boundaries of Windeport. Getting utilities out to UEM was a one-time thing; building anything next door would have cost the developer dearly. Building here would have meant the Village would have picked up the cost of getting the infrastructure extended. Damn.*

Finally, I thought. *The pieces are all here. Just one more to tie it all together...*

Switching screens on the phone, I dialed Charlie. To her credit, she picked up on the first ring. "I thought I would hear from you today. I bet you want that info on the infamous Windeport egg farm."

"How very prescient of you," I chuckled.

"Well, we *are* descended from the same stock."

"Duly noted," I laughed harder. "'Infamous' makes me think you found something. Something juicy."

"I did," she replied. "I must admit, doing this research for you has been quite interesting. Takes me right back to when I was in graduate school and spent those long, glorious hours scanning microfiche at the campus library for obscure facts."

I felt myself frowning. "I can't tell if you're being sarcastic."

"Good," she chuckled. "Your timeline was right on the money — there was an agenda item for a Village Town Council in the fall of 1985. A proposal was being made to shift the zoning along a stretch of Maple Street—"

"Also known as Route 203."

"Exactly," she continued. "The zoning change would have allowed commercial development on a one-hundred-acre parcel; included in the plan was extending what was then the Maine Central Railroad line using the former right-of-way that connected to the property."

"As I am currently standing in an empty field that would have presumably sprouted a business, could I assume the vote didn't go the way the business wished?"

"No," Charlie surprised me by answering. "It was unanimously approved."

My frown came back. "And yet, I am standing in an empty field," I reminded her.

"That's because the zoning change came up again at the *next* meeting."

"If it had already been approved, what was there to talk about?"

"The sale apparently fell through," Charlie said. "The minutes are a little vague as to why, but since the property was no longer being considered for commercial use, one of the Council members moved to rescind the earlier zoning changes. He apparently also waxed poetic about possible environmental concerns from developing the property, which was enough to convince a majority of the members present to reverse their earlier vote. So, effectively, the project that had been planned for the site was cancelled."

"The egg farm?"

"The egg farm," she replied.

"And Walter Guernsey was the Council member?"

"Bingo. There are also two interesting postscripts to the story, though I'm not entirely sure how they relate to your case."

"Oh?"

"Yes. First, it came out later that the plot to be purchased had been incorrectly surveyed; apparently, the border along that portion of the line between Windeport and the county is a little fuzzy based on some unusual measurements when the Village was founded back in the early 19th century."

"I've had a look at the deed," I said. "Even in 1972, the language was quite vague."

"Hence the problem. There was some legal wrangling over it in '85, which led to the State stepping in and rectifying the line through a targeted use of eminent domain. In the end, it shrunk the original property just enough that the right-of-way no longer touched the property." She chuckled. "According to the transcripts, the owner of the property in question was quite upset but had little recourse at that point."

"Targeted—" I started before my eyes widened.

That second deed for this address. It wasn't eminent domain! Walter sold just enough of a sliver to the State to make his land less attractive. But the State didn't need it — what use would a tiny slice of pasture be to them...? My head snapped around suddenly in the direction of the UEM campus. *Oh, hell. Of course.*

You're one smart cookie, Walter.

I felt myself smiling slightly as I continued. "They gave that entire plot to UEM, didn't they?"

"You catch on fast," she laughed. "I was curious what the school wanted with that area but couldn't dig anything relevant out of the archives."

"Well, it explains why there's no development out here. What was the second postscript?"

"A nearly identical situation happened in the early 1990s," she said. "A car dealer wanted to build a new location where the egg farm had intended to go."

"Identical? Like it was approved and then not?"

"Close," she replied. "The transcripts from the Village Council meeting indicated there was a spirited discussion, and initially it looked like the zoning change was going to go through. The vote took place after a brief recess, and shocked everyone when it came up short."

"Did Walter vote against it?"

"He did, in fact."

"Charlie, he owns the property in question."

There was a long silence. "Well, that makes things interesting. None of the sources I found listed him specifically; instead, it was a holding company by the name of ROH Properties involved. A lawyer from Steinman, Steinman and Sorrentino represented the firm at all the meetings, both in '85 and again in the 1990s."

"Where are they located?" I asked; as I did so, I remembered seeing incorporation papers inside the storage box back at the hobby store. It took another moment for the name to click.

ROH Properties? Holy shit - it's hiding in plain sight.

"All I could find was a post office box in Fort Fairfield," Charlie was saying. "You might have more luck using your magic police databases."

"Yeah," I sighed. "Good point. Thanks for getting me what you did."

"You want copies? I can drop them off at the station, so long as you are willing to pay for the printing."

I paused. "I'm not working for Windeport PD at the moment," I replied.

There was a stunned silence at the other end of the line. "What the fuck happened?"

"The short version is the Village Council accepted the Professional Board's recommendation of a suspension. So, I'm suspended for the next two months, though it seems pretty clear they are working on making it permanent."

"Didn't you say you were standing in a field?" she asked. "Sounds like you *are* still working."

"Norm hired me back as a consultant."

"Smart man," she replied. "You want to swing by for dinner tonight?"

I smiled at the invitation. "Let me see how it goes," I said. "I've got to touch base with Norm and see where he wants to go with this. I also need to prepare for my interview tomorrow."

"Interview?"

"Yes."

"I'm confused," Charlie said. "If you aren't technically a cop, can you even do that?"

"Probably not."

"Isn't breaking the rules what got you into hot water in the first place?"

"Yes."

There was another pause. "There are times when I don't understand you, Cousin."

"I feel the same way," I replied honestly.

"That... is a confusing answer," she sighed. "Are you *sure* you don't want to come over? I've got a nice Pinot Noir you'll love."

"I'll let you know."

"All right." She paused again. "Who exactly are you interviewing?"

"The son of the car dealer," I replied. "Thomas Levant."

That shocked silence appeared again. "I didn't give you the name of the dealer."

"No, you didn't," I smiled.

"And he's connected to this?" Charlie asked.

"Yes. Along with his partner, Ernie Stables."

"Sean," Charlie said, her voice serious. "You're actually going after a noted columnist?"

"I am."

"Are you sure?"

"I am now," I replied.

"If you're wrong, it'll end your career."

"What's there to end?" I asked. "I'm essentially out already."

"Let me get this straight. You think Walter was killed over nixing a property deal... that he would have benefited from?" Charlie asked. "And that Thomas and Ernie are behind it?"

"Yeah, that's about right," I replied.

"Jesus, Cousin."

"No argument there," I sighed. "But I'm right. And I think I know *why* Walter held out."

"Okay, I'll bite. Why?"

"For his daughter, and grandkids. He was betting that ultimately this end of Windeport would either get developed, or worst case, UEM would come knocking. The longer he waited, the more valuable it would become."

"That's pretty thin."

"It is. But I'm right."

I could almost hear Charlie putting her head into her hands. "May all your guesses be right."

"Amen to that."

Eighteen

"We did do some work for a Walter Guernsey, yes," Arabella said. "It was well before my time here at the firm; the notes on the file indicate it was my grandfather who did the initial intake."

"And it dates back to 1972?"

"Yes," she replied after a moment. "With some additional work here and there right up to this year."

I nodded, more to myself than the lawyer who couldn't see me; after getting off the phone with Charlie, I'd started back to the station to recap my findings only to remember halfway there I was no longer welcome. It was a harsh reality check that brought with it a slew of emotions I'd no experience dealing with, so instead I called Norm and filled him in on my literal field study. I was surprised to hear he was still at the doctor with Raphael and unsure of how much longer they would be waiting, so I did my quick rundown and then let him go — but not without a promise to let me know if the labs had finally been started. With nothing else on my own agenda, I'd returned to the bungalow with the intent of coming up with something more substantial than a sandwich for dinner but had instead grabbed a cold Samuel Adams from the fridge and walked out my screened-in back porch to watch the sunset as it reflected off the gentle swells in the harbor. That netted me about five minutes of peace before I'd begun stewing about the case; calling Arabella to confirm the connection between Walter and her law firm seemed like a logical next step, though I'd been surprised to catch her so late in the day. Then again, it always seemed to me that much like police officers, lawyers seemed to always be working. Arabella was apparently no exception.

Picking up the bottle of beer from the small table beside my wicker chair, I nodded again. "Was the work in '72 to create a new company?" I asked.

Arabella hesitated. "Technically, that would be privileged information between the firm and its client."

"Even if the client is deceased?" I asked. The last glimmers of light from the setting sun were highlighting the tall dune grass between my bungalow and the harbor as they swayed in the onshore breeze. If I'd been a photographer, it would have made for a frameable snapshot.

"That wouldn't mean the organization in question isn't still our client," Arabella replied carefully.

I tried not to smile at the backhanded confirmation. "Good point," I said, then took another sip from my beer. "Could I ask in general terms if Walter asked for advice regarding the sale of some property?"

"I can't really tell you that," Arabella replied after a moment. "On the other hand, that information is available to the executor of the estate. And whoever might be running your hypothetical organization."

I sat up in the chair, which creaked a bit at the movement. "There was a succession plan?"

"All I can say is that any organization we create on behalf of a client always includes one," she replied tactfully.

"That's quite a prudent move."

"We like to think so," Arabella said. "Look, I'm sorry to cut this short, but I've got a client arriving at the top of the hour. That only gives me, like, twenty minutes to deal with any unexpected phone calls I might receive."

I smiled at the not-so-subtle message. "Then I'll let you go, Counselor. Thanks for your time."

"Always."

The phone had barely beeped the ending of the call before I had dialed Caitlyn; she picked up immediately. "Chief? What's up?"

"I need you to call this number," I said before reading her the cell number from Arabella's business card.

"Okay," Caitlyn replied. "Why?"

"She's the lawyer for your father's companies," I replied.

"Companies? *Plural*?" she asked. Her tone was incredulous.

"Yes," I said. "That deed we found in the basement earlier today ties to a plot of land owned by ROH Properties. I suspect strongly your father set that up back in 1972, but I am not entirely certain why — yet."

"And you think this lawyer can tell me that? Because *I'm* now the owner?"

"You catch on fast," I chuckled. "Give her a call and then call me right back."

"On it."

I held the phone for a moment before putting it down beside the bottle of beer; checking my watch, I found myself at loose ends for the first time in years. Glancing back at the main portion of the bungalow, I realized just how empty it felt without Suzanne's presence; walking in that evening, it felt far bigger, and far lonelier, than any place I had ever lived. Picking up the beer, I drained what was left and then stood to consider the long shadows now being cast across the dunes. They felt like a metaphor for decisions I had made in my life, and their resulting aftereffects.

Grabbing my phone, I went back into the bungalow in search of another beer; a fresh one was still waiting for me in the fridge. I'd just pulled it out when my iPhone abruptly burst to life. Setting the beer down on the kitchen counter, I wasn't sure what to make of the fact that Caitlyn had called me back so quickly. Tapping at the answer button, I tried not to put the concern into my voice.

"That was fast."

"We're just getting started," was her reply. "I've got Arabella conferenced in; as the President and Chief Operating Officer of both ROH Properties *and* Route One Hobbies, I have authorized her to speak to you about our legal work with her firm."

My eyebrows went up. "Indeed."

"I'm still getting used to the notion," Caitlyn admitted. "But it does have a nice ring to it."

"I can't deny that — unless it means you're leaving the department."

"We'll have to talk about that," she hedged. "Right after you get your position back."

"Deal." I paused for a moment. "By the way, that was nicely played, Arabella."

"I have my moments," she chuckled. "Now, I still have that client coming in at the top of the hour. What can I tell you in the short amount of time I've got left?"

Every fiber in my body told me I was on the cusp of having the answers I needed; still, being under the pressure of time forced me to be judicious in my questions. Sorting through them, I decided on the best one to get the conversation going. "Does your firm act in a management capacity for ROH Properties?" I asked.

"We do," Arabella answered. "The official address for the firm is here in Fort Fairfield; we monitor the post office box and refer anything to Walter as needed."

"Did ROH Properties ask the State to take a section of their property by eminent domain?"

"It was more complicated than that," Arabella confirmed. "ROH offered the State a small, irregularly shaped parcel on the western edge, according to the lawyer who handled the negotiation. Part of the deal was to list the transaction as Eminent Domain for the purposes of record keeping."

"Hot damn," I smiled. "*That's* how he stopped the sale. He disconnected his property from the right-of-way."

"You're referring to the 1985 sales agreement?" Arabella asked. "I don't have any information on that other than to say the offer was contingent on access to both city utilities and a rail corridor. If neither existed, the sale could be cancelled."

"Do you have a copy of the 1985 sales agreement on file?"

"I'm looking at it now," she replied.

"Who was it with?"

"Levant Limited Partners," she answered. "I've had some dealings with them over the years — they're a holding company running multiple different concerns."

"Such as?"

"I don't know all of them off the top of my head, but that egg farm of theirs outside of Hampden was in the news recently; some sort of environmental fine for polluting the local groundwater. And they also own a string of auto dealerships between Bangor and Portland."

That feeling of the final pieces locking into place hit me, hard. "They wouldn't happen to have been the organization who tried to purchase that same plot of land in the mid-1990s?"

There was a moment of silence while Arabella tapped at a keyboard. "As a matter of fact, it was. Looks like that didn't go anywhere, either, though we did rack up some impressive billable hours on it."

"I can imagine," I said.

"Do you need anything else?" Arabella asked, bringing my attention to the clock.

"Not right now," I replied. "I might have some followups later, though, if you don't mind."

"Until Caitlyn revokes your authorization, I'm happy to chat," she replied. "Talk soon."

I heard her click off and then waited a moment more before speaking again. "Thank you, Caitlyn. That helps immensely."

"Good," she said. "You sound like you're close."

"I'm beyond that now," I chuckled. "Will you be in the office tomorrow?"

"I wasn't planning on it. Why?"

"No reason."

"Shit," she breathed. "I'll be there mid-morning. I've got to sort out the kids with Nic anyway; he's in deep trouble for taking them out of state without my permission."

I frowned. "Are you arresting him?"

"I'm thinking about it," she chuckled. "But it would only feel good for a few minutes."

"I hear you," I nodded. "See you tomorrow."

"Night, Chief."

I slipped the phone into my pocket and then continued the process of getting the cap off my beer; I'd just tossed the small piece of metal in the recycling bin when there was a knock at the front door. Deciding it might not be best to greet a visitor with my second beer of the evening, I put it back down on the counter and ambled through the living room and to the door; to my surprise, Norm was standing on my front porch, holding multiple canvas tote bags. Raphael was beside him, carrying what looked like a bottle of wine.

Pushing open the screen door, I invited them in. "To what do I owe this unexpected pleasure?"

"I didn't want you to be alone tonight," Norm replied as he moved into the living room.

I caught the smell of lasagna and fresh rolls as he passed. "Is that... Olive Garden?"

"Yes," he said. "At least, in the form of what you can find in the frozen food aisle at the IGA. Raphael made the rolls, though."

"From scratch," he added with a slight smile. "Where's your oven?"

I pointed to the kitchen, a bit taken aback. "That way."

"They just need to be warmed slightly and then we can eat," he said as he disappeared around the arch.

I stared at Norm. "What is this, really?"

"You never called Vasily back," he said after a moment. "So, he called me."

I felt the color rising on my cheeks. "Ah. He must have told you what happened in Portland."

"More or less," Norm nodded. "Enough that we both decided you could use some company tonight."

I nodded toward Raphael. "Does he...?"

"Yes."

"Lovely."

Norm put the bag holding the lasagna down and then gripped my shoulder. "You said earlier you hoped I considered you a friend. I do. This is what friends do."

"Get drunk over losing a girlfriend?" I asked, trying for humor, and suddenly feeling anything but merry.

The way Norm's eyes widened told me Vasily had left that part out from my text to him. "I don't do well when I'm drunk," he reminded me. "I imagine you don't, either."

"No," I sighed, "I don't. Come on, let's get this served up before it gets cold."

Truth be told, it was nice having the bungalow come alive once more; in short order, we had the lasagna served up on dishes Suzanne had found on one of our trips to Boston and glasses of wine all around. I was favorably impressed by the frozen dish, though it wasn't as close to the actual version served in the restaurant as the package would have had you think. Still, considering I'd pretty much planned on going to bed without eating, it was a far better alternative.

After washing up the dishes — and sneaking yet another of the amazingly good rolls Raphael had baked — the three of us wound up out on my back porch, watching the moon slowly rise over the ocean. The gentle onshore breeze was a welcome respite to the heat of the day, bringing with it the complex fragrance of the sea. Taking a deep breath, I relished the tang of salinity for just a moment, then took another sip from the excellent wine the duo had brought.

"What is this?" I asked, holding the wineglass up.

"A sauvignon blanc from California," Raphael said. "I was surprised to find it at your small grocery store here. It's one of my favorites, and it goes well with Italian."

"That it does," I smiled as I took another sip. "Thank you."

"My pleasure."

I looked at Norm, then back to Raphael. "How are the two of you doing?"

Raphael smiled. "Tonight is about you, not us."

I waved at them. "There's plenty of room for everyone's problems out here in the night air," I said. "And no small amount of comfort in numbers."

There was a long silence that Norm finally broke. "I'm petrified, frankly," he said before looking at Raphael. "Not to mention being appalled that I might have—"

"No," Raphael said forcefully. "This is not — and will not *ever* be — your fault. If I come back positive, that's on me."

"But—"

"No," he said again, interrupting Norm. "I'm a gay man; as I hesitate to remind you, I've been around a lot longer than you have. I knew better. I chose to do what I did." He shrugged and then looked at me. "I won't deny I'm concerned, but I'm also pragmatic enough to understand that I didn't take precautions."

I smiled slightly. "That can happen when feelings run high."

For the first time, I saw a tinge of something on Raphael's face. After giving a look of such fondness to Norm that it melted my heart, he smiled back at me. "They certainly were that evening."

"And still are, I would wager."

Norm reached for Raphael and interlaced his hands with what I was starting to think was not just his boyfriend. "I would agree with that," he said softly. "I'm just worried you won't have me—"

"I'm here," Raphael said firmly. "Regardless of what happens next, I will *still* be here."

"You can't stay here forever," Norm sighed. "Your career is in Arizona."

"Not any longer," Raphael said.

Both of us turned to look at the handsome latino; shock had to be clear on our faces. I managed to find my voice first. "You... you *quit* the park service?"

"No," he smiled. "But I did take the gig based out of Bar Harbor. I start in September; I just need to fly back to Arizona and get my stuff packed up so it can be shipped out." Raphael looked at Norm. "I'd planned on telling you when I saw you at the airport, but other things seemed more important at the time."

Norm was staring at Raphael with this sort of dreamy look that I'd never seen before. "You're... moving out here...?"

"Yes," Raphael replied. He glanced at me before adding somewhat quietly: "I hope that's okay?"

"It's more than okay," Norm replied. He hesitated for a moment. "Do you have a place in Bar Harbor lined up?"

"I should clarify, I'm technically posted at Acadia National Park, but I can live anywhere in the state within a few hours drive. My beat as an officer covers all the National Park Service assets in Maine."

Norm looked at me, then back at Raphael. "I should have bought a bigger place."

Raphael swallowed. "It's perfect... for two," he said quietly. "Assuming you are okay with that."

"I would be," Norm said. "Holy sweet Jesus, I would."

"Sounds like it's settled, then," I smiled before reaching to shake Raphael's hand. "Welcome to the Village."

"Thanks," he replied.

"And with that, I am shooing the two of you out of here," I said as I stood. "I've got an appointment in the morning with our prime suspect, and I still need to get prepped for it."

Norm remained seated. "What on earth are you talking about?"

"I'm speaking with Ernie and Thomas in the morning," I reminded him.

His eyes widened. "You connected the dots?"

"Just before you arrived," I nodded. "All that's left is to get them to confirm it."

Standing himself, Norm arched an eyebrow. "How do you expect to do that, now that you're no longer a police officer?"

I looked at him for a moment and realized just how much he had grown over the past few days. "Not without some help, I think," I replied with a sheepish smile. "Old habits die hard."

"Apparently." He looked at Raphael. "What were you planning on doing?"

"Talk to them," I shrugged. "Just like I always do."

"Without a Miranda warning?" Norm actually glared at me. "That's what landed us here in the first place."

I felt myself bristling slightly but tamped down the anger. My number two was right; storming in there without a way to ensure whatever evidence I collected was admissible would allow any decent defense lawyer free reign to get the case dismissed. "I was thinking of wearing a wire, actually," I said, hastily grasping at straws.

Norm just looked at me.

"Fine," I sighed. "I'll pick you up on my way over there. You can read them the damn warning, so long as *I* get to ask the questions."

"Deal," he said. "Are you going to practice in the morning? If so, I'll just pick you up on my way in. Then we can go together from the pool."

I felt an eyebrow arch at the inference I might sneak over to interview the suspects but decided not to comment on it. "That would work."

"Then I'll see you in the morning."

"That you will," I smiled as I walked them back through the house and to the front door.

Standing on my front porch, Norm paused. "You should probably call Vasily," he said. "He wasn't very happy that you'd left him hanging the way you did."

A slight shiver of embarrassment rolled over me. "I suppose he wasn't," I nodded. "And with good reason. I'll call as soon as you pull out of the driveway."

"Good," he smiled.

"Thanks for dinner. And... the company. I don't think I knew how badly I needed it."

"Everyone needs a lift from time to time," Norm said softly. "Even the great Sean Colbeth. See you in the morning."

I nodded, then waited on the porch to watch them drive away in his SUV. Glancing upward, I was surprised to see that the storm clouds had completely vanished without deluging us with rain; looking at it through the prism of the events of the evening, it felt like another sign that things were finally going in the right direction. Pulling out my iPhone, I dialed Vasily, intent on continuing the trend. He picked up on the first ring.

"There you are!" he exclaimed, his voice full of concern. "You certainly know how to make a guy worry."

"I... didn't want to burden you with my woes, honestly," I said as I watched the stars sparkle against the dark night sky.

"You've always been there for me in my lowest moments," Vas replied softly. "Let me return the favor. Just this once."

"Okay," I said. "I hope you have plenty of time."

"For you?" Vas said fondly. "Always."

Nineteen

Despite his being nearly identical to the one that I drove, somehow the passenger seat in Norm's SUV felt cramped and uncomfortable on the ride from the pool to the seaside mansion Ernie shared with Thomas. I knew it was all psychological, a manifestation of my frustration at not being — literally — the driver of the case any longer, but knowing didn't seem to make it feel any better. As I attempted to stretch out a calf that had grown tight in the aftermath of our extended weekend workout, I silently cursed the automaker behind that particular vehicle despite neither the cramp nor my feelings of claustrophobia being their fault in any way. Sighing, I continued to rub away at the muscle while watching the world go by outside the window; the day had dawned overcast and had only grown darker in the hours since. Rain had begun to pelt us as we'd pulled from the parking lot at the aquatics center; by the time we'd made the turn onto northbound Route One, it had become a steady downpour thick enough it was hard to see more than a few feet in front of us. I wondered how many tourists had been suckered into spending the weekend in Maine based on a faulty long-range forecast; in all my years of watching the station out of Bangor, rarely had the chief meteorologist gotten the weekend right. After his retirement, the station had closed shop in Bangor and shifted their broadcast to their main studio in Portland. Predictably, the new guy down there hadn't turned out any better; at least he had the excuse of being much further away, for whatever that was worth.

Norm managed to deftly navigate the growing puddles along Route One; the dirt road that led to Ernie's place was still passable, but as we turned onto it, I frowned at how soft it was becoming. After the near-constant rain from the past few weeks, the dirt was showing signs of being completely saturated; some spots bore ruts where the surface had finally become something closer to mud. I didn't think our SUV would have any trouble navigating back out again, but besides Ernie, there were more than a dozen cottages along that tract; most were summer visitors and unlikely to have a four-wheel drive vehicle capable of contending with the mess that was to come.

The SUV tilted slightly as Norm tried to get around a particularly nasty rut, and I turned toward him. "I bet the Real Estate agent didn't tell you about this aspect of the road when you were looking at your place down here."

I caught the slight smile as he wrestled with the steering wheel. "No, she didn't," he replied. "But by that point, I didn't really care. I'd looked at so many places only to get outbid by someone; this was the first one I saw and still had time to sign on the dotted line."

"I'm glad you finally found a place to land." I paused, then frowned. "Damn."

"What?" he asked, shooting a concerned look at me.

"You wanted to take yesterday off," I sighed. "And you wound up working because of me."

"It's not a big deal," he replied easily. "Especially now that Raphael is not going anywhere."

"Still, I owe you the day. I'll make sure you get it... assuming I am in a position to do it."

"You will be," he said with a certainty I didn't feel.

We lapsed into another silence as he navigated around an even larger rut, and then the driveway for the cottage appeared to our right. The first time I was there — during the Davies investigation the winter prior — I'd had a hard time calling it a *cottage*, for unlike all the other homes along that dirt road, it was a two-story monster on land that had been cleared right down to the ocean. It might have been sheathed in white clapboards, but that was where the resemblance to anything else in that area ended. Don Davies had kept the place pristine despite it being his second home and an infrequent getaway at that; as we pulled up the driveway and came to a stop at the front steps, it appeared Ernie and Thomas had not had time to put much of their own stamp on it yet. From my perspective, it looked very much like it had back in February, save for the lack of snow that it had been wrapped in at the time.

Turning off the SUV, Norm looked at me. "Ready?"

"In more ways than one," I smiled as I opened the door and hopped out.

I waited for Norm to round the bumper, then the two of us walked up the short flight of prefab steps; for whatever reason, I'd assumed Ernie had watched us pull up the driveway and had expected the door to suddenly be pulled open in a burst of exuberance. When it became apparent there was no welcoming party, I reached over and pressed the button for the doorbell, then stepped back as the tri-tones of the electronic chime echoed in the space beyond. I glanced sidelong at Norm when that failed to raise anybody and had begun to reach over to ring a second time when we finally heard the deadbolt to the door disengaged. Ernie's face appeared in the opening and initially wore an expression of worry; that quickly changed to a brilliant smile when he recognized me.

"Chief!" he cried. "You're early. I expected you at eight."

I glanced at my watch and noted it was ten to eight. "I dallied at the pool as long as I could, but there comes a point when even an Olympic swimmer is no longer welcome," I replied with a smile. "I hope this is all right? If not, I'm happy to return later."

"No—no, this is fine," he replied as he pulled the door open wider and gestured for us to step in. "The muffins are still in the oven, that's all. I'm afraid you'll have to wait a bit to get them."

"As long as you have fresh coffee to go with them...?" I asked.

"I just brewed a pot," he said proudly.

I had the strangest feeling he was excited to be entertaining, even if his company happened to be two police officers. *Well, one police officer,* I quickly amended. *And whatever I've become.*

"This way to the kitchen," Ernie continued as he led us down the main hallway toward the back of the mansion. "I'm afraid I didn't catch your name the other night, young man," he added as he glanced back at Norm.

"Norm," my number two said.

"Are you new to the department?"

"I've been working with Sean for a while now," he replied easily. "Before that, I was part of the South Windham Police Department."

"That's outside of Portland, isn't it?"

"Yes," Norm nodded.

We entered the kitchen at that point, which looked exactly as I had seen it that winter. The presence of the uniquely patterned china sitting on the counter seemed to be a clue that the sale of the mansion had included all the furnishings; while it wasn't all that unusual, for whatever reason, seeing the china reused in that way made it feel as though the duo were just renting the space and would be moving on just as soon as they could. Glancing at the wooden clock over the stove reinforced the idea; I wondered if the books out in the small den we'd passed were the same ones I'd pawed through for clues back in February. Ernie busily pulled two mugs out of the counter and poured each a full measure of caffeine before handing them to Norm and me; as he topped off a third one that had been on the counter, it dawned on me Ernie had been chattering on about something the entire time. Blinking, I chided myself for momentarily checking out and tried to pick up the thread of the conversation.

"—-windy enough that we had to take them down," he was saying as he gestured for us to take seats at the pleasantly sized kitchen table. "I quite liked the random notes, but Tommy positively grew to dislike them immensely."

"I imagine the onshore breeze is near-constant," I said.

"That it is," Ernie replied, nodding. "Which has been something of a godsend in all of this heat." He looked over at Norm. "I resided in Bangor for more years than I care to admit; you haven't lived until you've suffered through a summer in the heart of Maine."

"I had a friend go to the University of Maine," Norm said. "I heard how bad it was."

"There's this tiny smidgen of time in late April or early May when it is *gorgeous*," Ernie sighed. "That's it."

"I hope you find Windeport more hospitable," I smiled.

"So far, so good," Ernie smiled back.

"Well, thanks again for letting me steal a few minutes this morning," I continued, gently shifting the conversation back to the business at hand.

"Oh!" Ernie exclaimed as he leapt out of his chair. "The muffins!"

Norm and I exchanged a glance as the rotund form of our host moved with more grace than I would have imagined in the small space, pulling a tin of muffins from the wall oven, and then setting them out to cool on the counter. Wiping his hands on the apron I'd not realized he was wearing, he deftly snatched each muffin out of the tin and placed them on a wire rack, something I'd seen Charlie do a hundred times back at her farm. The space quickly filled with the comfortably domestic fragrance of blueberries, sugar, and butter; it was hard not to take a deep breath and feel the sense of peace it brought with it. The investigator part of me was cynical enough to wonder if that had been Ernie's intent all along, especially when he made quite the show of selecting the best specimens from the batch to present to us at the table.

"Enjoy," he entreated as he plucked a third one for himself.

For form's sake, I managed to peel away the wrapper very slowly from the muffin as I tried once more to move into the interrogation portion of the program. The first bite nearly had me gagging, though; I didn't know a ton about cooking, but it was clear there was a tad too much salt in the mixture. Chewing delicately, I glanced at Norm long enough to confirm that suspicion. Wiping my fingers on the small napkin beside the plate, I wondered how to dispose of the muffin without having to eat it in a way that wouldn't offend our host.

"Is Thomas here?" I asked as I picked away at a blueberry on the top of the muffin.

"Why?" Ernie immediately replied, his eyes wary for a moment before shifting into something gentler.

"I imagine he'd like one of these," I answered, pointing to the muffin. "I'd hate to eat all of them before he has a chance to get one."

"He's not a fan of my baking. Never has been," he replied.

I watched as Ernie took a huge bite from his own muffin, then tried not to laugh as his face contorted through multiple expressions; ultimately, it landed on something close to embarrassment, though I could also see he was trying to determine whether we had noticed anything ourselves. As it appeared Norm had also gone to the same school of manners as me, neither of us gave him any trace of our distaste; it wasn't lost on me how Ernie had subtly pushed his plate away.

"Well, I'd still like to talk to him, too," I continued to smile. A quick sip of coffee washed away the worst of the salty taste. "Can you get him?"

"Sure," Ernie replied as he stood. "He's just down in the basement."

We both turned and watched him go down the hallway and then open a door set into the staircase leading to the second story; even though he closed it behind him, we could hear Ernie as he descended below us. I glanced at Norm and saw he'd prepped his tablet for recording the conversation once our host returned; after years of seeing Vasily do that on his phone, I was having a hard time getting used to the larger device. My eyes snapped back to the basement door when it reopened again; Ernie emerged with an apologetic smile and walked back toward us after closing the door behind him.

"He'll be right up," he said as he took his seat once more. "Your arrival caught him in the middle of a delicate assembly step for his latest addition to Walter's layout."

I felt my eyebrows go up. "He's still building something?"

"Yes," Ernie replied, looking surprised. "Why wouldn't he?"

"Well, the status of the store is kind of in question at this point," I said. "Which would include the layout."

"Oh," Ernie said. The way he frowned made me think he'd not considered that. "Well, hopefully it will fit on his layout, then."

I smiled slightly. "I'd forgotten that members of the group all had their own layout. You'll have to give me a tour of yours before we go."

"Maybe another time," he demurred. "Ours is kind of torn up at the moment." He looked at Norm and shrugged. "He's never really done with it, you know?"

"I've heard that," Norm nodded as he placed the iPad down on the table. Ernie looked at it, then back to me.

"If you don't mind, I am going to have Norm record our conversation," I said by way of explanation.

"Why?" The wariness was back in those eyes of his, which were starting to look beady to me.

I smiled in the most self-deprecating way I could. "I'm not as young as he is," I answered. "My memory isn't what it once was. Besides that, no one can read my handwriting back at the station. It'll be far easier for us to take notes from later."

"Oh," he replied, his mouth forming the letter O as he said the word. "Makes sense. Sure."

"Good." I looked at Norm and we exchanged a glance; the moment of truth had arrived. "Now, since Norm is an officer with the department, in order to record you, we will need to officially get your permission to do so."

"Okay."

I nodded to Norm; he pressed the button to start the recording, then began the well-worn phrases. "Ernest Stables, you have the right to remain silent," he said. "Anything you say—"

"Hang on," Ernie interrupted. "That sounds like what they say to suspects on *Law and Order*. Just before they arrest them."

"Is that one of those television cop shows?" I asked, knowing full well it was.

"Yes," Ernie nodded. "Am I suspect?"

I smiled again. "Isn't everyone?" I chuckled. "It's just a formality the department requires. I bet they never say that on the show," I added as an aside to Norm. "Those Hollywood types have no idea the paperwork we have to go through."

"That they don't," Norm nodded before looking at Ernie. "Can we continue?"

"I wrote an article about the police back, oh, twenty years ago I think," Ernie was saying, his eyes slightly unfocused. "There was some sort of issue in the Bangor Police Department I was investigating, but it escapes me what it was."

"Ernie?" I asked, dragging him back to the here-and-now. "Are you willing to keep going?"

He looked at me, then Norm; for the first time since I'd met him, he looked ever bit of his age and then some. "Yeah," he nodded curtly. "Go ahead."

Norm began again, and this time got all the way through the Miranda Warning. "Do you understand these rights?" he asked at length.

Ernie took a long moment, long enough I thought we had lost any chance of getting him on the record. Then he looked at Norm and said clearly: "Yes. I do."

Masking my relief behind my best retail smile, I took a sip from the excellent coffee. "You grew up in Windeport, didn't you?"

"Yes," Ernie replied, running a hand through his hair. The act exposed the slight gray at the roots, answering one question for me. "I graduated from Windeport Regional High School, then got my degree in Journalism from UEM a few years later."

"When did you move to Bangor?" I asked, though I knew the answer from having read his bio earlier.

"1985," he replied. "The *Bangor Daily News* bought the *Windeport Observer* and essentially folded the staff into the mothership." Ernie smiled slightly. "Those that they retained, that is; I was one of the few reporters they kept on."

"Ouch."

"Yeah," he nodded. "I met Thomas a few years later — he'd just returned to Bangor after getting his Doctorate in Dentistry from some school in Massachusetts — and we've been together ever since. Got married the year Maine made it legal."

"I read the article you wrote about Walter's layout in the 70s," I continued.

"Oh my God," he chuckled. "I'd forgotten that was still around. Where did you find it?"

"The library had it in the archives."

"That figures."

"I had no idea you and Walter were the same age."

Ernie nodded again. "We graduated the same year. I was one of maybe four kids from the high school that used to hang out with Walt's dad and work on the layout at the store with the adults. It was pretty cool."

"Were the two of you close?"

"Not particularly, no," he replied just a bit too quickly.

I tried not to arch an eyebrow. "Considering how much time you spent together at Route One Hobbies, you must have gotten to know him pretty well?"

Ernie got up and took his dish to the sink; in a swift movement, he dumped the remains of his muffin into a trashcan just below it before rinsing the surface. "I suppose I did. We were in different circles back in high school, and then I was gone for nearly forty years; we weren't of the generation that had email growing up, so we didn't really speak after I left. It was pure happenstance that I wound up back in the group."

"Oh?" Norm asked.

"Yeah," Ernie said as he leaned against the kitchen counter. The way his hands were twisting the front of the apron spoke volumes. "Small town coincidences, right? I ran into him at the IGA and just started chatting; it was like the years dropped away from us. Before I knew it, he'd invited me to attend the next session the following week. I've gone every week since."

"Did you have a layout back in Bangor?" I asked.

"Thomas did. I worked on it with him." Ernie smiled slightly. "Honestly, I was so busy writing I hardly had the time to spend on it like my partner. For him, it was almost a spiritual release from the day-to-day grind of being a dentist."

My eyebrows went up at the past tense. "I thought you said he had a layout *now*?"

Ernie looked startled. "He still does. Sorry, I've only had one cup of coffee today; my brain is a little slow."

"I can fully relate to that." I tapped at the side of my mug. "Are you sure Thomas knows we want to talk to him too?"

"Oh yes," Ernie nodded. "He'll be along. The glue he uses for the roadbed to the layout is sometimes unpredictable."

I cocked my head. "Roadbed?" I asked, looking at Norm. He'd caught the shift in the explanation as well. "Expanding the track, is he?"

Ernie frowned for a moment and looked like he was searching for what to say. "Tommy was never done," he finally said. "Ever."

"Ah," I nodded as though that explanation made sense to me. It didn't. "I don't blame him for getting into a hobby; I imagine running Levant Limited Partners is all consuming."

"Oh, he has people for that," Ernie replied. I kept my expression neutral at his backhanded confirmation that Thomas was nominally connected to the organization at the heart of the case. "He focused on the dental practice — well, right up until he sold it to a national outfit last spring. Tommy wasn't really into running the investment portfolio the way his father did."

I nodded. "They had auto dealerships at one point, right?"

"Yes, I think so," Ernie replied. "Used to be all over the state. After the 2008 crash, though, they sold everything off but the original dealership in downtown Bangor."

"Did Thomas ever mention his father wanting to build a new dealership here in Windeport?"

The twisting at the ends of the apron became more pronounced. "Maybe in passing," he said, glancing out the kitchen window. Normally breaking eye contact was always a tell the person being interviewed was being less than truthful, but the rest of Ernie's non-verbal cues had long since been screaming *liar* to me.

I made a point of looking toward the basement door. "I was wondering a bit about that, actually," I said as I turned my attention back to Ernie. "Especially since it was slated for the same land Levant Limited Partners had planned on building an egg farm upon."

"Was it?" Ernie asked. A bead of sweat had begun to roll down his temple. "You're talking about that egg farm on the layout? I thought that was just a joke from Walter."

"It was anything but," I said before choosing my next words extremely carefully. "Especially since Walter was the one who killed it."

The color drained out of Ernie's face completely. "Really?" he managed to say. "I... I was under the impression the State of Maine was responsible for scuttling the deal."

This time, I couldn't prevent an eyebrow from arching. "I thought you didn't know about the egg farm deal?"

Ernie walked to the fridge, opened it, stared inside for a moment, then looked to me. "Cream? For your coffee?"

I glanced down at my empty mug. "No, thanks," I replied after looking at Norm.

"I usually offer it to people first. I forgot. Again."

He closed the door to the fridge; as he did so, for the first time I saw the whiteboard that was hanging on the door presumably with magnets. It held a series of reminders that seemed basic, including *shut the door to the oven* and *brush teeth after eating*. My eyebrows went up a bit more when I finally registered the little square notes that had been posted discretely throughout the kitchen; they all seemed to continue the same trend of reminders, but were even stranger, bearing missives such as *salt in here* or *use the oatmeal downstairs first*. While I was by no means an expert on aging or dementia, I had worked in Windeport long enough to know the signs of someone on the cusp of needing more help than they could get at home; looking at Ernie in a new light, I began to re-evaluate his role in everything and found myself even more disgusted.

"Are you sure you don't want cream?" Ernie asked.

"Yes. But I would love more coffee."

"Sure," he said before whisking off to the coffee maker and retrieving the pot; with a flourish, he refilled me, topped off Norm and then refilled his own mug before returning the pot to the hotplate. Turning back to me, his smile faltered for a moment before he spoke. "Chief," he said, almost like it had been an unspoken mantra. "I'm glad you came."

"Me, too," I replied easily. I felt like something had reset inside the brain of our host, and hoped I'd not lost any momentum as a result. "Did you help build the egg farm?"

"Thomas said they couldn't build it," Ernie frowned. "And his father very much wanted to."

I shot a glance at Norm, for that hadn't been my actual question. "Why?" I asked.

"The plant in Hampden was getting old and needed to be replaced. And *that* county was starting to get ornery about how the chickens were being treated." Ernie snorted. "I think I wrote an article about it; the insanity that something like a chicken would have 'rights' was too delicious not to deal with."

"And moving it to Windeport would alleviate that?"

"That was the idea," Ernie said before his expression went to surprise. "Maybe?" he added before starting to backtrack. "I don't really know. I wasn't around then. And Tommy never talked about it."

There's that past tense again, I thought. For some reason, it was triggering all sorts of alarm bells. I didn't quite dare ignore them, but I also knew I had one last shot to get the tangential connection I needed. Looking at Norm again, I steadied myself and asked pleasantly: "Was Tommy upset about Walter nixing the egg plant?"

"Oh yes," Ernie said solemnly before suddenly taking a quick breath. "I don't think I should have told you that."

Feeling my heartbeat picking up, I smiled slightly. "Is that why Walter had to die?"

"Walter?" Ernie's face faltered again as his eyes went unfocused. "Walter... he ran the hobby store."

"Yes," I nodded.

Ernie went back to the sink; it seemed like a safe spot for him. "This has been nice, but I've got to run some errands this morning," he said as he started to run his hands beneath the water. As he slowly started to scrub them, I realized he'd not used any soap. "Can you find your way out?"

"Why did you help Thomas kill Walter?" I asked quietly. "He used your friendship to get close to Walter, didn't he?"

Ernie continued to scrub, his face bent to the task; slowly, he nodded as a single tear appeared and rolled down his cheek.

"Why did you help him?" I asked, though I feared the answer.

Ernie looked up and out of the window, still mindlessly scrubbing his hands. The tears were flowing more freely as he nearly whispered his answer. "I don't want to be alone. Or go to that memory center in Portland." He looked at me, his face awash with fear. "I wanted to stay in our home. With him."

"Did he threaten to send you away if you didn't help?" I asked gently.

Ernie looked away, then nodded curtly.

"I think we should talk to Thomas now," I said as I stood.

Ernie swung around and looked at me, terrified. "If you do, I'll lose everything."

"We play the cards we are dealt," I said, not unkindly. "Work with us and that might not be the case."

"No!" Ernie cried.

Before we could act, Ernie rushed past us and over to the basement door; flinging it open with a *bang*, he shot down the steps faster than was probably prudent for a man of his age. As I was already standing, I recovered slightly faster and bolted to the door; Norm was right behind me as we started down the steps into the basement. My hand immediately went to the sidearm that wasn't there; grimacing, I paused long enough to allow Norm to squeeze around me, then carefully followed him as he continued down, his Glock at the ready.

Unlike the basement at Route One Hobbies, this one was a modern, well-lit marvel. A state-of-the-art workbench was along one wall, with tools and equipment that I barely recognized; along the other was a much larger layout in various stages of construction. Part of it appeared to have been disassembled from its earlier location in Bangor, and was sitting against the wall, awaiting reunification with the other sections that had been erected already. Aside from track, though, it didn't appear much in the way of scenery had been added; even the track seemed half-complete at that. Facedown in front of one of those standing sections was the body of Thomas Levant, wearing pressed khakis and what might have once been a white button down; it was hard to know for sure, since the blood spatters from the massive blunt force trauma at the back of his head had been absorbed into the fabric, creating a morbid tie dyed-like pattern. I presumed the rather sizable mallet just beside the body was the offending weapon; sitting just inside the pool of blood beneath the corpse, the business end of the tool was covered in brain matter and streaks of crimson. Ernie was standing with his back to us over the body of his partner, his shoulders slumped forward.

Going into full police officer mode, I went to one side and Norm, the other, allowing a careful approach to Ernie; he didn't put up much resistance when Norm gently placed his wrists together and handcuffed him. Turning toward me, I could see the tears had started again, though this time his face was a study in pure terror. For despite whatever memory issues he had been dealing with, some part of Ernie's brain had finally registered that his worst fear — being alone — had suddenly come true.

"Why?" I asked.

Ernie sobbed slightly, then inclined his head toward the concrete. Following his direction, I stepped around the dead body of his partner and knelt to retrieve a trifold pamphlet just a few inches away from Thomas's outstretched hand. Turning it over, I found the anger bubbling up again as I scanned the text.

Heron Shores Memory Care Center - For All Your Dementia Needs at a Price You Can Afford!

I shook my head as I looked at Norm. There wasn't much more to say at that point, and he seemed to intuitively understand that as well. Turning back to the still-sobbing Ernie, I suddenly felt world-weary as I pulled out my iPhone and called it in.

Twenty

Suzanne's absence at the funeral for Walter Guernsey wasn't a complete surprise that Monday afternoon; I'd not made any further attempts to contact her after she'd ignored my texts from Saturday evening letting her know about the service and that the case had come to a resolution of sorts. For once, I found my love of Apple devices severely challenged, for their unique messaging system had allowed me to see that my girlfriend — or was that *ex-girlfriend*? — had read what I'd sent; the longer I went without seeing those three little dots indicating she was replying increased my anxiety that the worst case scenario had come to pass. As I'd driven past her medical practice on the way to the service at St. Catherine-By-The-Sea, I'd tried to console myself that a For Sale sign hadn't yet appeared in the front window; it wasn't much of a lifeline, but it was enough to help box up my emotions so I could appear as the stoic, compassionate Chief of Police the assembled crowd in the cathedral were expecting.

Or rather, soon-to-be-former Chief of Police.

As I entered the vestibule for the cathedral and waited to be taken to a pew inside the sanctuary, I tried to put aside a second, far different wave of emotions that threatened to overwhelm me each time I thought about my position with the Village. I'd received a hand-delivered invitation at the bungalow Sunday requesting my presence at an emergency meeting of the Windeport Village Council; I harbored no illusions that the session being held that evening was nothing more than a formality, putting the finishing touches on their years-long effort to remove me from the Police Department. All that remained was to agree on how the exit would take place, and how much it would cost them financially to make me go away. Arabella had offered to drive down from Fort Fairfield and represent me at the Council when I'd called to inform her of the package and ask what my options might be; oddly, there was a peace to knowing the end was at hand, and I'd decided against her attending.

"Chief?"

Pulled from my thoughts, I turned my attention to a teen from the local high school who was serving as an usher. His expectant face and slight look of hero worship made my heart ache. "Sorry."

He smiled. "I've got a spot for you up with the family. Follow me."

We slowly made our way down the wide polished-wood aisle in a manner befitting such a solemn occasion; the pipe organ in the loft above us was playing something appropriately funereal, but soft enough so as not to overwhelm the magnificent space. The pews were comfortably full, but the conversations were mostly in muted whispers that were barely audible. Flowers in an extraordinary array of colors were everywhere, including a significant concentration arrayed around a freestanding poster-sized headshot of Walter just to the side of the raised dais for the priest. Two tiers of candles sat on either side of the dais, flickering quietly in the late afternoon sunshine slanting through the stained-glass windows.

My usher paused at a row two down from where Caitlyn and her kids were seated; her ex-husband, Nick, was sitting beside her, along with a guy I didn't recognize. Caitlyn happened to be looking in my direction and nodded at me as I moved into the pew; as I settled in, I mused as most people do during such times about beginnings and endings. After my own brush with mortality back in February, I'd found myself truly considering the unthinkable for the first time. What would my funeral look like? Would I even *have* a funeral? Where would I be buried — in the family plot beside my mother, there in Windeport? Or someplace more exotic that I'd not yet considered? I'd done some estate planning when I'd bought the bungalow, but that had only covered the assets I owned; it wasn't until that past February I'd actually begun thinking about the spiritual end of things. I wasn't particularly religious, but that didn't forestall my belief there was something more — something *beyond* — the short lives we lead on Earth. Looking at the smiling picture of Walter Guernsey, I hoped he had found *his* something, and wondered if it included an intricately detailed model railroad for him to spend eternity tweaking.

As much as I tried to get into the celebration of the person Walter had been, I found my thoughts drifting; my attention was so distracted that I'd had to be nudged to get up for the final hymn of the service. It was with some relief that we began to file out of the sanctuary and over to the Fellowship Hall for coffee and light refreshments, though in all honesty I wasn't sure I was completely up to the small talk necessary for such a function. Still, I put on a brave front and greeted as many people as I could on my way through the line for coffee, then retreated to a distant corner of the space in the hopes my presence would not be missed while equally not sought after. The plan worked until I saw Norm enter the room, with Raphael beside him; almost like a finely-honed radar-guided missile, once his eyes locked themselves on mine, he quickly crossed the room to where I was attempting to blend in with the wallpaper.

"Hey," he said as he stopped beside me. "Tough day."

"Yeah," I nodded, knowing he wasn't entirely referring to the funeral. Though he'd not directly told me, I'd intuited that he was already aware of portions of the pending transition plan and was extremely unhappy about it. I looked out across the crowd and saw Caitlyn speaking with a crowd of well-wishers, flashing a tired smile every now and then. "At least you'll have an excellent number two."

"Maybe not," he sighed, indirectly confirming everything for me in the process. "She's asked for an indefinite leave of absence while she figures out what to do with the store."

"I'm not surprised," I replied. "There are a lot of memories there. It could take a while to sort through it all."

"I don't relish the work ahead of her," Raphael said. "Digging through the past is never easy."

I looked at him, knowing that in some ways the Park Service Police Officer was speaking from experience. "It's not," I nodded. "I went into a veritable fugue after my mother passed; it drove my fiancé away and nearly wrecked my relationships with everyone else I held dear."

"Death can do that," Raphael replied softly.

"Speaking of death," Norm said before glancing meaningfully at the double-door exit to the hall. "Want some fresh air?"

"More than anything."

We carefully made our way through the crowd and then out in the afternoon July heat. While not as oppressive as it had been earlier in the month, the humidity was still intense enough for us to seek shade beneath the wide leafy limbs of a massive oak tree. Just being out of the sunshine dropped the temperature enough to make it bearable, though based on how my undershirt was sticking to my back already, I wasn't certain how long that would be the case. I unbuttoned my collar and loosened my tie, glad that such accoutrements had not been part of my normal business wardrobe up to that point.

"I heard back from the Crime Lab this morning," Norm said as we huddled beneath the tree. The dappled sunlight across his face made him look like a teenager with freckles. "There was enough left of the circuit board inside the transformer that they were able to track down the manufacturer that had made it."

"I presume it wasn't original to the device?"

"No," he said. "It was a custom job. There's a company in New Mexico that you can ship electronic plans to; they outsource the actual work to a plant in Asia, then send back the completed circuit board.

When the techs read them the serial number they located, it matched one in their databases from an order Thomas Levant had placed almost a year ago."

My eyebrows went up. "That's somewhat premeditated."

"Yeah." Norm smiled slightly. "Heather's team found shipping boxes in the Thomas's basement about the right size for the transformer; we'll see if the tracking numbers connect the rest of the dots."

I thought back to the massive workbench I'd seen during my visit. "I didn't know dentistry included electrical engineering."

"Doctorates in Dentistry don't," Norm replied. "But the sort of Bachelor's program Thomas graduated from at the University of Maine *does*. While he obviously never used it in his actual vocation, he appears to have retained enough to have designed his weapon of death."

"Well, how about that," I replied. "Did Ernie confirm our theory on how the device was swapped in?"

"To a point," he replied with a slight frown. "It's probably wise we're not going to trial on this one, for his dementia is actually quite advanced. The poor guy thinks he's still working for the *Bangor Daily*; when we called over to verify, his editor disclosed — off the record, of course — they'd forced him to retire more than a year ago."

"That explains why the columns appear to be repeating."

"It was part of the deal to get him to go. He still gets paid for them to be published, at least for the next few years." Norm shook his head. "Anyway, as far as we can tell, Thomas used Ernie's prior relationship with Walter as the way for the two of them to join the weekly work group. After that, it was just a matter of distracting Walter long enough to install the replacement transformer and controller; from what Ernie recalls — and this is sort of vague — the transformer went in about two weeks before Walter's death."

"And the controller?"

"Last week," he replied. "Ernie actually asked Walter to test it; Thomas appears to have told Ernie he'd ordered it for his own layout but was having trouble getting it to work and asked him to take it to Walter on one of the nights the group wasn't meeting."

I nodded. "Hence why he was on the calendar we found."

"Exactly. Walter must have bought the story since he plugged it into the compromised transformer. The techs at the lab were able to determine it, too, had a replaced circuit board; if the dial went past seven, the capacitor unloaded its deadly cargo."

I felt an eyebrow arch. "And that's why the calendar went missing: to try to hide the fact Ernie had been there."

"Yes."

"That doesn't explain the POS system being fried, though."

Norm frowned. "No. Our working theory is that Ernie messed up Thomas's plan and bought something before the transformer killed Walter; Thomas found out about it and was forced to return later to remove the evidence of the transaction."

"Clever by half," I said.

Norm frowned. "Unfortunately, with Thomas dead and Ernie's memory issues, it's just informed conjecture at this point. But it fits."

"That it does," I replied. "What sort of plea did Ernie accept?"

"Involuntary incarceration at a long-term care facility for people with dementia," Norm replied. "Exactly what he *didn't* want, but given his condition..."

"Yeah," I nodded.

"I'm still struggling with the notion that this murder was retribution for a failed real estate transaction decades ago," Norm said. "Levant Limited Partners is still a multimillion-dollar organization without having either the egg farm or the auto dealership."

"Businessmen aren't always logical when it comes to those sorts of things," I said. "I imagine Thomas' father wasn't used to being told *no*, and that stuck with him enough to try again; when that failed, he passed his frustration on down the line to his son."

"But *murder*?" Norm pressed. "I could see underhanded tactics to drive Walter out of business, maybe."

"Thomas was obsessed with the revenge, buried beneath ever mounting layers of years. As he grew older, I imagine the intensity of the desire to right the perceived wrongs became far more pronounced." I looked out across the parking lot and toward the Fellowship Hall; a steady flow of people exiting told me it was slowly ending. "People can convince themselves that murder is the only way to rebalance the scales of justice. Thomas was likely no different." I looked back at Norm. "We'll probably never know at this point."

"No," he sighed again. "The postmortem essentially confirmed that Ernie killed Thomas less than thirty minutes before our arrival. Lou thinks the initial blow was fatal; the rest were... unnecessary to the job."

"It depends on your perspective," I said, thinking that Ernie may have been attempting to right his own wrongs that morning.

"I suppose," Norm agreed. He looked at me. "Are you all right?"

I caught the intent behind his words. "About what is going down this evening?" I asked with a shrug. "It is what it is."

My number two seemed unsure of how to respond to that. Instead, he nodded quickly. "I'll see you tonight, then."

"Until then," I smiled. "Raphael."

"Sean."

I watched the two of them go and smiled when Norm's hand sought out that of Raphael's; they had a long road ahead of them, possibly longer if Raphael's HIV test came back positive. For some reason, I had the strangest sense it wasn't going to, though I had no earthly reason to support it. Turning away from the disbursing crowd, I started down the sidewalk and home; assuming the worst was about to come, I'd driven the SUV back to the station on Sunday night and locked the keys inside it. While it had been a churlish thing to do, it had given me a momentary bit of satisfaction at the expense of one of my officers who'd need to jimmy the lock open later.

Popping in my ear buds, I was on the cusp of firing up some workout music for the walk back to the bungalow when my phone rang.

Smiling when I saw it was Vasily, I answered. "Hey. You caught me out for a walk."

"In *July*?" he asked, astonished. "What on earth is *wrong* with you?"

"Well, I don't have wheels for starters."

The sudden silence put a pin into the balloon of good humor created by the conversation. "Shit," Vasily said. "They're actually going to go through with it."

"I think so, yes."

"And you're not going to fight it?"

"No."

"Why?"

"I don't want to," I replied. "I'm tired of dealing with these jerks. So," I smiled slightly, "now I have to look for some slightly *better* jerks who will hire a washed-up former Police Chief."

"My offer still stands," Vasily said.

"I may take you up on that," I replied. "At the very least, I'll want a few weeks away from here."

"Come to California," Vasily said. "We've got plenty of room so long as you don't mind sharing your couch with our cat. Though if I tell Rosie you're headed in this direction, you may wind up at her mansion again."

"As nice an offer as that is, I think I'd prefer something else."

"I'm hurt, but I understand," Vas said with a laugh before going silent for a moment. "You've not heard from Suzanne yet, then, have you?"

"No," I answered. "I thought she might come to the funeral, but she didn't."

"Damn, dude," he breathed. "This has been the week from hell for you."

"No argument there."

"What are you going to do now?"

"Charlie's agreed to lend me her former husband's car for a few days; first stop is Bangor and seeing about purchasing my own car. I have no idea what to get, other than I want something in navy blue or black."

"Black," Vasily said without hesitation. "Black would suit you perfectly."

"I'll take that under advisement," I chuckled as I crossed the street and started down the Sea Road. "Do they still make Mustangs?"

"Yes," Vasily replied. "But that's not what you want. Get a Dodge Charger. That is *totally* you."

"All right," I laughed.

"Then what?" Vas pressed.

"Maybe I drive to California in my new Dodge Charger," I replied easily. "Nothing like an old-fashioned road trip to clear the mind."

"True," Vasily replied thoughtfully. "Having made that trip myself a few times, I can tell you it has cathartic properties."

"Just what I need, then," I said.

"You want me to fly out? No reason for you to drive it alone if...?" he asked, trailing off before mentioning the proverbial elephant in the room.

"I expect I will be alone," I said, obliquely confirming for him what I thought my status with Suzanne was. "I can't ask you to do that. That's a ton of time to take off, plus I can't imagine the flight would be cheap."

"The department owes me for cutting into my July 4th vacation," he reminded me. "Let me check on what's available — when do you think you'll leave?"

"Depends on what the dealer has in stock," I hedged, suddenly realizing that driving cross-country – even if it was to see my best friend – was the last thing I truly wanted to do. "Give me a few days. I'll let you know."

"Okay."

I crossed again and started down Ocean View Lane, and then frowned when I saw a pickup truck in my carport. As I drew closer, my frown deepened at the logo for the Village of Windeport stenciled on the side. "Vas, I've got to go," I said. "I'll call you later?"

"Sounds good."

Sliding the phone into my pocket, I walked to the end of my driveway, and then paused; the doors to the truck opened and two men I recognized from Facilities Management greeted me. The taller of the two took an extra step forward and then stopped; the embroidered name badge on his work shirt said he was Rick. The shorter of the two seemed extremely anxious to be anywhere but there in my driveway. I didn't blame him when I finally understood why the two of them were there.

"Chief," Rick greeted before nodding toward the bed of the truck. "Where would you like these?"

I moved to the tailgate and immediately saw the top of my Keurig peeking over the edge of a large cardboard box; beside it were other boxes of various sizes, presumably holding all my personal items. The small fridge was in the back; it was a thoughtful gesture that a small cooler was beside it, hopefully full of the items that had been stashed inside. A long, rectangular shape carefully wrapped in a white sheet brought a lump to my throat; the Gold Medal from my Olympics had been the first thing I'd hung in my office when I'd been promoted to Chief. Seeing it prone against the bed of the truck brought me up short; it took a full minute for me to find my voice.

"This way, gentlemen," I managed to say as I fished my house key out of my dress pants. "I think I can find room inside."

Twenty-One

In the end, the emergency meeting of the Village Council lasted — gavel to gavel — less than seventeen minutes by my watch. While my presence had been required, my voice was not; I was forced to sit and listen to the long litany of grievances multiple members of the leadership group had apparently been harboring from the earliest days of my tenure. It wasn't lost on me how more than a few of them had been acquaintances of Yvette Bedard, the former head of the College of Agriculture at UEM I'd put behind bars two years earlier for murdering a colleague over patent proceeds. I'd not believed in her ability to reach beyond the prison walls to extract her revenge, but clearly, she had; my issues with Shelly West had only provided the opening she'd been looking for.

I wasn't surprised when the pronouncement of my contract's termination was finally made by the current head of the Council, Violet Kepler; seeing my career arrayed across the floor of my den in boxes large and small earlier that same day had pretty much inured me from feeling anything beyond relief at that point. What *did* surprise me was the rest of the department similarly being shown the door; in a move that nearly had me vaulting the railing from the gallery and throttling each member of the Council in turn, they'd decided to outsource the law enforcement function of public safety to the County, which, apparently, already had enough staff to handle our small Village. It was a spectacular misunderstanding of what our role had been within the community, a decision barely justified through cherry-picked budget savings and promises that the State would backstop anything the County was unable to provide. To say steam was coming out of my ears as I exited the Council Chambers was an understatement, made worse when I realized I had no leverage to reverse *any* of it.

Norm met me on the sidewalk outside of the main administrative building; the look on his face told me he was devastated. "I didn't expect that," he said as we started down the sidewalk and toward the Public Safety building. "I'd hoped they'd keep you on, but figured, like you, it was a forgone conclusion. Getting fired too wasn't on my Bingo card."

"Nor mine," I said, still seething. "Me, I get. Taking their frustrations out on everyone else? Not in the least. The County can't cover us, and the State won't unless there's a compelling reason to do so. They'll regret this decision right after the next cruise ship docks, I assure you."

Norm smiled slightly. "That happens to be the end of the week," he reminded me. "Just after we all punch out for the final time."

I shook my head again. "One week's notice! Not *even* a full week. That's insane."

"That is politics. At least we are all getting six weeks' salary."

"The politics of retribution, maybe," I said. "Damn. I am so sorry; I've destroyed both of our careers, it seems."

Norm shrugged. "Maybe. Something will turn up, I suspect."

I looked at him and was horrified all over again. "The medications you need—-!"

"I can afford COBRA for a few months," he said, referring to the Federal law that required Windeport to offer him access to healthcare after he left the department. "Maybe I can get something on the exchanges afterward. I'm not worried."

I smiled slightly. "Oh, to be young again."

Norm shrugged. “I’m just pragmatic. Windeport wasn’t the only department I applied to originally. I’ll find something.”

“What about Raphael?” I asked.

“He doesn’t know yet,” he replied. “I’ll have to tell him tonight.”

“Damn. I’m sorry.”

“Quit apologizing,” he smiled. “And join me for a drink to celebrate what we had.”

“I’m tempted,” I said, “but I don’t think I’m going to be good company tonight. Raincheck?”

“Raincheck, then,” he said. “Want me to pick you up for practice in the morning?”

“I wouldn’t refuse,” I smiled. “Thanks.”

The walk back to my bungalow seemed to be faster, perhaps owing to the fact it was both the second time I’d done it that day *and* that with the sun slowly sinking in the west, the temperature had gone down enough that a more rapid pace was possible. I’d left my porch light on assuming the Village Council meeting would go far longer than it had; as I went up the steps to my front door, it seemed like a silly affectation in the golden rays of sunset. Sighing, I unlocked the door, tossed my keys on the small side table just inside, then walked all the way through to the back porch to watch the ocean for a bit. I’d long found that the gentle swells brought a unique sense of calm; even the more robust whitecaps from a Nor’easter had their own special way to distract me from my thoughts. It was part of the unique spirit of the house I had purchased — a house that I now wondered if I might need to sell far sooner than I’d anticipated.

Slowly, the shadows grew longer over the tall grass of the dunes; as I stood there, I waited for the moment when twilight turned to dusk, then began to seek out the few constellations I could recognize. At that time of year, Venus was particularly bright and easily identifiable; scanning a bit more, I thought perhaps I could *just* see Mars, which the paper had said would appear fleetingly for a few days in our hemisphere. Squinting, I wasn’t entirely convinced I’d located it; maybe now that I had time on my hands, I could get a few books on Astronomy and finally decipher the starry code above.

Once it had become dark enough, I could see the lights on the horizon from various fishing vessels plying the open water, I went back inside and paused at the threshold of the kitchen. It was just late enough to consider going to bed, but I was so keyed up that I knew my brain would never let me drift off to sleep. Having missed afternoon swim practice due to the funeral, I decided a quick evening run was just what I needed and zipped down to my bedroom to change into my running gear. A few moments later, I stepped onto my front porch in my reflective tights and compression muscle t-shirt and sat down on the steps to pull on my running sneakers. I'd just gotten one laced up when I caught headlights from a vehicle sweeping across the entrance to my neighborhood; pausing my efforts, I watched with fascination as the recognizable shape of a Maine State Police SUV pulled into my carport.

In a dramatic scene worthy of a major motion picture, the driver's side door opened, triggering the dome light inside the SUV. The harsh yellow glare backlit the form of State Police Captain James Roberts as he emerged from the truck; he stood beside the door for a moment as he took his bearings, then moved up the walkway to where I was sitting on the steps to my bungalow. Standing just inside the small circle of light from the lamps on my porch, I could see he was still dressed in his Class A uniform; given the hour, that usually meant he was on duty and — in better circumstances — needed my help for something. The wry smile that hit my face was hard to stop.

"Whatever it is, Jimmy, I'm no longer available."

Roberts smiled, a slash of brilliant white against his tanned face. "Right to the point this evening, I see."

"It's been a long day," I replied.

"So I heard," he nodded. "Got a moment?"

"I'm just about to go for a run," I replied, thinking I was stating the obvious.

"At this hour?"

"It's as good a time as any," I snapped, feeling more than a little irritated at the interruption.

"This will only take a minute," he replied, ignoring my tone. "Then I'll be on my way."

"Nothing you have *ever* brought to me has been that short," I reminded him.

He smiled again, this time a bit sheepishly. "Yeah, I suppose that's true. Give me thirty minutes. And maybe a beer if you have one; it was a long drive from Portland."

I put a hand on my Spandex-covered knee. "Maybe I wasn't clear earlier," I said. "I'm no longer employed by the Village of Windeport."

"Last time I checked, that didn't mean you weren't still a Law Enforcement Officer," Roberts countered.

"Jimmy—"

"*Dammit*, Sean," Roberts finally exploded. "I know you're angry, but I'm not the fucking enemy here."

In all the years I'd known him, Roberts had rarely lost his cool; even rarer was his use of foul language. My eyebrows went up as I considered him anew, then slowly began to nod. "Sam Adams okay?" I asked as I stood. "I've got a few in the fridge."

"Sounds perfect," he replied.

I pulled open the screen door and held it for Roberts to enter. When he paused just inside the threshold, it dawned on me it was his first time at the bungalow. "Kitchen's just through here," I said as I led him across the living room and under the archway in question.

"Nice place," Roberts said as I went to the fridge and pulled out two bottles of beer.

"Thanks," I said as I went to the counter and used the opener I'd left there. "I'd forgotten you'd not been here before."

"No," he confirmed as I popped the tops off. The slight hiss as the pressure was relieved from each bottle seemed to reflect how the mood had shifted once I'd invited Roberts inside. "I'd forgotten you were no longer at the pharmacy. When I pulled up and saw the lights were out, I had to call back to the office to get your actual address."

I smiled slightly as I held a bottle to him. "You could have just called *me*."

"And miss seeing you pissed off?" he laughed as he took the bottle. "Not in a million years."

"Was it that obvious?" I asked as we stood there in the kitchen.

"You might as well have a klieg light aimed at your wounded ego," he replied. "One that is visible from space."

"What ego?" I smiled slightly.

"Exactly," he chuckled.

I waved him toward the back porch. "Come on, it's cooler out back. We can talk there."

The light onshore breeze from the harbor did indeed drop the ambient temperature a few degrees, making it reasonably tolerable to sit outside. Bypassing the wicker couch and the implied companionship it represented, we instead each took one of the wicker chairs angled on either side of a small side table. As dark as the night had become, the ocean itself was impossible to make out other than the occasional set of dancing lights from the ships on the far horizon. Instead, I took a moment to close my eyes and let the gentle sound of the waves crashing on the rocky shore behind the bungalow perform their soul-salving magic. Roberts seemed similarly enthralled, allowing the moment to stretch to a few minutes; by some unspoken agreement, neither of us felt the urge to pick up the thread of the earlier conversation before we'd made a dent in our bottles. When the gentle buzz from the alcohol appeared on the fringes of my senses, I finally felt capable of facing whatever it was Captain Roberts had brought to my doorstep.

Putting my half-full bottle on the glass surface of the table, I turned to Roberts. "You drove here from Portland?"

"Yeah," he nodded. What little light we had was escaping from the living room lamp I'd left on; it was just enough to make him seem slightly more solid than a mirage. "I was saying goodbye to a friend."

I sat up a bit. "Did someone die?"

"Not in the traditional sense," he chuckled. "You remember Zachary Holland?"

I frowned slightly at the name. "That name seems familiar," I said slowly. "Isn't he part of your Major Crimes unit?"

"Statewide Commander," he nodded. "I think you worked with him on that case in Fort Kent."

I frowned deeper. "Oh, *shit.* I forgot about that one. It took me a long time to eat potato chips again after seeing how that poor woman died."

"Right up there with a woodchipper, that," Roberts replied. I thought maybe he'd shuddered, but it could have been a trick of the weak light (or the alcohol I'd had). "He's wanted to retire for a few years; up to now, I've managed to talk him out of it, but his eldest just had her first kid. Zach is ready to be the kind of grandfather that dotes on his grandkids."

"Good for him," I said, eying Roberts. "Why were you in Portland?"

"That's where Zach was based," he replied.

"Not in Augusta?"

"No," he shook his head. "Zach moved south to be closer to his family a few years ago. Remote work is all the rage now."

"I'm surprised the brass allowed that," I said. "Especially with that Taj Mahal of an office in Augusta," I added, flashing back to my recent visit there for the Professional Standards meeting.

"Oh, hell, what's left of the support staff is still there, of course," Roberts sighed. "The Legislature has whacked our budgets so badly over the years, we're essentially down to Zach and a handful of detectives that rotate between other divisions. Often, we've had to bring in experts as consultants to fill the gaps." He looked at me. "People such as yourself."

"If this is a recruiting pitch," I said, "I'm not interested in replacing him. Or moving to Portland."

"I'm not saying you would have to move to Portland—"

"So, this *is* a recruiting pitch," I interrupted, looking away in disgust.

"If you'd let me explain—"

"Explain *what*?" I snapped, turning toward him. "That you're using the excuse of getting my ass thrown out on the sidewalk to finally get me to work for you? Fuck, Jimmy. That's low."

"Now hang on just a damn minute," he bristled. "That's not what I'm doing at all! I admit that I value your expertise highly enough that I want you on my team, but I'm not using this situation to pressure you into something."

"Like *hell*."

"God *dammit* Sean, we've known each other for *years*," Roberts said. "Long enough that I would have expected you to at least *listen* to me before—"

"There are nearly two dozen people *besides* me that got the axe today," I interrupted angrily. "Two dozen of the finest law enforcement officers I have ever had the privilege of working with. Two dozen people that I'm responsible for throwing out of work. What the fuck about them?"

"I want them, too."

I felt a bit like a needle had suddenly skipped on one of those old vinyl records; my anger suddenly shifted to puzzlement. "What did you say?"

"I want them, too," Roberts repeated. "I'm rebuilding the department."

"You're... *what*?"

"Rebuilding the Major Crimes department," he said calmly. "I've made some adjustments to our budget, while also receiving some additional dollars from the Legislature in this year's funding bill. I was already in progress when Zach decided to retire — and you suddenly made yourself available to replace him."

The attempt at gallows humor made my mouth quirk. "Happy to

be of service," I replied with the faintest touch of sarcasm. Roberts' eyebrows dipped.

"What happened to you here, today, is unconscionable," Roberts said as he leaned toward me. "And I can't overlook the fact that the higher ups in my own area were complicit. All of it makes me angry enough to try and right things in whatever way I can."

I looked at my friend, and immediately felt miserable for having been so antagonistic. "Jimmy—"

"Yes," he continued. "I *am* recruiting you to be the Commander of the statewide Major Crimes unit. And I want *you* because, quite simply, you are the best damn person for the job. I don't give a fuck what these chuckleheads in Windeport think; I could care even *less* what Professional Standards has to say on the matter. I want you. And if these idiots are willing to let you go, then, yes," he said, "I *am* using the excuse of them throwing your sorry ass out on the pavement to make sure the taxpayers of the Great State of Maine have the single most qualified individual for the job on the payroll."

I stared at Roberts. "You're... *serious*?"

"I am," he nodded. "This has actually been in the works for some time; my single biggest regret has always been letting you take the Windeport job instead of encouraging you to stay with the State."

Somehow, that made me feel even worse about my attitude. "And you'll take *everyone* that worked for me?"

"You'll be running the division," he said. "Who you want to hire is completely up to you."

I cocked my head. "I'll need office space," I said. "None of us will want to go to Portland. Or Augusta."

"The support staff would remain in Augusta," Roberts said. "The bean counters and Human Resources folks, mostly. The detectives working with Zach in Portland will be able to rotate back to their home units for good once you get going." Roberts smiled at me slyly. "As to the office space, well, as it happens the State has recently come into possession of something that I think might work for you and the team."

I felt an eyebrow arch. "I haven't said I'll take the job."

"Haven't you?" he chuckled.

Shaking my head, I sighed. "You're incorrigible, Jimmy."

He shrugged as he polished off the last of his beer. "How soon can you start?"

I thought about that. "I think I need a few weeks to adjust to my new situation," I said. "Besides, I've not had a proper vacation in years; this might be my only chance before you put my nose to the grindstone."

"Then we'll say September 1," he smiled, confirming my suspicion without saying another word. "The paperwork should already be in your email."

I cocked my head at him. "You couldn't have known I'd say yes. Hell, I haven't *actually* said yes."

Roberts put his empty bottle down on the table and reached a hand over. "Welcome to the State Police, Commander."

Eying his hand, I sighed and rolled my eyes before taking his hand and shaking. "Dammit. I hope I don't regret this."

"You won't," he smiled as he stood. "I've got to get back."

"To Augusta?" I asked as I stood, too. "This late? Stay the night and go first thing."

"I wish. I must cover a suspicious death in Bangor — it came in as I was turning onto Route 203." His eyes danced merrily. "Until my new Commander reports for duty, we're a little thin in that area."

"Shit."

"Never a dull moment," he chuckled. "I'll see you in a month and change."

"All right," I nodded.

I walked him back to his SUV, my mind reeling; while I had the acute sense I'd not fully thought out the implications of our conversation — and my essential acceptance of his offer — a significant portion of me had already shifted into manager mode, thinking through the next steps. The rollercoaster of emotions was even harder to ignore, having gone from desolation to anger to optimism over my future in the space of just a few hours. Suddenly my unexpected time off felt like a genuine opportunity to reset, a far cry from its original purpose of allowing me to quietly lick my wounds well away from the glare of the spotlight. By the time Jimmy had slid into the driver's seat of his SUV, it was clear to me I had already accepted my new reality.

"Jimmy, two things before you go."

"Okay," he said.

"I'll need wheels."

"I thought you were missing something when I pulled up," he chuckled. "I can have something to you next week; earlier, depending on what motor pool has available."

"Even before I start?" I asked. "Officially?"

"I'm the Captain," he shrugged. "I can make it happen."

"Unmarked?"

Jimmy smiled. "Sure," he said before getting a sly look. "Unless you want to rub it in that you landed on your feet."

I thought about that. "Let me get back to you on that."

"Okay. What was the other thing?"

"*Where* is my new office?"

Roberts closed the door, started up his SUV and rolled down the window. Smiling he replied. "Right where your old one was. By the way, it came fully furnished, too. Hell of a deal."

My eyes widened. "You *bought—*"

"The Windeport Public Safety Building? Yes, and then leased the part the Fire Department was using back to them. I'm not sure they realize how expensive that will be in the long run, though," he said before smiling wider. "I thought you might appreciate the delicious irony."

"That won't go over too well."

"Not their choice," he replied. "The Village sold it to the State for cash. What we do with it is our business."

I looked at Jimmy and slowly smiled. "Remind me to never get on your bad side."

"A wise policy," he chuckled as he put the SUV into reverse. "See you in September."

Epilogue

I watched Jimmy back out of my driveway and then accelerate down Ocean View, all the while wondering why I had so willingly agreed to his proposal. As his taillights disappeared into the night, I thought perhaps he'd known me far better than I'd realized, for the chance to continue the work I knew I was exceptional at was too good to pass up. At the end of the day, only the scope of my job would change; my life in Windeport would — *could* — essentially remain as it had been. Hiring back everyone who had originally worked for me would go a long way toward making me feel less guilty about getting them fired in the first place; that I would be operating mere yards from the people who had tried to eliminate me was something of a cherry on top of the sundae.

As I continued to stare down the street in front of my bungalow, the turbulent nature of my thoughts reinforced the idea that a quick run would still help take the edge off. I wasn't sure it was the wisest of options, though, given how two beers were sloshing around in my stomach — and not much else; fortunately, prudence intervened, and I instead went back up the steps and entered my home, my mind momentarily focused on rustling up some sort of late dinner. Halfway through warming up some leftovers from the depths of my fridge, my eyebrows went up in surprise at the tentative knock against the door for the carport.

Wiping my hands off on a towel, I wandered across the kitchen and wondered who my second mystery guest of the evening might be; I was wholly unprepared to see the gorgeous form of Suzanne standing there when I pulled the door open. Her blue Subaru Forester was behind her, parked in her usual spot; it wasn't lost on me that, one, she'd knocked instead of coming straight into the bungalow and, two, she wasn't toting the luggage she'd likely had for her trip to Portland. Suzanne's expression was calm but also expectant, though it *was* odd that she'd not changed out of her scrubs for the drive to Windeport. We stood there at the door staring at each other for an uncomfortably long time before she finally spoke.

"Can we talk?"

Those were *not* the three words I'd wanted to hear out of the gate.

My heart began beating forcefully in anticipation of a conversation I'd never wanted to have with Suzanne; trying to ignore it, I nodded and moved to the side to allow her into the bungalow. Suzanne stepped past me and into the kitchen, then moved over to the small dining table in the corner. Pulling out a chair, she sat down and then carefully placed her phone on the surface. I felt a bit rooted to the spot, my fear at continuing the conversation nearly palpable; somehow, I regained my motor abilities and managed to close the door to the carport. Turning away from her for a moment, I returned to the microwave and the dish I'd been reheating.

"Can I get you anything?" I heard myself ask. For some reason, I felt like I was a third party watching the process unfold from the corner of the room.

"Wine if you have it," she said.

"I have that bottle we—there's a half a bottle left from the other night," I said, pulling open a cabinet door and retrieving a wineglass.

"That sounds great. It was a long drive."

"I can imagine," I said.

Retrieving the bottle of red from the fridge, I poured her a healthy amount before putting it back; against my better judgement, I grabbed another Sam Adams out, then closed the door. My hands were shaking so badly, it took me three tries to get the top off the bottle; taking a deep breath to steady myself, I turned and brought my wares to the table. The tension in the room only seemed to grow thicker as I placed the wineglass in front of her; she smiled her thanks before taking a quick sip of the enflamed liquid. I considered taking my usual spot on the other side of the table but couldn't quite bring myself to do that; instead, I returned to the counter and carefully leaned my back against it, trying to cover the insane roiling in my gut with a casual attitude. I may or may not have also desperately needed the support the counter was providing; otherwise, I was likely to crumble on the spot.

Suzanne took another sip from her wine, then put the glass down. "I owe you an explanation," she said as she turned her beautiful blue eyes on me.

"I wouldn't mind one," I replied. From how her eyes widened, I realized it had come out harsher than I'd intended.

Ignoring the barb for the moment, she continued, tapping an elegant finger at her wineglass as she spoke. "I never expected to love anyone again, not after surviving my ex-husband." Looking at me, I could see that this was not an easy conversation for Suzanne, which knocked my ire down a few notches. "I don't talk much about him, and for good reason."

I nodded, no longer trusting myself to say anything.

"When I fell for the bastard, I thought it was going to be forever; our romance was fierce and fast, and before I knew it, we were married and living in a three-bedroom ranch on the outskirts of North Conway. And, within weeks, it was clear all the plans we'd hatched up during our courtship had been nothing more than fantasies meant to lure me into a reality that was far from being a fairy tale."

The pain was evident on her face as she sorted through memories of her former marriage. I wanted nothing more than to move over to her and wrap my arms around her in comfort, but my wounded heart stilled my movement.

"I didn't think much of his suggestion that we sell my place after I moved in with him; I'd bought a small two-bedroom close to the ski slopes that I loved, but I had to agree we didn't need it. Then he told me how much easier it would be to have joint accounts at the bank; that, too, seemed reasonable."

A creeping horror began to overwhelm me as I recognized the signs of a controlling personality; it was matched by intense frustration I'd given her any cause to put me into the same category. The urge to scream out *I'm not him* was almost too great to ignore, but somehow, I managed to instead grip the beer bottle just a bit tighter while keeping my face impassive.

"Somewhere in there, I thought I had misplaced my credit cards only to discover he'd taken them; the same went for the checkbook. The explanation for that was something along the lines that it was simpler, *easier* if I went through him for anything I needed. For a while, I accepted that, until the morning I woke up and realized I had no access to anything. That, in fact, I was putting in eighty hours a week at the practice only to come home and have to beg him for twenty bucks to go to lunch with the nurses."

Sipping from her wine again, she smiled sadly. "And still, for years, I accepted that. I loved him so much, I willingly subjugated my own wants and desires to his own. Until I didn't."

All I could do was nod.

"You already know the divorce was messy; about the fact he'd been carrying on an affair with another woman while he essentially subjugated me. What I didn't tell you was just how violent he became the day I kicked him out and reclaimed what little I still called my own. You know about the gun I bought for protection, and, of course, why I moved as far away as I could." She looked at me. "After all of that, I vowed never to fall *that* in love with anyone again."

I swallowed hard. "And then you did." My voice sounded alien to me.

"And then I did," she sighed.

"I am not your ex-husband," I finally pointed out, so softly I wasn't sure she'd heard it.

"No," she said before smiling slightly. "Given our age difference, you're more like my boy toy."

I felt my face flush slightly. "Even knowing that, you still got scared."

"I never got over the fear of possibly losing who I was," she said, her eyes glistening slightly. "Of losing control."

"I don't want to control you," I said forcefully. "I never have. You're not some object, some *property* I wish to own. I love you with every fiber of my being — I only want you to be happy. That's it. That's all it's *ever* been."

Suzanne shook her head. "That is exactly the language my ex used," she sighed. "And part of the reasoning he gave for moving in together. With him, 'taking care of me' was less of a euphemism and more of an outright obsession."

I slowly nodded. "I... I had no idea talking about merging our homes would be a trigger," I said. "How *could* I?"

"I figured I'd given you enough subtle clues," she replied.

"I can see that *now*," I said, hardly able to stop from rolling my eyes. "Why didn't you just say something?"

Suzanne gave a quick sarcastic laugh. "Oh, that conversation would have gone *great*. 'Hey, Sean, I love you to pieces but will never *ever* move in with you.'"

"It would have been honest," I said. "And I could have handled it. Far better than you abruptly dropping out of my life for a week with no explanation." I waited a moment before adding, quietly: "You should have trusted me."

"Trust," Suzanne replied softly, "is not something I am terribly good at."

"I thought we'd covered this ground when you spent that Christmas in Portland," I said quietly, somewhat shocked. My heart skipped a beat or two as I flashed back to that lonely holiday when I'd feared I'd lost her before I'd even gotten started. "Have I... given you reason to doubt me?" I asked, genuinely concerned. "Doubt my intentions? If so, it wasn't—"

"You haven't," she answered before I could continue. "And honestly, you're not the part of this equation that's a problem. It's me and my bruised and battered heart."

"Let me help you heal those wounds," I said, taking a tentative step toward the table. "Let me remind you why you are the most wonderfully unique person in the universe — and the one who has captured *my* heart and soul completely."

Suzanne looked at me, her eyes watering. "I'm not sure I *can* be healed."

"Someone I care very deeply for told me not long ago that *everyone* can be healed," I replied softly. "Maybe not all at once, for sure, and perhaps not as completely as we would hope. But enough that we can get to the next chapter of our lives without the baggage from the last."

A single tear slowly emerged and rolled down Suzanne's cheek. "I can't move in with you," she said so softly I had to move closer to hear her. "Not yet. Maybe not ever. Can you live with that?"

I dropped to a crouch beside her chair and took her hand into mine; my heart was in my throat, but somehow, I found a way to speak around it. "I love you, Suzanne. I want to be with you every moment of every day, but I get it. You need a safe space you feel you can retreat to if the world goes into the toilet again." I looked at the kitchen, then the living room. "I won't lie, I've got this romantic notion it would be here at the bungalow, with me as your protector. Maybe, with time, you'll feel that way, but if you never do, I won't love you any less."

"You'll always be welcome at the apartment," she said. "But for now, it's got to be my place. My sanctuary."

I nodded and tried not to think of the engagement ring sitting at that very moment on top of my dresser in our – *my* -- bedroom down the hall. I thanked my lucky stars I'd not had a chance to propose to her in Portland as I had planned, for it was quite likely that would have been the end of everything. It was clear to me now she wasn't ready for such a bold step forward in our relationship; reaching a hand up to brush back her hair, I nodded slowly at the recognition that Suzanne had put on a brave face for the world when in fact her emotional foundations had been hollowed out and dangerously close to collapse. No, this was going to take some time — time to delicately repair what her ex had so cruelly destroyed.

And I knew beyond a shadow of a doubt I was the man to do it.

"I'm here for you," I said softly. "I always will be. I hope you can believe that."

She took my hand and placed it on her chest. "My heart is all in, but my brain is going to have to work at it."

I looked at her and finally saw the fear just behind those beautiful eyes; for the first time in my life, I actually felt my confidence falter. There was so much hurt in there – enough that I wasn't entirely sure my love *alone* would be able to bring her back to me. Scanning her face, my heart ached at the thought we might be at the beginning of the end. It was a destination I had no interest in getting to; at least, not without a fight. Taking her hand back into mine, I summoned my last bit of courage, smiled gently, and risked what was left of my own bruised and battered heart on a future I knew beyond a shadow of a doubt I desperately wanted.

"It's a start."

Acknowledgments

I started off thinking that this book would be somewhat easier for my hero; after all, over the past three books, he's watched his friend nearly drown, been critically wounded by a suspect, and then had to investigate the murder of his former high school flame. That's quite a bit for anyone to handle, so *Vengeance* was *supposed* to be a nice, quiet little mystery that would allow him to recover and regroup. But, like so many of my books, as I began to get into the story, little threads from all of the early *Sean Colbeth Investigates* were hanging out there, just begging for me to tug at them. The most intriguing one was Suzanne's backstory with her ex-husband, though honestly, I had no idea that pulling slightly on *that* thread would lead to their entire relationship unraveling. I guess it just goes to show you that I may write these characters, but I don't control them in the least.

(The upshot of all that chaos was the creation of my first-ever short, *Snow Drifts*, where we get a little more insight into Suzanne's feelings about love and relationships – and (hint, hint) how she *actually* feels about Sean. It's worth a read if you missed it originally if for no other reason than to give you the tiniest bit of hope for our star-crossed lovers when we see them again in *Solitude*.)

The model railroad that features prominently in this story is partially based on one that I helped my father bring to life when I was a kid. I have so *many* cherished memories of nights and weekends spent in the basement of my childhood home in Maine building – and rebuilding – a scale empire with long, sweeping curves designed to showcase the rolling stock my father had collected over a lifetime. We never seemed to *finish* any of the many designs we came up with; that, honestly, seems like a feature of the hobby, not a bug. While it horrified me to stage the tragic death of our victim in the midst of such a work of art, please note that I took great pains to preserve the layout with minimal damage. My one true regret in moving to Arizona is the serious lack of basements here; I've long rumbled about taking over the dining room, but so far haven't made good on my threat.

Once more, my wife, **Paula**, was with me every step of the way on yet another crazy adventure. Coming off the emotional lows that *Bewitched* presented, I wasn't entirely certain I had it in me to dig deeper and rock Sean's world further; with her patient guidance, I got there with far more aplomb than I have any right to. As always, my best only comes to light when she teases it out from beneath whatever rock I've hidden it.

—C

February 21, 2023

About the Author

Born and raised in Maine, Chris has spent nearly three decades as an IT nerd, writing just about everything other than a novel in the process. That changed in early 2019 when he was advised to find a way to wind down from his day job; sifting through his options, he recalled a childhood ambition to become a writer and quickly found himself weaving an entirely new world from the comfort of his laptop. *Vengeance* is his twelfth book, part of the series featuring Sean Colbeth and Vasily Korsokovach.

Despite his love for the Northeast, the author escaped the cold for Arizona, where he currently resides with his beautiful wife and an American Staffordshire Terrier rescue who thinks any time is a good time for a nice, long walk.

Keep up with all of the latest information on the author's website, chrisjansmann.com, where you'll find whimsical blog posts, in-depth podcasts on each novel and an exclusive reader newsletter with hints about upcoming books in both series.

facebook.com/christopherjansmann
instagram.com/chrisjansmann
amazon.com/author/chrisjansmann
bookbub.com/authors/christopher-h-jansmann
goodreads.com/chrisjansmann
mastodon.coffee/@chrisjansmann

www.ingramcontent.com/pod-product-compliance
Lightning Source LLC
Chambersburg PA
CBHW020609310726
48979CB00008B/1404/J
9781960914118